5P

HARDCASTLE'S SPY

HARDCASTLE'S SPY

Graham Ison

severn
House

This first world edition published in Great Britain 2004 by
SEVERN HOUSE PUBLISHERS LTD of
9–15 High Street, Sutton, Surrey SM1 1DF.
This first world edition published in the USA 2004 by
SEVERN HOUSE PUBLISHERS INC of
595 Madison Avenue, New York, N.Y. 10022.

British Library Cataloguing in Publication Data

Ison, Graham
    Hardcastle's spy
    1. Police - England - London - Fiction
    2. Murder - Investigation - England - London - Fiction
    3. Spies - England - London - Fiction
    4. Detective and mystery stories
    I. Title
    823.9'14 [F]

    ISBN 0-7278-6018-6

Typeset by Palimpsest Book Production Ltd.,
Polmont, Stirlingshire, Scotland.
Printed and bound in Great Britain by
MPG Books Ltd., Bodmin, Cornwall.

One

Thinking that the body lying near the railings was that of a tramp, the policeman pushed at it with his foot. 'Come on now, you can't doss down there,' he said. 'It's Rowton House for you, my lad.'

But the body did not stir. The constable shone his bullseye lantern. 'Oh my oath!' he muttered, and stooped to examine the still figure. Then, sweating beneath the glazed, oilskin cape that the sheeting rain forced him to wear, he hurried towards the nearby Old Street police station to report that he had found the dead body of a woman in Hoxton Square, Shoreditch.

It was two o'clock on a Sunday morning in July of 1916.

The following Tuesday was, in many respects, a sombre day: an unseasonable chill wind swept a London overcast by scudding clouds, and rain was never far away.

But the weather was as nothing compared with news of the losses at the Battle of the Somme. Eighteen days previously, thousands of British soldiers had left their trenches and almost strolled towards the German lines. By nightfall, nearly 60,000 of them had fallen victim to German machine guns as effortlessly as corn falls to scythes. And that was only the beginning. Throughout the country, every day since that terrible first of July, widows and bereaved mothers had stared, in stark disbelief, at tear-stained telegrams.

In Whitehall, motor buses and taxi cabs, exuding noxious fumes, toiled between Trafalgar Square and Parliament Square, their passengers seemingly uninterested in the passing scene. Pedestrians thronged the pavements, but now there were as many men in uniform as in civilian dress. Most were officers whose duty lay either in the War Office or at the Admiralty, and whose grave faces bore testimony to the serious situation in which the British Empire now found itself.

In Downing Street, the two policemen standing at the door of Number Ten hunched their shoulders under their capes and stared at the handful of sightseers who were gathered beneath shining, wet umbrellas opposite them, hoping for a glimpse of the Prime Minister.

Just off Parliament Street, at Cannon Row police station – an awesome building which, like Scotland Yard opposite, was constructed of Dartmoor granite hewn by convicts – Divisional Detective Inspector Ernest Hardcastle, senior CID officer of A Division of the Metropolitan Police, stood up, walked to the window of his office and yawned.

The previous evening he had taken Mrs Hardcastle to see George Robey in *The Bing Boys Are Here* at the Alhambra Theatre and they had been late getting back to Kennington, but the night had been interrupted when Mrs Hardcastle had woken at two in the morning. Rousing her husband and swearing that she could hear engines and the sound of artillery, she had insisted that they look out of the window. For the next five minutes they had watched, spellbound, the sight of a Zeppelin hovering over London, its sausage-like shape, nearly seven hundred feet long, held, as if on ghostly stilts, by the probing shafts of the searchlights mounted on Apsley Gate at Hyde Park Corner.

Hardcastle had taken the opportunity of telling his wife that all the gilt had been stripped from Prince Albert's statue opposite the Royal Albert Hall to prevent the moon from reflecting on it and thus attracting Zeppelins.

At last the giant airship had escaped the unwelcome attention of the staccato anti-aircraft guns and made for the coast at sixty miles an hour. For the remainder of the night, Hardcastle had dozed only fitfully, but his wife, her head covered in twisted rags to give her hair 'a good curl', had slept soundly.

As a result of his disturbed night, Hardcastle had risen at six o'clock and was in his office by eight.

Irritated that, since 1914, Big Ben's chimes had been stilled for the duration of the war, Hardcastle sighed, took out his chromium-plated hunter, clicked open the cover and looked at the time: it was five minutes to ten. Absentmindedly he wound the watch before dropping it back into his waistcoat pocket. He had little to do now that the murder of a prostitute, whose body had been found in St James's Park, had been solved. The soldier who had strangled her was awaiting execution in Pentonville Prison.

There was a light knock at the door and Detective Sergeant Charles Marriott entered the room. 'Excuse me, sir.'

'What is it, Marriott?' Hardcastle turned from the window. Far below, an underground train rumbled out of Westminster station, the noise amplified by the gap between the buildings.

'There's a detective sergeant from Commissioner's Office to see you, sir.'

'Where in Commissioner's Office?'

'He wouldn't say, sir.'

'Send him in.' Hardcastle picked up his pipe from the ashtray and began to search his pockets for matches.

'Good morning, sir. Detective Sergeant Drew from Special Branch.'

'Oh, and what would Special Branch be wanting with me?' Hardcastle expelled a cloud of smoke into the air. Special Branch was the political wing of the police and was concerned, nowadays, with German espionage in addition to the Fenian threat which they had been formed to combat.

'Superintendent Quinn sends his compliments, sir. Would you be so good as to see him as soon as possible.'

Inwardly surprised at this request, Hardcastle gave no indication to the sergeant that this summons was in any way out of the ordinary. 'Is he there now?'

'Yes, he is, sir.'

'Good,' said Hardcastle, 'then you can show me to his office.'

Despite the fact that Special Branch had its offices in New Scotland Yard, just across the courtyard from the police station, Hardcastle donned his bowler hat and lifted his umbrella from the hatstand.

3

Superintendent Patrick Quinn, head of Special Branch since 1903, was seated behind a huge oak desk set across the corner of the room, in which all the windows were tightly closed. He was a tall, austere-looking man with a grey goatee beard, an aquiline nose and black, bushy eyebrows. He looked up, studying the inspector, who now stood in front of his desk. 'Sit down, Mr Hardcastle. I shan't keep you a moment.' And for the next five minutes, Quinn continued to write a letter in his fastidious copperplate hand. 'Mrs Maclaughlin's pension,' he said, as he put down his pen. 'I've written to tell her that arrangements have been made.'

'Mrs Maclaughlin, sir?' Hardcastle was puzzled that an officer as senior as Quinn, beset as he was with affairs of state – particularly onerous in time of war – should be troubling himself with such a comparatively trivial matter. He wondered, briefly, if he had been sent for to discuss a widow's pension.

'Her husband, Detective Sergeant Maclaughlin, was Lord Kitchener's protection officer. He went down with him when HMS *Hampshire* was sunk off Orkney.' The Secretary of State for War had been drowned the previous month when the ship carrying him had struck a mine less than two hours out of Scapa Flow.

Quinn placed the letter carefully on the corner of his desk, from whence it would be collected by the duty constable the moment the superintendent summoned him. 'Now then, Mr Hardcastle, you are to be attached to Special Branch from today. In a manner of speaking.'

Hardcastle, a detective who had spent all his career investigating crime, was aghast. 'But I know nothing of political matters and spying, sir,' he protested.

'And we know little of murder here in Special Branch,' said Quinn, his level gaze still surveying Hardcastle with a stony glare. 'I understand that your enquiries into the murder of Annie James are complete.'

Hardcastle was amazed that Quinn, with so many responsibilities, should know of the prostitute's murder. 'That they are, sir. The man's due to be hanged shortly.'

A wintry smile crossed Quinn's face. 'Perhaps he'll be

topped the same day as Roger Casement, then,' he said. Casement had been arrested in County Kerry the previous April as he stepped ashore from a dinghy, intent on recruiting disaffected Irishmen to the German cause, and Quinn had been in charge of the case at the Old Bailey.

'Perhaps he will, sir,' said Hardcastle, still wondering why he had been sent for.

Quinn stood up and crossed the room to the large steel safe that stood next to the fireplace and withdrew a file. 'Early on Sunday morning' – he sat down again and placed his hand flat on the unopened file – 'the body of a woman was found in Hoxton Square, near Bowling Green Walk. She'd been murdered. There was nothing about her person to indicate who she was and at first it was thought that she was a prostitute. But yesterday morning the DDI at City Road had the newspapers publish details of a laundry mark found on her clothes. Within hours, the manageress of a collecting shop in Strutton Ground had identified the mark as one of hers. Furthermore, she was able to furnish the name and address of the dead woman. She's called Rose Drummond.'

'Excuse me, sir, but why are you telling me all this?' asked Hardcastle.

'Because you are going to investigate it, Inspector.' Quinn frowned. He did not like being interrupted and his usually soft Mayo accent became a little sharper.

'But, sir—'

'Just listen, man,' said Quinn irritably. 'Rose Drummond was a woman about whom we have harboured suspicions for some time. MI5 were supposed to have had her under observation, but she seems to have given them the slip.' Again he permitted the briefest of smiles to cross his face. 'In short, Mr Hardcastle, she was suspected of having been a German spy.'

'Ah, I see,' said Hardcastle. 'Might I ask, sir, why the DDI on G Division is not investigating the matter, as he started it off?'

'Certainly,' said Quinn. 'As you seemed skilled at solving murders of women found in parks, the assistant commissioner, Mr Thomson, on my advice of course, has directed that you

5

will investigate this one; secondly, I shall need to be informed of your progress daily; and thirdly, you will need to speak to officers of MI5 from time to time. And you will only do that in this office and under my supervision. As your own office is just across the road, it will be convenient for me to have a DDI who I can get hold of in a hurry.'

'I see, sir.'

Quinn stroked his beard. 'I'm not sure that you do, Mr Hardcastle,' he said. 'Although the woman was dressed like a prostitute when she was found, we know that she was not one. At least, not in the sense of being a streetwalker. In fact, she was well educated and usually well dressed. She lived in rooms in Artillery Mansions, down the road in Victoria Street, and it is known that she has entertained prominent persons, politicians among them.' He looked piercingly at the detective inspector. 'And I mean entertained in the widest possible sense.' He now opened the file and turned a page. 'It is possible that she was a German national but our enquiries had not reached that stage when she was murdered. We would be interested to have it confirmed.' MI5 had, in fact, already established that the woman was a German, but Quinn was being his usual circumspect self.

'Of course, sir,' said Hardcastle, and wondered how he was expected to discover something that had, so far, apparently eluded the combined resources of Special Branch and MI5.

'If that is the case, then there are sure to be others involved and it is in our interests to find out who they are. So, Mr Hardcastle, the situation is this: you will take over the investigation of the murder but bear in mind what I have said. I don't want you spoiling it all. Apart from the request for information about the laundry mark, there has been nothing in the newspapers and Colonel Kell has threatened Fleet Street with the Defence of the Realm Act if they publish a single word about it. Particularly about her identity.'

Hardcastle found it all very difficult to take in. First Quinn had mentioned Basil Thomson and then this Colonel Kell who, he rightly presumed, was the head of MI5.

But Quinn had not finished. 'I need hardly say,' he went

on, 'that both the Prime Minister and the Home Secretary will be greatly interested in the outcome of your enquiries.'

'Yes, sir,' said Hardcastle. There was little else he could say.

'I shall attach my Detective Sergeant Drew to your investigation, Mr Hardcastle,' said Quinn. 'He's the fellow who brought you here, and he is to be made privy to everything that occurs. You understand?'

'Yes, sir, of course.'

'He's a very good detective, incidentally.' Quinn closed the file. 'Very well, Mr Hardcastle, you'd better get started,' he said.

'Er, may I have the file, sir?' Hardcastle stood up.

'No, Mr Hardcastle, you may not.' Quinn put the document back in the safe and locked it. The interview was over.

As a matter of courtesy, Hardcastle called first at City Road police station in Shepherdess Walk, next to the Eagle public house in Shoreditch where draymen were unloading great barrels of beer. Hardcastle gave wide berth to their ponderous horse, seemingly intent upon mounting the pavement.

'Aha!' said Detective Sergeant Drew. '*Up and down the City Road, in and out of the Eagle*, eh, sir?'

Hardcastle ignored the Special Branch sergeant's lame attempt at humour and sought out the office of the divisional detective inspector of G Division, who was only too glad to be relieved of what promised to be a protracted and difficult murder enquiry.

'Well, Ernie,' said the City Road DDI, 'it's a right bugger's muddle and no mistake. I don't know why the assistant commissioner wants you to handle it, but I'm not sorry to be letting you have it, and that's the truth.'

'Thanks a lot,' said Hardcastle cynically; he was far from happy about investigating a crime that had occurred well off his ground. For the next ten minutes, he and Drew examined such documents as had, so far, been prepared, and gleaned from the City Road DDI what steps he had already taken in the investigation.

From City Road, Hardcastle went to Old Street police

station opposite Shoreditch Town Hall, and it was here that his enquiries began in earnest.

Police Constable Tom Willerby, the officer who had found Rose Drummond's body, had been roused from his bed in the police quarters near Bunhill Fields and told to report to the station urgently.

'I'm DDI Hardcastle, Willerby.'

'Yes, sir.' The young PC had dressed hurriedly after an equally rushed shave; a small piece of tissue paper still adhered to his chin where he had cut himself.

'Well, don't stand there, lad. Tell me what you know about this woman.' Hardcastle felt for his pipe, but realized that it was still in his ashtray at Cannon Row police station.

'Yes, sir.' Willerby plucked his pocket book from somewhere inside his tunic and opened it. He coughed and then began. 'Sir, on Sunday, 16th of July 1916 at approximately two a.m., I was patrolling Seven Beat, night duty, in an anti-clockwise direction—' he broke off and glanced at Hardcastle '—it being an odd day of the month, sir, when I started duty like. On the Saturday, that is.'

'Don't bother with all that fiddle-faddle, Willerby. Just tell me.' Hardcastle was familiar with the police practice of changing the direction of patrolling beats on a daily basis. 'I suppose you were going into the gardens in Hoxton Square for a crafty smoke, were you?'

'Oh, no, sir.' Willerby looked offended.

'Come off it, lad,' said Hardcastle. 'I started out at Old Street. I know what young coppers get up to. Done it myself in the past.'

'Yes, sir. Well, sir, I was walking across the square towards the hut in the middle of the gardens when I sees this bundle against the railings, like. Well, first off, I thought it was a tramp, so I gives him a bit of a poke with me foot, like, and told him as how he'd be best off going to Rowton House. T'ain't much of a stride down Whitechapel, sir, and I might even have given him tuppence meself, seeing as how it was such a night.'

Hardcastle gazed sceptically at the constable. 'I'm sure

you're a very charitable sort of fellow, Willerby, but can we get on with it?'

'Yes, sir. Sorry, sir. Well, like I said, I thought it was a tramp, but it turned out to be this doxy, sir. She had this bit of thin rope tight around her neck and her tongue was poking out and she'd been bleeding from the nose.'

'Did you touch the body before the divisional surgeon got there?' Hardcastle asked. 'Apart from kicking it, that is,' he added drily.

'No, sir, not beyond feeling her wrist for a pulse, like. But there weren't nothing. Then I legs it up to the nick and reports to the station officer, sir.'

'How wet was this body, Willerby? You say it was raining at the time.'

'Coming down in stair rods it was then, sir. She was wet but not soaked through.'

'How long had it been raining?' asked Hardcastle.

Willerby considered the question for a moment. 'Well, I made a point with the sergeant at half past one, sir, at Pitfield Street junction of Haberdasher Street. He'd just signed me book when it started to come down. That's when I—'

'That's when you decided to make for the hut in the centre of Hoxton Square and have a spit and a draw, was it?'

Willerby grinned. 'Yes, sir.'

Hardcastle turned to Detective Sergeant Drew.

'What did the divisional surgeon say about it in his report, Drew?'

'Said that the ground under her was wet, sir. Looks as though she'd been dumped there after it started raining.' Drew spoke hesitantly; he had yet to measure the gauge of the DDI.

'Who said she'd been dumped there, Drew? More likely to have been topped there, I'd've thought. Still, we'll see what the post-mortem reveals.' Hardcastle turned back to Willerby. 'And you never heard or saw anything as you were approaching Hoxton Square?'

'Nothing untoward, sir, no,' said Willerby.

'Was that the first time you'd been to Hoxton Square that night duty?'

9

'Yes, sir,' said Willerby. 'I got called to a fight down the Crooked Billet about a quarter after eleven. Nicked a drunk. Never got round me beat proper, like, till after grub. I was early grub, you see, sir,' he added.

'What time was that?'

'Quarter to one, sir.'

'And I suppose that was after you'd had a pint off the licensee of the Crooked Billet for your pains, eh, Willerby?'

'Oh, no, sir.'

'No?' Hardcastle shook his head in wonderment. 'Well, things *have* changed at Old Street nick since I was here. Mind you, that was getting on for twenty-one years ago.' He stood up and gathered his papers together. 'Get your helmet, lad, and take the sergeant and me up there. Show us exactly where you found the body.'

It was still raining as the caped figure of Police Constable Willerby led the way to Hoxton Square. Hardcastle, immaculate in navy-blue serge suit, a bowler hat and drab, box-cloth spats over his shoes, had raised his umbrella against the penetrating rain. Drew wore a bowler hat too, but pursued the modern practice of abandoning the wearing of spats.

They passed a column of soldiers marching back to Finsbury Barracks in City Road. The rain ran off their caps and down the gas capes they wore over their packs and reversed rifles, so that they looked like khaki-clad hunchbacks. A wag in the ranks who asked Hardcastle what he had been arrested for had his name taken by a sergeant with a fierce, waxed moustache.

A brewer's dray ground its way eastwards and turned into Hoxton Street. High on their box, the driver and his mate – clad in waistcoats, leather aprons and brown derbies – had covered their shoulders with sacks to protect them from the rain. Overhead, a droning Farman biplane started its long glide downwards towards the Royal Flying Corps airfield at Sutton Farm in Hornchurch.

'It was just here, sir,' said Willerby, pointing to the place near the railings where he had sighted Rose Drummond's body. 'Her head was towards the north' – he gestured in

10

the direction of Bowling Green Walk – 'and her feet was towards Old Street itself. She was sort of lying on her right side, facing the railings. That's what made me think she was a tramp having a kip, sir.'

Still shielding himself with his umbrella, Hardcastle squatted down on his haunches and studied the ground closely. Although the DDI at City Road had assured him that the scene of the killing had been examined, Hardcastle preferred to make sure for himself, even though it was now Tuesday and the murder was two days old. For five minutes or so, he brushed at the grass. He stood up and poked in the nearby bushes and wandered around the immediate vicinity of where Willerby had found Rose Drummond's body. 'Can't see anything that's likely to help us there, Drew,' he said to the sergeant. 'Have a look yourself. Your eyes are younger than mine.'

But Drew had no greater success than the inspector. 'If there were any footprints they've been wiped out by the rain, sir,' he said. 'Looks like we've drawn a blank here.'

Hardcastle nodded. 'Let's hope the post-mortem will have told us more than this does,' he said. 'But I don't suppose it will,' he added, with a cynicism born of years of experience. 'Right, we'll get back to Old Street.' He glanced at Drew. 'Where are the woman's clothes?'

'I don't know for sure, sir,' said Drew.

'Well, you're supposed to know, Drew. That's why a DDI's given a detective sergeant to help him. So's he'll know all the answers.'

Drew was unsure whether Hardcastle was being facetious or was in earnest, but he determined to take no chances. It was obvious that he would have to keep his wits about him. The investigation of murder was a new world to Drew, but Hardcastle was soon to discover that the world of espionage was not exactly familiar territory to him.

Two

Rose Drummond's clothing had been placed in a paper sack and locked in a cupboard in the property store at Old Street police station for safe keeping. Detective Sergeant Drew took it up to the detectives' office on the first floor and spread it on a table. 'God, what a smell,' he said, as the musty odour of the still-damp clothing rose to his nostrils.

'Stay with me and you'll soon get used to it, lad,' said Hardcastle. 'It's the smell of murder.' He cast a withering gaze at the sergeant as he began to sort through the garments that Rose Drummond had been wearing at the time of her death. 'Where's the body?' he asked suddenly.

'St Mary's, sir,' said Drew. Since returning to the police station, he had rapidly acquainted himself with the main details of the murder, sketchy though they were.

'Why St Mary's? Why not St Leonard's? It's nearer.'

'Apparently they don't have the facilities there, sir,' said Drew. 'Not according to Dr Spilsbury, so he directed that the body be taken there for the post-mortem apparently.'

'Oh!' said Hardcastle, and lapsed into thought. For a few moments he continued to pick over the cheap apparel on the table. Then he looked up. 'Well, we'd better go and talk to Dr Spilsbury, then.' He paused to glance at the clothing again. 'And you'd better bring that lot with you.'

'Yes, sir.' With an inaudible sigh, Drew began to bundle the clothes back into the sack.

Bernard Spilsbury was a dedicated and skilled pathologist who enthused about his work, so much so that only a year previously he was said almost to have killed a nurse at the Old Bailey while demonstrating to the court how George Joseph

12

Smith had drowned three of his seven wives in a bath. In fact, it was Detective Inspector Neil who had shown how the murder had been committed, but the near-fatal outcome of the demonstration had quickly been attributed to Spilsbury. It was a feature of the doctor's character that he had never denied it.

'What can you tell me about the Drummond woman, Doctor?' asked Hardcastle as Spilsbury looked up with a frown.

'Death was as a result of asphyxiation by means of a ligature, Inspector,' said Spilsbury abruptly. 'Just stand over there, out of the way, there's a good fellow.' He was conducting another post-mortem as he spoke.

'Is that her, Doctor?' asked Hardcastle, gazing at the body on the slab in the centre of the austere, white-tiled room, and wrinkling his nose at the overpowering smell of chlorine.

Spilsbury glanced up, a look of mild amusement on his face. 'Good heavens no. This is some woman they pulled out of the river.' He put down his scalpel and turned. 'I attended the scene, of the Drummond murder that is,' he added, so that there would be no confusion in this rather stolid inspector's mind, 'and there was evidence of lividity implying that the murder took place where the body was found. What happens, you see, is that the blood—' He broke off, frowning. 'Perhaps I'd better put it into layman's language for you. In short, once the heart stops pumping, the blood obeys the laws of gravity, where it can, and will subside to the lowermost part of the body. This is represented by a livid staining on the surface of the skin. But this will only happen during the—'

Hardcastle held up his hand. 'Dr Spilsbury,' he said, 'if you tell me that the woman was murdered where she was found, I'm perfectly prepared to take your word for it.' He was amazed that the pathologist could accurately describe the cause of death in one case while searching for the cause in another.

Spilsbury nodded slowly and gazed at Hardcastle as if to imply that the detective would be ill-advised to adopt any other attitude. 'The woman had engaged in sexual intercourse shortly before her death, apparently a willing participant. That's to say, there were no signs of her having been forced.'

He turned back to the body on which he was working. 'Swing that light down here, Donald,' he said to his assistant. 'This looks interesting.' Spilsbury extracted some part of the cadaver's viscera and peered at it before placing it in a white enamel bowl. He turned again, apparently surprised to see Hardcastle still there. 'Well, the rest is up to you, Inspector,' he said, 'but if I can be of any help, you have only to ask.'

Artillery Mansions was a red-brick block of elegant apartments in Westminster that dominated the corner of Victoria Street and Artillery Row. A few members of parliament lived there during the weeks when the House was in session; within walking distance of the Commons, they found it a useful and convenient pied-à-terre. But among the other residents who used it as a London dwelling were to be found peers, lawyers, an admiral, two generals, and several high-ranking civil servants. And Rose Drummond.

Hardcastle hammered on the door marked 'Porter' and waited. Eventually a short, stocky individual of about thirty or so, wearing a green baize apron, opened it. 'Yes?' His manner was surly and he seemed annoyed at having been interrupted in whatever task he was presently engaged in.

'Are you Perkins, the porter?' asked Hardcastle.

'I'm *Mister* Perkins, yes.' The porter stared nervously at Drew and then, once more, at Hardcastle. He knew instinctively that they were police officers.

'I'm Detective Inspector Hardcastle of the Whitehall Division, and we need to see into Miss Drummond's flat.'

Perkins looked doubtful and Hardcastle assumed that the police were no friends of his. 'I dunno about that,' he said. 'What would she say if she knew I was letting you in? I mean she might turn up, mightn't she?'

'She'll not do that,' said Hardcastle shortly.

'What d'you mean?' Perkins showed no signs of acceding to the policeman's request.

'I mean she's dead,' said Hardcastle, 'and if you breathe a word of it to anyone, I'll have you up in Bow Street Court in a trice. There are penalties for obstructing a police enquiry, especially in time of war. Now get on and open up.'

'Strewth!' said Perkins, suddenly contrite in the face of this threat. 'What happened to her then?'

'None of your business,' said Hardcastle. 'Now come along with you.'

Muttering about having work to do, Perkins disappeared into his apartment and returned with a bunch of keys. Leading the two detectives in an exhausting climb, he eventually admitted them to Rose Drummond's flat on the fourth floor.

Hardcastle took off his hat and placed it, with his umbrella, on the table in the narrow hallway. 'Just you hold on,' he said, as Perkins made to leave. 'I want to talk to you.'

'What about?' asked Perkins churlishly.

'When did you last see Miss Drummond?'

'She were *Mrs* Drummond, not miss,' said Perkins, 'and I reckon it must have been Saturday, around about dinner time.'

'What d'you mean by dinner time?' asked Hardcastle.

Perkins looked momentarily puzzled. 'About one o'clock, I s'pose. That's when folks usually have dinner, ain't it?'

Hardcastle let that pass; Mrs Hardcastle always insisted on calling the midday meal 'luncheon'. 'What was she doing? Coming in or going out?'

'She were coming in. She nodded and said "Good day, Mr Perkins". She always called me Mr Perkins.' Again he emphasized the 'mister'.

'What sort of accent did she have, when she was calling you "mister"?' asked Hardcastle.

Perkins considered that and then said, 'It was sort of foreign.'

'What sort of foreign? French, German, Dutch?'

'More American, I'd say.'

'Was she on her own when you saw her coming in last Saturday?' Hardcastle slid his watch from his waistcoat pocket, opened the cover and gazed briefly at it.

'Yes.'

'What about Mr Drummond?'

'What Mr Drummond?' Perkins raised his eyebrows.

'You said she was *Mrs* Drummond, so that means she must have a husband.'

15

'Well, if she had, I never saw him,' said Perkins.

'Did you see her go out later on that day?'

'No, I never. But I has other things to do. I don't just stand around clocking people coming in and out, you know.'

'What time did you have your supper on Saturday, Perkins?'

'About seven, same as any other day.'

Hardcastle nodded. 'So, she could have gone out while you were having your meal,' he said, half to himself.

Perkins shrugged. 'Search me, guv'nor. Like I said, it's not my job, watching the comings and goings of them what lives here.' And then curiosity got the better of him. 'Dead, you say?'

'That's right,' said Hardcastle.

'What she die of then?'

'None of your business, and not a word to anyone. You understand?'

'It's murder, ain't it?' Perkins glanced at Drew as the truth dawned on him. 'Otherwise you and this other rozzer wouldn't be here.'

Hardcastle stepped closer to the porter. 'I said it's none of your business, my lad, and I'll say again, if you mention this to anyone you'll be down the nick quicker than you can say Jack the Ripper. You got that, have you?'

'All right, guv'nor, all right.' Perkins took a pace back. 'I was only interested. What's going to happen about this place now then?' he asked, anxious to change the subject.

'It'll stay locked up until I say otherwise,' said Hardcastle. 'After that, I don't know and I don't care. And while I think of it, you can give my sergeant that key you've got in your hand. But no one else comes in here, no one at all. Is that clear?'

Perkins nodded his head. 'Whatever you say, guv'nor.' He took the key from the large ring and handed it to Drew.

'There's one other thing,' said Hardcastle. 'Has anyone been here, asking for Mrs Drummond, or has anyone, to the best of your knowledge, been into this apartment?'

'No, guv'nor, no one as I knows of,' said Perkins.

'Right,' said Hardcastle, 'you can go now, but I'll likely want to talk to you again.' And with that he and Drew

16

carried out a brief tour of the apartment before returning to the sitting room.

'Looks like there's a bob or two here, Drew,' said Hardcastle, gazing around the opulently furnished room. It was richly carpeted and the furniture was of good quality. Over the fireplace hung a large oil painting of a bucolic scene reminiscent of the style of Constable.

Drew nodded approvingly as he too appraised the contents of Rose Drummond's flat. 'That there is, sir. A few genuine antiques among this lot.'

Hardcastle shot a sideways glance at his subordinate. 'I suppose you Special Branch fellows know about that sort of thing, eh, mixing with the cream.' He walked across to a glass-fronted bookcase, took out a book and riffled through it.

'Er, what exactly are you looking for, sir?' asked Drew hesitantly.

Hardcastle paused and stared at the sergeant. 'Blessed if I know, Drew,' he said. 'Evidence, I s'pose. Have you got a better idea then?'

'I've had quite a lot of experience of spies and spying, sir, and I think we should concentrate on finding any personal correspondence there might be about the place.' Drew spoke respectfully, aware that although Hardcastle was a practised criminal investigator, he knew nothing of espionage.

Hardcastle replaced the book and closed the bookcase. 'Well then?'

Drew made his way across the room to a rosewood davenport and tried the side drawers. 'All locked,' he said, as Hardcastle joined him. 'Wouldn't take much to force them open though, sir.'

Hardcastle shook his head. 'I'd rather not,' he said. 'Looks to be quite a valuable piece, that.' He glanced at Drew as if seeking confirmation. 'The keys must be here somewhere.'

'There weren't any among her effects, sir,' said Drew unhelpfully. 'Unless they got lost somewhere in the struggle.'

'If there was a struggle, Drew.' Hardcastle looked sharply at the sergeant. 'For all we know, she might have got took by surprise, and whoever topped her made away with the keys and her money. There wasn't a handbag found. If she was carrying one,' he added.

'You mean it may have been nothing more sinister than a robbery, sir?' asked Drew.

Hardcastle, back on the familiar territory of mundane crime, nodded. 'Aye, lad, it's possible,' he said thoughtfully. 'Just because Mr Quinn and MI5 think she was a spy, don't stop her from being robbed like ordinary folk.'

'That doesn't answer the question of why a woman who lives in a place like this was wandering about Hoxton in the middle of the night dressed like a doxy, though, does it, sir?' asked Drew thoughtfully.

'No, it don't,' said Hardcastle. 'Let's hope there's something here that'll tell us.'

The two detectives searched the flat but found no trace of any keys or anything else of help to their enquiries. But Hardcastle was puzzled that, apart from clothing, there was little of a personal nature anywhere in the flat.

'Right, Drew, we've wasted enough time here. If memory serves me correctly, there's a locksmith across in Palmer Street. Slip over and get him here, smartly.' Hardcastle turned to a side table and picked up a copy of the *Star* newspaper. Dated Saturday the fifteenth of July, its headlines announced: MAMETZ WOOD FINALLY TAKEN – 7,000 PRISONERS. 'At last,' he murmured, well versed in the struggle and the loss of life that had preceded that small victory at the Somme. 'Well, that seems to confirm Perkins's statement, that she was here the day she was killed,' he said, but Drew had gone.

The locksmith, an elderly man with a walrus moustache and a mournful expression, put his bag of tools on the floor and scratched his head as he surveyed the task the police had set him. 'Should have 'em open in a trice, guv'nor,' he said, and promptly set to work. 'There's nothing to these locks,' he went on, as he opened one drawer after another as quickly as if he had the proper key. 'Only meant to stop the servants meddling, you see. Wouldn't stop a cracksman for half a minute these wouldn't.' He stood up. 'Shall we say half a dollar, guv'nor?'

'Sounds fair,' said Hardcastle but, ill-disposed to part with his own money for official purposes, added, 'Send your account to the Receiver at Scotland Yard and put a note with it saying it was incurred by Divisional Detective Inspector Hardcastle of . . .' He paused. 'Of Special Branch. And,' he continued, as the locksmith, muttering, turned to go, 'not a word to anyone, understood?'

'If you say so,' said the locksmith, unhappy that he would probably have to wait several days if not weeks for his two shillings and sixpence.

'Right, Drew,' said Hardcastle, once the door had closed behind the locksmith, 'as spying's your business, you'd better see what dark secrets Mrs Drummond had in her desk.'

Out of the four drawers in the davenport, three proved to be empty and Drew removed them and placed them on the carpet. The bottom drawer, however, contained an American passport, a bundle of letters and a bank statement, inside which were folded a number of cancelled cheques. While Hardcastle was examining this find, Drew attempted to remove the drawer, but it refused to shift.

Hardcastle looked up. 'What's up with that?' he asked.

'It's stuck, sir,' said Drew. 'Won't come out.' He knelt down on the carpet and peered inside the drawer. 'Aha!' he exclaimed, and fiddled about with a home-made wooden catch that prevented the drawer from being fully withdrawn. 'That's done it.'

Triumphantly, he pulled the drawer right out and then peered closely in the aperture. Reaching in, he brought out a bottle marked *eau-de-cologne*, a couple of pens and a small book bound in red leather. 'This looks more interesting.'

Hardcastle took the book from the sergeant and flicked through its pages. 'Empty,' he said. 'There's not a word in it.'

'I'd not wager on it, sir,' said Drew. 'If this eau-de-cologne bottle contains what I think it does, that book could be full of information.'

Hardcastle frowned. 'What are you talking about, Drew? The damned book's empty, I tell you.'

'I think this bottle might contain a substance that's used

19

for invisible writing, sir, and these two pens would seem to confirm my theory.'

'Invisible ink?' Hardcastle scoffed. 'That's Sexton Blake stuff.'

'So it might be, sir,' said Drew, 'but it wouldn't be the first time the Germans had used it. I'll be very surprised if tests don't bring up some interesting reading.'

Hardcastle shook his head. Despite having been a policeman for nearly twenty-five years, it was obvious that he knew little of the world in which his Special Branch colleague worked. 'What d'you suggest then?'

'We'll have it examined, sir. MI5 have got the facilities. Best thing's to get this lot across to them as quickly as possible.'

'You'd best deal with that, then, as you know all about it,' said Hardcastle a little peevishly, and turned to examine the letters. After a moment or two, he bundled them up again and handed them to Drew. 'You'd better let them have a look at those too, I suppose,' he added. Then with an inspired thought, he said, 'If there's secret writing in there, mightn't there be some in those books?' He waved a hand towards the bookcase.

'Might very well be, sir,' said Drew. 'I reckon our best bet's to get some of the MI5 chaps round here to give the place a good going over.'

'What and have them interfering in a murder enquiry?'

Drew placed the bundle of correspondence in a neat pile on top of the davenport and turned to face Hardcastle. 'If you'll forgive me for saying so, sir, I think the espionage aspect is more important than the topping. After all, if she was a spy she'd have been hanged anyway. But if this' – he tapped the pile of paper – 'means anything, it might lead us to others in the same game.'

Hardcastle nodded slowly. Not only had he been plunged into a world of which he knew nothing, but here was a smart young sergeant telling him what to do. 'Aye, lad, well we'll see about that,' he said sharply. But he knew, instinctively, that Superintendent Quinn and the faceless moguls of MI5 would get their own way, despite anything that he might have to say, murder or not. 'But before we leave here,' he went on, 'I think it might be a good idea if we posted an officer in these rooms.'

'What for, sir?' Drew was genuinely puzzled by the suggestion.

'We've not found her keys, have we, Drew?'

'No, sir.'

'Neither here nor on the body. And, like I said, we don't know whether she was carrying a purse or handbag or whatever.'

'No, sir.'

'It's just possible that there is something here that we haven't found, something incriminating. According to the porter, no one's been here since the murder, so it's possible that someone might yet decide to pay the place a visit to remove that evidence, and we could save ourselves a lot of time if we can capture him when he comes here.'

'Or her, sir,' said Drew, determined not to be outdone in the matter of investigation.

'As you say, Drew, or her,' said Hardcastle, 'but strangling ain't usually a woman's game. In my experience they're a bit taken with poison as a method. However, I think it might be as well if you telephoned the Yard and got them to send one of your bright young constables round here to sit on the place until we decide what to do next.'

'Very good, sir.' Drew paused. 'And what *are* we going to do next?'

Hardcastle slipped out his watch and peered at it. 'I think we've done enough for one day,' he said. 'But first thing tomorrow morning, we'll start on the cabs. There's a good chance that whoever topped Rose Drummond took a cab, either to Hoxton, or from it. And another thing, Drew, have a word with that porter, Perkins, put the fear of Christ up him if he breathes a word, and tell him that we're putting an officer in here. Got it?'

'Yes, sir,' said Drew.

It was seven o'clock in the evening by the time that Hardcastle returned to his cramped office at Cannon Row police station.

But he felt at home there, despite its polished, wooden floor with just a small mat in front of the desk – an indication of his rank – and the cast-iron fireplace that, in the winter, was kept stoked by a constable, often filling the office with fumes, but still leaving Hardcastle's back frozen. Settling in his wooden armchair, he removed his spats and his shoes and began to massage his feet. 'Well, I don't know about you, Drew, but I could sink a pint.' He glanced at the clock as he replaced his footwear and then strode to the door of his office. 'Marriott!' he shouted, and sitting down again, began to fill his pipe.

Detective Sergeant Marriott appeared in the doorway. 'You wanted me, sir?'

'This here is Detective Sergeant Drew of Special Branch,' said Hardcastle. 'You and he will be working together from now on.'

'I see, sir,' said Marriott, who did not see at all. He nodded a brief acknowledgement to the Special Branch sergeant.

'Good. Now then, Marriott, there's a piece of rope sculling about somewhere, either at City Road or Old Street. Might even be at St Mary's Hospital.'

'Rope, sir?' Marriott looked puzzled.

'Aye, lad, rope. Sergeant Drew and I are investigating the murder of a woman called Rose Drummond and she was strangled with the rope in question.'

'Where was this, sir?' Marriott had heard nothing of a murder on the division.

'In Hoxton Square last Sunday morning,' said Hardcastle. 'So get hold of the rope and get it looked at. I want to see where it came from.'

'Yes, sir.' Marriott hesitated. 'But what are we doing looking into a murder that took place on G Division's manor?'

Hardcastle stood up and sighed. 'Because the powers that be have said we will, Marriott, that's why. So do what I did when the assistant commissioner directed that I take it over: ask no questions and you'll hear no lies.'

'Right, sir,' said Marriott, somewhat mystified as to how he was expected to conduct an investigation without asking questions.

'Good, and not a word to another soul. Not even the others here on the division. This is secret Special Branch work.' Hardcastle spent some seconds getting his pipe going. 'Now then, DS Drew and I have been legging it about all over the place today, so we're going for a pint in the Red Lion. Come with us and I'll get Drew here to explain what we're about.' And half to himself, added, 'Then you can tell me.'

Three

It was obvious that neither Drew nor the officials of MI5 had wasted any time following the discovery, in Rose Drummond's rooms, of the passport, the letters, the bank statements and cheques and, above all else, the little red book.

At two o'clock the following afternoon Hardcastle was summoned to Superintendent Quinn's office at Scotland Yard. Flanking the head of Special Branch were two men.

'This, as you know, is Mr Thomson,' said Quinn, indicating the older of the two men, 'and this is Colonel Kell.'

Vernon Kell, the head of MI5, gazed, unblinking, through a pair of pince-nez. 'It looks as though you have uncovered some very interesting documents, Hardcastle,' he said.

'Is that so, sir?' said Hardcastle, slightly overawed by the august company.

'Oh yes.' Kell leaned forward and thumbed through the documents that rested, now, on Quinn's desk. 'This for instance.' He picked up the red notebook. 'We had our people subject this to a scientific analysis and it proved to be a list, written in invisible ink, of people Mrs Drummond had met. Unfortunately she did not name most of them.' He glanced down at the book. 'For instance, she talks about meeting a Scots Guardsman near Wellington Barracks from whom she extracted some innocuous information, and a bombardier from Finsbury Barracks with whom, she notes for some reason, she had sexual intercourse and who told her something unimportant about troop movements.' He moved the book away with a brushing motion of his hand as though dismissing it as of no value. 'It is not a very long list, I hasten to add, and it contains very few names, but there are some interesting, er, biographical notes, I suppose one might call them. The information could be very . . .' he paused, searching for a suitable word '. . . compromising, shall we say.'

'You mean they're spies, sir?'

Kell gave Hardcastle a benevolent smile. 'Not necessarily,' he said, 'but I think that some of the people mentioned in this book would rather not have it known that they had met Mrs Drummond. I think you know what I mean, Hardcastle.'

'Yes, I think I do, sir.' Hardcastle was not greatly taken with Kell who, he thought, was patronizing him.

'However,' Kell went on, 'there are others mentioned who I am sure will be of great interest to us in military intelligence. The important thing, as far as they are concerned, is that they are prevented, for as long as possible, from learning that Mrs Drummond is dead. I think that Superintendent Quinn explained to you that we have put an embargo on Fleet Street's publication of any details of the murder?'

'Yes, sir, he did.'

'Good. Now then, I have arranged with Mr Thomson' – Kell shot a sideways glance at the assistant commissioner and received a nod of agreement – 'that three names be given to you, but nothing else that was found in the Drummond apartment—'

'But, sir—' Hardcastle was about to protest that he could not conduct a murder enquiry with only some of the evidence being made available to him, but Kell cut across him.

'It's not that we distrust you, Hardcastle, far from it, but we need time to investigate some of these matters ourselves. However, we are satisfied that these three are above suspicion, of espionage, I mean. Give you something to be getting on with, d'you see?' He passed Hardcastle a handwritten list of three names. 'Once we have investigated the others we may well be able to let you have their names too.'

In the face of his own assistant commissioner's agreement, Hardcastle could hardly object. 'Very well, sir,' he said, wishing he was back across the road investigating an ordinary murder. He knew, in his heart, that if he failed to identify

Rose Drummond's killer, it would be seen as his fault and not Kell's or Thomson's.

'I don't wish to teach you your job, Hardcastle,' Kell continued, 'but one of the people on the list I have given you may well know something of Mrs Drummond's death. It is our view' – once again he glanced at Thomson – 'that her murder was unconnected with her suspected espionage activities.' He smiled. 'You may find that they're not altogether willing to talk about her, but then you're an experienced detective and I don't think that will stop you.'

Thomson grunted in agreement. 'Given that she's turned out to be something of a scarlet woman, Hardcastle,' he said, 'it's entirely possible that her murderer saw his reputation at stake. I'm sure you know what I mean.'

'Yes, sir, I suppose so.' Hardcastle had the feeling that his investigation was already being steered in a particular direction, but he was hardly in a position to ignore the assistant commissioner's fairly clear hints about the course that it should take.

'As a matter of interest, Hardcastle,' said Kell, 'the United States passport you found is a forgery. We've had that confirmed by officials at the American Embassy.'

'So we don't know the woman's real name, sir.'

Kell smiled. 'Yes, we do,' he said. 'She's called Mia Elsheimer, an unmarried woman from Delmenhorst near Bremen. We discovered that from the other papers you and Sergeant Drew found at Artillery Mansions. It will certainly assist us, but I doubt that it will help you very much, so keep it to yourself, eh?' In fact, Kell had known the woman's real identity for some time and had certainly not learned it from the evidence that Hardcastle had recovered.

'As you wish, sir,' mumbled Hardcastle. 'But do we have any idea how old she was?'

'I think we can safely assume that she was thirty years old,' said Kell. 'In our experience, people using false passports tend to keep their own age. Avoids making mistakes if they're suddenly asked for their date of birth, you see.'

'Yes, I see,' said Hardcastle, and for a moment or two looked thoughtful. 'According to that passport, Mrs

26

Drummond landed at Liverpool in September last year. D'you think that's true, sir?'

Kell opened the passport. 'I've an open mind about that, Hardcastle,' he said, 'but that entry may well be as false as the passport itself.'

'What are you proposing to do next, Mr Hardcastle?' asked Quinn.

'I'm having enquiries made of the cab trade, sir, to see if I can trace a driver who might have taken Mrs Drummond or a suspect to Hoxton, or who had taken someone from the scene.' Hardcastle thought that to the trio facing him the statement might have sounded crass, but as a dedicated and experienced investigator, he knew that every possibility must be considered.

Quinn made a note on the pad in front of him. 'Is one of your people doing that?' he asked, without looking up.

'I have assigned one of my own officers from Cannon Row to that enquiry, sir,' said Hardcastle stiffly. 'Detective Constable Henry Catto.' There was really no need to mention the officer's name; it was of no interest to Quinn, and the superintendent emphasized it by interrupting.

'I think it would be better if you let Drew take that over.' Quinn made another note. 'He'll know how to make the enquiries discreetly.'

'The divisional CID can be discreet too, sir,' said Hardcastle defensively. He was irritated by the occasional hauteur of the Scotland Yard branches.

'I'm sure it can, Inspector,' said Thomson soothingly, 'but we are dealing with very sensitive matters here. You are the investigator best qualified to deal with murder, and Mr Quinn's men are experienced in matters of espionage. That's why I arranged for you to be put together. The best of both worlds, you might say.'

'Yes, sir.' But Hardcastle was not really placated, nor did he follow the reasoning behind Quinn's instruction.

Quinn glanced at the officials on either side of him and then directed his gaze at Hardcastle once more. 'Very well, Mr Hardcastle,' he said, 'we'll not detain you any longer, but keep me informed.'

'Yes, sir.' Hardcastle rose, nodded briefly to Thomson and left the room.

Detective Constable Catto was in the CID general office when Hardcastle returned to Cannon Row police station. 'How's that cab enquiry going, Catto?' he asked irritably.

'I spoke to a sergeant in Public Carriage Branch, sir,' said Catto, 'and he's promised to circulate the enquiry urgently.'

'Well you can forget about it now. Detective Sergeant Drew'll take it over from you.'

'But it's all in hand, sir,' said Catto, as though he had been found wanting in some way.

'Nothing to worry about, lad. It's been decided across the road.' Hardcastle shrugged but did not criticize the decision, a decision with which he disagreed. It seemed to him that he was being forced to investigate this murder with one arm tied behind his back, and what he saw as the condescending attitude of Thomson, Quinn and Kell had done little to improve his temper. 'Just let Sergeant Drew know what you've done so far.' He turned and marched back to his own office.

'I'm sorry about that, sir,' said Drew when he joined the inspector a few moments later. 'I don't know why Mr Quinn wants me to do it. I'm sure that your men are just as good, if not better, at doing that sort of thing.'

Hardcastle scowled at the sergeant. 'I sometimes wonder whether you Special Branch people are in the same police force as me, Drew,' he said, but then lapsed into silence. It was not Drew's fault. 'Now, we'll have a look at these names that were found in the red book. Your Mr Quinn, or rather Colonel Kell, has not seen fit to release all of them, so we'll just have to do the best we can with what we've got.' He took a pair of wire-framed spectacles from his pocket and carefully hooked the arms around his ears. 'Charles Smith, MP,' he said, reading aloud from the list. It was the only name that interested him, but he read out the other two: 'Mr Donald Hollins and Mr Lawrence Foster.' He glanced up. 'Well, the first one shouldn't be too difficult to track down, but I've no idea who the other two are. Have you, Drew?'

'No, I haven't.'

'And we don't know what notes Mrs Drummond put alongside their names because these MI5 people didn't tell us.'

'Perhaps you'd care to leave that to me, sir,' said Drew. 'In view of who the first one is, I've a rough idea who the other two might be.'

Hardcastle stared at the detective sergeant. 'Are you not telling me something I ought to know, Drew?' he demanded.

'Not at all, sir.' Drew looked a little offended. 'I'm just as much in the dark as you are.'

'Hmm!' Hardcastle continued to stare at Drew for a moment or two longer, wondering whether he was telling the truth. Although the Special Branch officer had ostensibly been assigned to assist him, he was beginning to wonder whether Quinn had put him there to spy. 'It seems strange to me that there were so few names in the book,' he went on. 'Very strange indeed.'

'You did say that Colonel Kell had—'

'I know what I said, Drew, but there can't have been that many more. How many informants d'you think this woman had? Hundreds?' Hardcastle scoffed. 'If that's the case, the Empire'll likely fall before supper.' He did not intend to let these shadowy figures at MI5 have it all their own way. He stood up. 'Well, don't dally, Drew. Better get out and start talking to some cabbies.'

'But I thought that Catto had—'

'All Catto did was to speak to the Public Carriage Branch, Drew, but detective work, real detective work, means getting out on your feet and talking to people. So get on with it.' But as Drew left the office, Hardcastle realized that he was being unfair by making the sergeant take the brunt of his irritation with Superintendent Quinn, Basil Thomson and the smooth-talking Colonel Kell.

Next morning, events moved quickly. Detective Constable Catto appeared in Hardcastle's office to tell him that Public Carriage Branch had traced a cab driver who had some interesting information.

More importantly, the *Daily Mail* had published an article

about 'a shocking murder in Hoxton', but luckily did not publish the victim's name.

'What the hell's this?' demanded Hardcastle, brandishing the newspaper as Drew arrived in the DDI's office. 'Your people said there'd be nothing in the linen drapers about this.' He grabbed the newspaper from his desk and took his hat and umbrella from the hatstand. 'Catto's found a cabbie. Get hold of him and bring him here. I'm going to see your Mr Quinn.'

Superintendent Quinn gazed at Hardcastle. 'Yes, I saw the report, Mr Hardcastle,' he said mildly.

'But Colonel Kell said that nothing would be published, sir. He said that the Defence of the Realm Act would be brought to bear on anyone who printed a word about it.'

'There's no good to come out of crying over spilt milk, Mr Hardcastle.' Quinn spoke blandly as though the matter was of no great consequence.

'Don't concern me, sir,' said Hardcastle. 'In fact, if anything, it might help. But I shouldn't think it'll help with Colonel Kell's spying investigation.'

'Yes, well you leave that to us,' said Quinn. 'At least no mention's been made of espionage.' He nodded briefly. As far as he was concerned there was nothing more to be said. And he certainly had no intention of telling Hardcastle that Kell had deliberately released the information to the press.

It was nearly midday before Detective Sergeant Drew returned with the cab driver. He was a melancholy-looking fellow with a Kaiser Bill moustache, a cloth cap that he twisted constantly in his hands and a long overcoat that reached almost to the ground. His name, he said, was Arthur Cubbins.

'Well, Mr Cubbins, I understand that you have something to tell us,' said Hardcastle, settling himself behind his desk and beginning to fill his pipe.

Cubbins watched Hardcastle packing tobacco into his briar and then produced a clay pipe from the recesses of his overcoat. 'I s'pose you couldn't spare me a fill, guv'nor, could you?' he asked. 'Come out without me baccy this morning.'

Hardcastle shook his head at the cab driver's audacity and slid his tobacco pouch across the desk. 'What d'you know about Hoxton, early last Sunday morning then, Mr Cubbins?'

Cubbins, having stuffed too much of the inspector's St Bruno into his pipe, had difficulty in making it draw. 'Well, guv'nor,' he began, pausing to strike another match, 'I'd just dropped an army officer at Finsbury Barracks and I was making me way to Shoreditch . . .' He struck yet another match and looked up. 'Live down that way, see. When this geezer give me a shout, like.'

'Where was this?'

Cubbins ran a hand around his bristly chin. 'Old Street, guv'nor, corner of Pitfield Street.'

'Yes, go on.'

'Says as how he wants to go to Sloane Square.' Cubbins shrugged. 'Good fare that. So I says to meself, can't look that in the mouth, Arthur Cubbins, I says, Zeppelins or no Zeppelins, so's off I goes.'

'And where did you put this fare down?'

Cubbins thought about that for a moment or two. 'Like I said, Sloane Square. On the corner of Kings Road.'

'What time did you pick him up?'

'Near as dammit a quarter to two in the morning, I reckon, guv.'

Hardcastle nodded. 'And what did he look like, this fellow?'

Again Cubbins appeared to give the question some consideration before replying. ''Bout the same height as me, I s'pose,' he said.

'Well there must be more to it than that,' said Drew, who was leaning against the fireplace.

Cubbins half turned to look at the sergeant. 'Well, I couldn't see a lot of him, guv'nor,' he said. 'He was wearing a coat with the collar turned up, see, and one of them new felt hats pulled well down over his eyes.'

'What did he sound like when he told you where to take him?' asked Hardcastle. 'Well spoken, or a Cockney? Foreigner maybe, or from up north?'

31

Cubbins shook his head. 'Nah, just ordinary. Like what you and me speak, guv. Mind you, he only said the two words: Sloane Square. That was all, see.'

With a sigh, Hardcastle put his pipe into the ashtray. 'Take a statement from him, Drew,' he said. 'For what it's worth.'

It did not take long for Drew to record Cubbins's recollection of what he had seen and heard on the morning of the murder. 'What now, sir?' he asked, when he returned to Hardcastle's office and handed him Cubbins's statement.

Hardcastle toyed briefly with the sheet of paper. 'I think we'll make arrangements to have a word with this MP, Charles Smith,' he said. 'You clever buggers in Special Branch know about these things, so you can fix it up.'

Because of the serious situation at the Somme, the House was still in session and Drew managed to arrange an interview with Smith for nine o'clock that evening at the Commons.

Four

It was only a short walk from Cannon Row police station to the House of Commons and Drew was surprised when Hardcastle paused at the bus stop in Bridge Street and peered closely at the young conductress on a Number 59 bus that had just pulled up there. He grunted and then began to cross the road. 'Thought it was my girl Kitty,' he said by way of a grudging explanation. 'She's working on the buses now. Mrs Hardcastle didn't approve' – he forbore from mentioning that it was because of what Mrs Hardcastle thought the neighbours might think – 'but Kitty said it was helping the war effort. Went on about releasing some young fellow to go off to the front. Too damned headstrong, girls today,' he muttered. He avoided a cab and glanced over his shoulder. 'Come along, Drew, don't dally,' he added.

The tall, distinguished figure of Charles Smith entered the crowded Central Lobby from the door at the back of the Speaker's Chair. He spoke briefly to the attendant at the desk and, following the direction in which the official pointed, strode across to where Hardcastle and Drew were standing. Smith wore a frock coat, had a neatly trimmed moustache and pomaded hair that was flecked with grey at the temples. Hardcastle estimated him to be between forty-seven and fifty years of age.

The MP pulled a watch from his waistcoat pocket and stared at it, as if to imply that he did not have too much time to waste on policemen. 'Well, Inspector, and what can I do for you?' he asked.

Hardcastle had thought carefully about how he was to question the MP. He knew that if he asked outright if Smith knew Rose Drummond, he would probably receive a flat denial, and he decided to introduce an element of shock. 'I'm investigating the murder of a woman in Hoxton last Sunday morning, sir,' he began.

Smith nodded. 'Yes,' he said, 'I saw a snippet about it in the *Daily Mail* this morning.' He gave the air of being aloof from such sordid matters.

'She'd been strangled, sir.' Hardcastle avoided being too specific about the cause of Rose Drummond's death.

'I'm sure this is all very interesting, Inspector,' said Smith in a tired voice, and took out his watch once again, 'but I really don't see what any of this has to do with me.'

'Her name was Rose Drummond, sir.'

Hardcastle had to admire Smith's reserve: there was only the slightest tightening of his jaw muscles to indicate that the name might have meant something to him. 'I'm afraid that I'm none the wiser, Inspector.' He looked over Hardcastle's shoulder and nodded vacantly to an acquaintance in the distance before looking at the inspector once more.

'I believe that you knew the lady, sir.'

'I've never heard of her,' said Smith.

'She seems to have heard of you, sir,' said Hardcastle flatly. 'She had your name written in a notebook which we found at her apartment in Artillery Mansions. That's a block of mansion flats just down the road from—'

'I know where Artillery Mansions is, Inspector,' snapped Smith. 'I have rooms there, and the fact that you find an MP's name in a notebook is not altogether surprising. People in all walks of life tend to note the names of MPs.'

'Were you *her* MP, sir? I mean, was she a constituent of yours?'

'Of course not. I sit for a Leicestershire constituency. Maplewood, as a matter of fact.'

'Yes, I know that, sir.' Hardcastle laboured on.

'Well then why are you bothering me with this? Because we both live at Artillery Mansions, is that it?' Smith was beginning to show signs of a shortening temper.

Hardcastle imagined it to be a device for avoiding further, and possibly embarrassing, questions. 'The book happened to contain the names of all those with whom the lady had a more . . .' He paused. 'Shall we say a more intimate relationship.' There was no evidence to support that statement, not yet anyway, but Hardcastle knew men and he knew prostitutes and, from what Colonel Kell had said, Mrs Drummond seemed to have been little more than a whore who used her body to extract information from unsuspecting men. Despite what Kell had also said about Smith being in the clear insofar as espionage was concerned, it was possible that the MP standing in front of him was simply one of Mrs Drummond's 'fancy men'. And that, in Hardcastle's book, made him a suspect.

'So that's it.' Surprisingly, Smith laughed and steered Hardcastle and Drew towards a more discreet corner of the lobby. 'I take it that you're a man of the world, Inspector?' he said. 'Yes, I knew Mrs Drummond . . .' He looked around, guiltily. 'And I have to say,' he continued, lowering his voice, 'that I enjoyed her company on several occasions. But I didn't murder her, if that's what you're driving at. In fact, on Saturday evening I was having dinner at Ten Downing Street. With Mr Asquith,' he added somewhat unnecessarily.

'Where did you meet Mrs Drummond, sir?'

'Here, as a matter of fact, in the House,' said Smith, 'at a political soirée. She was one of the guests. I've no idea who invited her, but I got into conversation with her and, well, once we'd discovered that we both had rooms in Artillery Mansions, one thing led to another.' He gave a rueful smile that seemed to imply a hope that the inspector was an understanding man.

'Was there anyone else that she paid particular attention to, sir, at the soirée?' Hardcastle asked the question in a casual sort of way, as though it was of no real interest or importance.

'Yes, there was as a matter of fact. Brigadier-General Humphrey Levitt – he's something at the War Office, I believe – and they were in animated conversation for quite some time. A week or two later, I met him again at Mrs Drummond's apartment. She held a small party there.'

'That's interesting,' said Hardcastle.

Smith looked across at the crowded centre of the lobby and then stooped a little so that his head was closer still to Hardcastle's. 'I'm a married man, Inspector,' he said, his voice barely more than a whisper, 'but my wife lives in Maplewood. Never comes to London because of the Zeppelin raids, you see. I would appreciate it if this matter could be kept quiet. I wouldn't like the newspapers to get hold of it. I'm sure you understand.'

'Oh, they won't, sir,' said Hardcastle. 'You see, we are dealing with matters far more important than murder. We believe Mrs Drummond to have been a German spy and there's evidence that on several occasions she had sexual intercourse with soldiers in order to extract information. She was certainly dressed like a prostitute when her body was found.'

'Good God, you mean that she was sleeping with common soldiers as well?' For the first time since the interview had begun, Smith showed signs of concern. He relinquished his hold on Hardcastle's arm and his hands fell to his sides, fists clenching. His jaw dropped, albeit slightly, and he diverted his eyes from Hardcastle's steady gaze. But it was sufficient to indicate that the information had frightened him.

'As well as generals then, it would seem,' said Hardcastle drily. Judging by Smith's reaction, it was apparent that he too had slept with the woman.

'D'you mean that General Levitt and she were—?' Smith broke off, appalled by Hardcastle's revelations. 'I mean what possible grounds can you have for saying that?'

'I'm sorry, sir, but as an MP I'm sure you'll understand that I can't possibly disclose that sort of information,' said Hardcastle, suddenly realizing how useful was the Defence of the Realm Act.

'No, I suppose not,' said Smith, his mind racing as he tried to formulate an excuse for speaking to Sir Herbert Samuel, the Home Secretary; and more to the point, whether he would be able to extract any information about the crisis with which he, Smith, was now faced. But then he wondered whether a greater priority should be to speak to a Harley

Street consultant of his acquaintance who specialized in the delicate business of socially infectious diseases.

'Well, thank you for your assistance, sir, and your frankness,' said Hardcastle smoothly. 'I don't somehow think that I'll need to bother you again.'

Hardcastle and Drew crossed New Palace Yard and out into Parliament Square. 'Well, that rattled him a bit, Drew, but I suppose we'll just have to take his word that he was with the Prime Minister on Saturday night. Can't very well call on Mr Asquith, can we?'

'No need, sir,' said Drew. 'I'll have a word with the inspector who's the Prime Minister's protection officer. He'll be able to find out.' He paused. 'But I can't see that a dinner party would have gone on until one thirty in the morning, even there.'

'The important question,' said Hardcastle, 'is how long it would take to get from Downing Street to Hoxton.'

Drew had not been idle. The following afternoon, a Saturday, he appeared in Hardcastle's office. 'I've had a word with the Special Branch inspector who does duty with Mr Asquith, sir,' he said, 'and Charles Smith was indeed at Number Ten for dinner a week ago. So was Lloyd George and the Chief of the Imperial General Staff. Seems they were discussing the war, which comes as no surprise. According to the waiters – they were complaining immoderate at being kept on so late – the Welsh wizard went on for hours. Now that Kitchener's gone and LG's Secretary of State for War it's reckoned he's after Asquith's job. However, none of them left until just after midnight apparently.'

'Presumably, Drew, the Prime Minister's man don't know where Smith went when he left Downing Street.'

'No, sir. Not his responsibility, you see.'

Hardcastle nodded thoughtfully and then strode to the door of his office. 'Marriott!' he bellowed down the corridor.

'Sir!' Marriott came out of the detectives' office and walked towards the DDI.

'Marriott, get hold of the uniform man who was on Number Two Post last Saturday, night duty. Him or the man on Number Three. I want to see either one of them urgently.'

As is always the case when such summonses come unexpectedly, the policeman who had been on duty at the front door of 10 Downing Street the previous Saturday night wondered what he had done wrong. 'All correct, sir,' he reported. 'PC 217 Emms, sir. You wanted to see me?'

'You were on the Downing Street fixed post last Saturday night, is that right?'

'Yes, sir, I was.' Emms's mind raced through all that had happened that night and wondered if he was guilty of some misdemeanour.

'There was a dinner party, so I'm told, Emms, at which, among others, Mr Lloyd George and General Sir William Robertson were present.'

'Yes, sir.'

'And an MP called Charles Smith.'

'That's correct, sir.'

'Tall chap, greying hair. Looks a bit of a toff.'

'Yes, sir, I knows the one,' said Emms.

'What time did he leave?'

Emms thought for a moment. 'Must have been about a quarter past midnight, sir,' he said. 'As a matter of fact, he and Mr Lloyd George stood on the doorstep for a few minutes, having a chat. Then Mr Smith got into his motor car and went, sir. Mr Lloyd George went a few minutes later. He and "Wully" Robertson were having a bit of a barney about munitions, I seem to recall, out there in the street.'

'How well d'you know Mr Smith's chauffeur, Emms?'

'Not all that well, sir. He don't often come to Downing Street. But I daresay the blokes on the Palace of Westminster would know him. They get to chat to all the chauffeurs.'

'Yes,' said Hardcastle pensively, 'I suppose they would. All right, lad, thanks.' He paused. 'And don't mention this conversation to anyone, understood?'

'Right, sir.'

When PC Emms had left, Hardcastle walked along to the detectives' office and spoke, once more, to DS Marriott. 'Have a word with the inspector across at the House, Marriott,' he said, 'and get him to find out from Smith's chauffeur where he took him when he left Downing Street last Saturday night. But tell him to be discreet about it. Tell him to make up some fanny to cover up what he's really asking. Got it?'

'Yes, sir,' said Marriott, who was becoming more and more mystified about the line Hardcastle's investigation was taking.

'And another thing, what about the rope?'

'The rope, sir?'

'Yes, man, the rope that was found round Rose Drummond's neck. What's happened about that?'

'Not got very far with that, I'm afraid, sir,' said Marriott.

'Well how far's not very far?' Hardcastle was beginning to sound exasperated.

'I went and saw an ironmonger at King's Cross—'

'What the hell did you go to King's Cross for? You found out something you haven't told me about, Marriott?'

'No, sir, it's just that this chap, Jess Walker's his name, is a member of my lodge and he can be trusted to keep his mouth shut.'

'I see.' Hardcastle gazed at his sergeant sceptically; he approved of the circumspection but not of freemasonry. 'And?'

'He reckons it's from an ordinary clothesline, sir. Says that you can buy them in almost any shop.'

'Looks like we've come a gutser on that one then, Marriott,' said Hardcastle, but was not surprised at the result.

He walked back to his office. 'Now then, Drew,' he said, rubbing his hands together, 'how are you getting on with tracking down those other two names in Mrs Drummond's little red book?'

Drew grinned at the DDI and flicked open his pocketbook. 'They're both senior civil servants, sir. Donald Hollins is at the Ministry of Munitions and Lawrence Foster works at the Admiralty.'

'Are they now? Right then, fix up appointments for us to see them as soon as you can. In the meantime I'm going to have a go at getting alongside this brigadier-general. What's his name again?'

'Brigadier-General Humphrey Levitt, sir.'

'That's the chap,' said Hardcastle. 'Playing hard to get, he is.'

'I doubt that we'll be able to get hold of any of them before Monday, sir,' said Drew. 'It is the weekend after all,' he added with heavy emphasis.

'Aye, so it is,' said Hardcastle. 'Wouldn't think there was a war on, would you? However, Drew, we've got a murder on our hands, so we can't rest, can we?'

'No, sir, I suppose not,' said Drew dolefully. 'Incidentally, I've come up with another cab driver.'

'Oh? Any good?'

'Might be, sir. He picked up a bloke in Sloane Square who fitted the description of the man that Cubbins took there from Hoxton.'

'How did you find him then?'

'Didn't have to, sir. He went into Chelsea nick. Said he'd read about the murder in the *Daily Mail* and heard we were making enquiries.'

'Did he now?' mused Hardcastle, and then, looking suddenly interested, said, 'I wonder how he worked out that picking up a bloke in Sloane Square had anything to do with a murder in Hoxton. What time did he pick this man up?'

'About half-past two on the Sunday morning, sir.'

'And where did he take him, this obliging cabbie of yours?'

'Chester Mews, off Grosvenor Place, sir.'

'Did he take him to a particular house there?'

Drew grinned. 'He did that, sir. I've got the exact address.'

Hardcastle nodded slowly. 'I think we'll have to have a chat with this mysterious occupant of Chester Mews then, Drew. Who is he? Any idea?'

Drew referred again to his pocketbook. 'Spurling, sir. Roger Spurling.'

'What's his line of business, this Spurling?'

'I don't know, sir, but living there, I shouldn't think he's short of a pound or two. Probably of independent means, but I haven't made any enquiries as yet. Thought it better to leave it and see what you had to say.'

Hardcastle stared at Drew and pursed his lips. 'Very wise, Drew,' he said. 'Very wise.' He took out his watch and glanced at it. 'Well, now, it's nearing seven thirty, so I think we'll pay your Mr Spurling a visit.'

The two detectives took a cab to Chester Mews but received no answer when they knocked at the door of Spurling's house. 'Oh well,' said Hardcastle, and glanced across the road at the Chester Arms. 'I suppose I'd better let you buy me a pint then, Drew.'

On Monday morning, with the murder now eight days old, Hardcastle and Drew set off to walk the short distance down Whitehall from Cannon Row police station to the War Office. A boot-black on the corner of Derby Gate looked despairingly at the highly polished footwear of the two detectives and thought how much more profitable would be the return of the rain. He said as much to the newspaper boy next to him whose placard – and his voice – shouted the news that the South Africans were attacking Delville Wood at the Somme.

A constable, patrolling his beat at the regulation two and a half miles an hour, came towards Hardcastle but in accordance with the rule that CID officers were not acknowledged in the street, walked on without a flicker of recognition.

It had been less easy to arrange an interview with Brigadier-General Humphrey Levitt than with Charles Smith, MP, and it had been some three days before – somewhat reluctantly, Hardcastle surmised – the general had condescended to be seen. The excuse which his secretary made was that the general was heavily involved in planning the operations now taking place on the Western Front and was constantly at the beck and call of General Sir William Robertson, the Chief of the Imperial General Staff.

With a world war on its hands, Hardcastle had assumed that the War Office would be a hive of activity. He was, therefore, somewhat surprised at the peace and tranquillity that seemed to pervade the nerve centre of the conflict when eventually he and Drew were conducted to Levitt's comfortable, carpeted office.

41

The general was standing behind his large desk, a desk that, Hardcastle noted, was devoid of paper. Levitt was a couple of inches under six feet tall, probably about forty years of age, and his face was adorned by the sort of moustache favoured by the General Staff. 'Well, Hardcastle, what's this all about?' he demanded truculently. 'I am very busy, you know.'

Hardcastle was not much taken with soldiers. 'It's *Inspector* Hardcastle, sir,' he said, 'and I'll try not to take up too much of your time.'

'All right,' said Levitt, with a little less hostility than he had displayed thus far, probably aware that he had been mildly rebuked and, by the same token, reminded that Hardcastle was not serving under his command. 'You'd better sit down, then,' he added, and sat down himself.

In much the same way as he had introduced the subject to the Liberal MP, Hardcastle explained about Rose Drummond's murder.

'Yes, of course I knew her, Inspector.'

'And how did you meet, sir?'

Turning his chair sideways, Levitt stretched out a field boot and looked reflectively at its toecap. 'It was at a sort of politico-military soirée at the House of Commons, as a matter of fact. There were MPs, admirals, generals and other people involved in the prosecution of the war. There are dozens of these functions actually, and quite frankly, they're a bit of a bore.'

'I see,' said Hardcastle, and paused. Given that Charles Smith had admitted, albeit obliquely, to having had an affair with Rose Drummond, the detective decided to save time by putting the same proposition to Levitt.

The general's reaction was predictably angry. 'How dare you make such a suggestion, Inspector.' His eyebrows shot up and he tugged at his moustache. 'You have absolutely no proof of such a preposterous allegation.' He moved a silver model of a field gun a couple of inches across his desk and for a fleeting moment, Hardcastle thought he was going to aim it at him. 'I happen to know Sir Edward Henry very well, Inspector,' he added menacingly.

The mention of the Commissioner's name did not frighten

Hardcastle in the slightest. 'In that case,' he responded mildly, 'I'm sure you will know that Sir Edward insists that his officers make the most thorough enquiries, particularly into a case of murder, no matter what embarrassment might be caused. After all, sir, only you and I, and of course Sergeant Drew here, know that I've asked you that question.'

Levitt appeared slightly mollified by that. 'Yes, well, I can assure you that I only met Mrs Drummond the once.'

'And you've never met her before or since, sir?'

'If you'd listened, Inspector,' said Levitt testily, 'you would have heard me just say that I only met her the once. And given that I told you that it was at a soirée at the House, that should answer the question for you.'

'Yes, I see, sir,' said Hardcastle, but he was loath to let Levitt off the hook. 'Did she suggest, at this soirée, that you should meet at some other time?'

Levitt turned back to face the inspector and leaned forward, linking his hands on his desk so that a shaft of sunlight glinted on the crossed sword and baton of the rank insignia on his epaulette. 'As a matter of fact, she did. She said that she would be holding a party at her place at Artillery Mansions and would like me to go.'

'What did you say to that, sir?'

'I declined, politely.'

'Might I ask why?' Hardcastle refused to be cowed by the general's overbearing attitude.

'Very simply,' said Levitt, 'because I had been warned off by military intelligence. They seemed to harbour some suspicions about the lady's *bona fides*.'

'What sort of suspicions, sir?'

'They had some notion that she might have been a spy, Inspector.'

'Well if that don't beat cockfighting, I don't know what does, Drew,' said Hardcastle when they were back in the DDI's office at Cannon Row. 'What's going on? That's what I want to know.' He was not in a good mood. Having spent some time arranging the appointment with Levitt, he was displeased to learn that the army officer had been advised against seeing Rose Drummond by, of all people, military intelligence.

'I don't know, sir,' said Drew, 'but I must say that it seems a bit odd.' He was beginning to like Hardcastle more and more. Despite the DDI's rough and ready approach, a marked contrast to the suavity of many of Drew's Special Branch colleagues, Hardcastle was a genuine man and a dedicated investigator. Knowing the ways of MI5, Drew was beginning to think, as indeed was Hardcastle himself, that something was being kept back from him.

'That's one way of putting it,' said Hardcastle gruffly. 'If General Levitt's name was in Rose Drummond's book and these MI5 fellows had tipped him the wink, why the blue blazes wasn't I told? There can't have been any more problems in me seeing him than in seeing Smith.' He sighed and then yawned. 'Well, Drew, we'll just have to get on with it, won't we. Time to speak to this Spurling chap, I reckon.' He stood up and thrust his pipe into his pocket. 'By the way, what's happening at Artillery Mansions?'

'Happening, sir?'

'You've got one of your men stationed there, haven't you?'

'Oh, yes, we have, sir. As far as I know nothing out of the ordinary's occurred.'

'What, no visitors? No one sniffing around the place?' Hardcastle looked suspiciously at the sergeant. He was beginning to think that he could not trust anyone from Special Branch who was involved in the enquiry into the murder of Rose Drummond.

'Not as of last night when I went off duty, sir,' said Drew. 'At nine o'clock,' he added pointedly.

Hardcastle grinned. 'Comes a bit hard, working on the Sabbath, don't it, Drew? Never mind, that's what real police work's all about. Well, I think I'll take your man off. No sense in wasting manpower. I daresay your Mr Quinn can find something else for him to do.'

'D'you want me to arrange that, sir?'

Hardcastle slipped his watch from his waistcoat pocket. 'Tell you what, Drew, you go across and see Mr Quinn about it now. Tell him I'm busy but I've no need of his man sitting in Rose Drummond's rooms any longer. Then you come back here and we'll go and see Spurling.' He closed the cover of his watch, swung it on the end of his Albert and dropped it back into his waistcoat pocket.

When Drew had gone, Hardcastle shouted for Henry Catto. 'Now listen, lad,' he said when the detective constable entered his office. 'There's a Special Branch officer holed up in Rose Drummond's place, but I've just told Sergeant Drew to have him pulled off. Once he's out, I want you in there, understand?'

'Yes, sir,' said Catto, 'but what am I looking for?'

'You're not looking for anything, lad. You'll be there in case some Johnny turns up and lets himself in with Mrs Drummond's keys.'

'And what do I do then, sir?'

'You arrest him, lad, that's what you do, because he's more than likely the man who topped her.'

'Blimey!' said Catto. 'Couldn't the SB man do that then, sir?' he asked with a grin.

'If he knew how,' said Hardcastle caustically, 'but I'm putting you in there because I don't altogether trust those clever buggers from the Yard. They're up to something, Catto, and until I find out what, I'd rather trust my own men and no one else.'

'Right, sir.' Catto preened himself slightly at the indirect compliment Hardcastle had paid him.

But Hardcastle promptly negated that. 'So don't go making a Mons of it, Catto,' he said, 'or I'll have you out in a helmet quicker than you can say Jack the Ripper. Got it?'

Five

Hardcastle raised his bowler hat and gazed at the man who answered the door of the house in Chester Mews. He was of medium height, and wore a dark suit and a wing collar. Hardcastle reckoned him to be in his mid-thirties even though his receding hairline and neatly trimmed beard gave him the appearance of a man much older. 'Mr Roger Spurling?'

'Yes.' Spurling examined the two detectives with a slight air of disdain as if he had already deduced that they were in a lower social class than himself.

'We are police officers,' said Hardcastle.

'Indeed?' Having had his original assessment confirmed, Spurling made no move to admit them.

'We'd like to talk to you about your movements on the evening of Saturday the fifteenth of July.'

'And of what possible interest could my movements, as you call them, be to the police?' Spurling lifted his chin slightly and looked down his nose at the two detectives, a gesture that was exaggerated by his superior position on the doorstep.

'We are investigating a murder, Mr Spurling,' said Hardcastle flatly.

'I see.' Seemingly mollified by the seriousness of that statement, Spurling took a pace back and opened the door wide. 'You'd better come in, then.'

The sitting room was furnished in typically Victorian fashion: a riot of floral chintz fabrics vied with velvet curtains and an amazing quantity of bric-à-brac. Fussy ornaments abounded on the mantelpiece and on the several small tables that were dotted around but, unusually for a room of that type, there were no framed photographs. Hardcastle took it all in but said nothing.

'Sit down, gentlemen.' Spurling stationed himself in front of the fireplace and pushed a forefinger into each of his waistcoat pockets. 'Well?'

'I am Divisional Detective Inspector Ernest Hardcastle of the Whitehall Division, and this here is Detective Sergeant Drew of the Special Branch.'

'Really?' Spurling raised his eyebrows slightly. This latter piece of information seemed to interest him.

Hardcastle took a chance. 'I have reason to believe that you took a cab from Hoxton to Sloane Square and another from there to this address last Sunday morning. That is to say, on the sixteenth of July.'

'And if I did, does that amount to a crime?' asked Spurling, a half smile on his face.

'Not in itself, no it don't,' said Hardcastle. 'But the facts of the matter are that a young woman was found murdered in Hoxton Square early on that Sunday morning. I am making enquiries of anyone believed to have been in the vicinity.'

Spurling laughed sarcastically. 'I see, and because I might have been in the area at that time you automatically think that I murdered this poor young woman, is that it?'

'Not necessarily. But you might have seen something.'

'Ah, very subtle, Inspector.'

'Were you in the area, Mr Spurling?' persisted Hardcastle. 'I might have been.'

'What d'you mean, you might have been? Either you were or you weren't.'

'Who was this woman, as a matter of interest?'

Hardcastle had no intention of telling Spurling, quite possibly a murder suspect, any more than he was obliged to. 'We think she may have been a prostitute' he said.

'You *think* she may have been a prostitute,' Spurling scoffed. 'Does that mean you don't know who she was?'

'Our enquiries are continuing,' said Hardcastle stiffly. 'However, Mr Spurling, were you or weren't you in the area at the time in question?'

'Well now, let me see.' Spurling stroked his beard and gave the detectives a pensive look. 'Yes, I was as a matter of fact.'

'And what were you doing there?'

'I'd been to the theatre with a friend.'

'Which theatre was that?' asked Hardcastle.

'The Brit in Hoxton High Street,' said Spurling.

'The Brit? I take it you mean the Britannia?' Hardcastle was more than familiar with the theatre from his beat-duty days, but saw some profit in appearing to be rather dim-witted.

'Exactly so,' said Spurling patiently. 'It's known as the Brit.'

'And what time did you leave there?'

'I suppose it must have been about eleven. Then we went to a chophouse in Pitfield Street for a bite of supper.'

'And you took a cab to Sloane Square at about a quarter to two,' said Hardcastle.

Spurling nodded slowly. 'Yes,' he said, 'it must have been about that time.'

'From where?'

'From Old Street, as a matter of fact,' said Spurling, a sardonic smile on his face.

'Why didn't you take a cab all the way home, then, Mr Spurling? Why dismiss your cab at Sloane Square and take another to Chester Mews?'

'I thought it might have been more than six miles, Inspector.'

'Six miles? What's that got to do with it?'

'I should have thought that you'd have known,' said Spurling, a supercilious tone creeping into his voice. 'If one hires a cab to take one more than six miles, the driver can charge what he likes. And there are some scurrilous fellows about in the cab trade, I can assure you.'

'You might be interested to know that it's less than six miles from Hoxton all the way to Chester Mews. It's nearer three and a half miles, in fact.' Hardcastle was no expert on such matters and had sent Catto to the Public Carriage Branch to enquire the exact distance. 'Anyway, you must have been pretty certain of getting another cab at half-past two on a Sunday morning in Sloane Square, Mr Spurling. Supposing you'd been stranded there, all for the sake of a few shillings?'

Spurling shrugged. 'Then I'd've walked, Inspector,' he said.

'What play did you see at the Britannia?'

'Hardly a play,' said Spurling dismissively. 'It was some nonsense called *The Crystal-Gazer*. I think it had failed at the Lyric and they tried it up there. Shouldn't have bothered really.'

'Did you walk past Hoxton Square at any time?'

'Of course. We strolled through Mundy Street and Bowling Green Walk to get from the theatre to Pitfield Street.'

'And what time would that have been?'

'As I said, about eleven. When we'd finished our meal, and more wine than was good for us, I went down to Old Street and hailed a cab. That satisfy you, does it?' It was obvious that Spurling was becoming impatient with Hardcastle's pedantic questioning.

'What was the weather like?'

'It was a fine night when we went to the theatre and it was still fine when we left it. But when we went from Pitfield Street to Old Street it was pouring with rain. It was as well I had my umbrella.' Spurling sighed pointedly. 'Look, Inspector, I don't really have the time to waste on this sort of nonsense, so if there's anything else, I'd be grateful if you'd spit it out.'

'Did you see or hear anything untoward at the time you were proceeding to Old Street?'

'Anything untoward at the time I was proceeding?' Spurling savoured the words sarcastically. 'What a delightfully policeman-like phrase. No, Inspector, I did not see or hear anything untoward as you put it.'

'And this friend you were with. Who was that?'

'Just a friend, Inspector. And if you can prove to me that it is necessary, I will tell you that person's name.'

'You mean that you're refusing to tell me now?'

'I mean exactly that, Inspector.'

'Why is that, Mr Spurling?' Hardcastle inclined his head, but he thought he knew.

Spurling looked at Drew and then back at Hardcastle. 'It was a lady, Inspector,' he said, lowering his voice. 'My wife, you see, is away quite often, nursing wounded officers at some grand house in Park Lane. I take it you understand the situation?'

'Perfectly,' said Hardcastle as he stood up. 'Presumably you didn't see this lady home?'

'I did not. I put her in another cab.'

'Thank you for your assistance, Mr Spurling. It may be that Sergeant Drew and I will need to see you again.' He paused at the door. 'What exactly is your line of business, sir?'

'I'm a property owner,' said Spurling with a frown. It was clear from the way in which he replied that he had no intention of expanding upon that loose description unless forced to do so.

Early on the Tuesday morning, Hardcastle knocked on Superintendent Quinn's office door to make his daily report.

'That's very interesting, Mr Hardcastle,' said Quinn when the inspector had finished telling him about his interviews with Brigadier-General Levitt and Roger Spurling. 'Very interesting indeed.' He crossed to his safe and took out a bundle of papers before sitting down again and riffling through them. 'Now then . . . Spurling. Let me see. Ah, yes, here we are.' He glanced up at Hardcastle. 'Spurling's name was in Mrs Drummond's little red book.'

Hardcastle stared hard at the Special Branch chief and frowned. 'I wasn't told that, sir,' he said.

'Were you not?' Quinn frowned too, and stared at the sheet of paper in front of him. 'That must have been an oversight. There's no reason to suppose that he was anything but one of her beaus. He certainly wasn't one of those whom Colonel Kell suspected.' He leaned back in his chair. 'Did you put Mrs Drummond's name to him, Mr Hardcastle?'

'No, sir, I did not.' Hardcastle was furious. It was only his natural reticence – a reticence based on years of experience – that had prevented him from mentioning the dead woman's name to the patronizing Spurling. Had he gone armed with the information that Quinn had just given him, he would have been in a much stronger position to question the man. In the event, he had found himself floundering like a probationer detective.

'Well, that's most unfortunate, Mr Hardcastle.' Quinn looked almost apologetic. 'D'you think that he's likely to be your man?'

Hardcastle sighed inwardly. Quinn, he thought, might know all about spying, but he was no great shakes at murder, that was obvious. 'There's no way of telling, sir, but clearly I shall see him again.'

Quinn nodded. 'Of course, Mr Hardcastle, of course,' he said. 'And perhaps you'd let me know the moment you have any progress to report.'

'Marriott!' Hardcastle shouted along the corridor as he entered his office. He put his hat and umbrella on the hatstand and slumped into his chair, reaching for the pipe he had left in the ashtray.

'Yes, sir?' Marriott knew the DDI's moods and had deduced, accurately, that he was not in one of his best tempers this morning.

'Get someone to get me a cup of tea, Marriott, and then come back here.'

'Yes, sir.'

'And where's Sergeant Drew?'

'I'm here, sir.' Drew appeared in the office door, bowler hat in hand.

Hardcastle related what he had just learned from Quinn and added a few pithy comments about what he regarded as Special Branch intransigence. 'I'm beginning to wonder if we're on the same side, Drew,' he added, puffing furiously at his pipe and filling the office with thick, dark smoke.

'I don't understand it, sir,' said Drew, 'but these things tend to happen when MI5 start interfering.' He was becoming increasingly concerned at Hardcastle's worsening opinion of Special Branch and was trying to offset the blame for this latest apparent lack of co-operation.

Marriott appeared, carrying a large cup and saucer. 'Your tea, sir,' he said, and turned to go.

'Don't you go running away, Marriott. I've got a job for

you.' Quickly, Hardcastle briefed the detective sergeant on the enquiries he wanted undertaken with, as he put it, all possible despatch. 'And take a cab.'

'Right, sir.' Marriott looked up from his pocketbook, an expression of surprise on his face. It was not often that the Metropolitan Police considered enquiries to be so urgent that the use of a cab by a junior officer could be justified.

When Marriott had left, Hardcastle told Drew to sit down. 'Now then, Drew, have you arranged to see these two civil servants that were on Rose Drummond's list of runners and riders?'

'Yes, sir, I have,' said Drew. 'For this afternoon.'

The interviews with Donald Hollins at the Ministry of Munitions and with Lawrence Foster at the Admiralty proved to be disappointing from Hardcastle's point of view. Both officials readily acknowledged having met Rose Drummond at the soirée attended by Charles Smith and Brigadier-General Levitt at the House of Commons, but each denied having seen her again, and vehemently rejected any suggestion that they might have enjoyed an intimate relationship with her.

'Well that was a waste of bloody time,' said Hardcastle, two and a half hours later, when once again they were in the DDI's office at Cannon Row police station. He opened his day book, his record of what he had done and what needed to be done in connection with Rose Drummond's murder. 'Now then, Drew, I have an enquiry in Hoxton I want done, and you're to take a cab too.'

It was nearly eight o'clock when Hardcastle returned from consuming a pie and a pint at the Red Lion in Derby Gate. Drew and Marriott were both waiting in his office. If Marriott had been surprised at being told to take a cab to pursue his enquiries, he was even more surprised by Hardcastle's genial mood, a marked contrast with his ill temper that morning. Paradoxically, it was the fact that Spurling's name had been in Rose Drummond's red book, and that he had perhaps lied about his visit to Hoxton, that had engendered Hardcastle's buoyant humour.

'Well, gentlemen, what news?'

'Roger Spurling is not married, sir,' said Marriott, 'and from my enquiries it would appear that the only properties he owns are the house in Chester Mews and a cottage in Hertfordshire. I gathered from what you said that he implied that it was a commercial arrangement, but everything points to him being a man of independent means.'

'Hah!' said Hardcastle triumphantly. 'Drew?'

'The Britannia Theatre was dark on Saturday night, sir.'

'Dark? What d'you mean, dark?'

'It was closed, sir. It's a theatrical term. Apparently they won't open with a new play until Monday week.'

'Interesting,' said Hardcastle. 'And there's no doubt about that?'

'No, sir,' said Drew, 'none at all.'

'Right then.' Hardcastle examined his watch. 'You and I will visit Mr Spurling again, Drew. I think it's time we dusted him with the frightening powder.' He grinned and stood up, rubbing his hands together.

'Very good, sir.' Drew also glanced at his watch. 'When, sir?'

Hardcastle affected surprise at the question. 'Well, Drew,' he said, 'there's no time like the present.'

Roger Spurling was wearing a black vicuna smoking jacket and carrying a cigarette in an amber holder. 'Oh,' he said, 'it's you again. It's a bit late, I must say, but I suppose you'd better come in.' He led the way into his sitting room and gestured at the chairs with a nonchalant wave of his hand. 'Can I persuade you to a glass of something, Inspector?' he asked.

Hardcastle ignored the offer. 'Mr Spurling,' he began portentously, 'when Sergeant Drew and I saw you yesterday, you claimed to have been to the Britannia Theatre in Hoxton High Street on the evening of Saturday, the fifteenth of July. You further stated that you subsequently went to a chophouse in Pitfield Street and left there to hail a cab at about a quarter to two on the Sunday morning. You also said that you were in the company of a lady and, on account of the fact that you were married, you implied that I should not pursue that alibi too closely.' Hardcastle paused for a moment and then added, 'But the theatre was closed that night and you're not married.'

Spurling threw back his head and laughed uproariously. 'Dear me, Inspector,' he said, 'it rather looks as though you've caught me out.'

'How long were you having an affair with Rose Drummond, Mr Spurling?' Hardcastle had no intention of avoiding the main reason for his investigation any longer.

'Oh, I say, now look here—'

'Just answer the question, Mr Spurling.'

Spurling made a business of turning and removing the cigarette from his holder before stubbing it out in a brass ashtray on the mantelpiece. Then, picking up a glass of port, he turned to face the two detectives again. 'All right, Inspector, I did know Mrs Drummond, although I can't for the life of me understand how you learned of it. But having heard that she'd been murdered, I was not going to tell you that I knew her. It was just bad luck that I was in the vicinity of Hoxton Square that night.'

'What makes you think that Mrs Drummond is the one who's been murdered?' Hardcastle asked the question mildly.

For the first time, Spurling appeared disconcerted. 'It was in the newspaper, surely?'

'No, it was not,' said Hardcastle. Although he was angry, he gave no indication of his annoyance. 'As a matter of fact, we've been at pains to keep it from Fleet Street. So, what were you doing there, Mr Spurling, given that you could not have gone to the theatre?'

Spurling looked down at his feet, a guilty expression on his face. 'As a matter of fact, I was looking for a . . . what shall I say . . . a lady of the night.'

Hardcastle could not resist repaying Spurling for his earlier taunt about police jargon. 'That's a nice euphemism, I must say,' he said.

Spurling looked mildly surprised that a police inspector should know the word. 'Well, that's what I was doing,' he said.

'Why there? You live in Chester Mews. You need have gone no further than Piccadilly for a half decent whore, which is more than you'd have found in Hoxton.'

'I know,' said Spurling, 'but I would have been unlikely to meet any of my friends in Hoxton.'

'Well, I'm far from satisfied with your answers, Spurling,' said Hardcastle, 'and I'm taking you to Cannon Row police station for further questioning with regard to the wilful murder of Rose Drummond.'

'I hope you know what you're doing, Inspector,' said Spurling mildly, apparently unperturbed by this turn of events.

'Don't you worry yourself about that,' said Hardcastle.

Six

The station officer at Cannon Row police station, a burly sergeant of some fifty years of age, had listed Roger Spurling's possessions in the huge occurrence book that rested permanently on the front office desk. He had returned the man's watch, but kept those items with which he might do himself harm: his Albert, to which was attached a silver match case, his braces, sock suspenders and bootlaces. Then Spurling had been placed in a cell for the night.

'He don't seem all that concerned, Drew,' said Hardcastle the following morning. 'In my experience, the shadow of the noose tends to throw even a bugger like him into a bit of a sweat. But he couldn't give a fig for any of it.'

'Perhaps he didn't do it, sir,' said Drew.

'Don't matter,' said Hardcastle. 'If you get knocked off for a murder, how d'you know that the jury's not going to believe you did it so's you get topped all the same. That ought to put the wind up him if nothing else does. But he ain't turned a hair.'

'He's a cool one and no mistake, sir,' said Drew.

Hardcastle felt in his pockets for his matches. 'Well, get him up, Drew. We'll see if we can't get him to break out in a sweat after all.'

Deprived of his braces and holding up his trousers, the tired-looking Spurling carved a pitiable figure as he shuffled, in his unlaced boots, into Hardcastle's office.

'I really must protest at this treatment, Inspector. I have been obliged to sleep on a wooden plank in a freezing cold cell, with just a single blanket. The breakfast was a disgrace, and as for taking my braces away . . .' Spurling tugged at the waistband of his trousers. 'Dammit, man, I'm being treated like a common criminal.'

'It's for your own good, Spurling,' said Hardcastle. 'It's so's you won't hang yourself in your cell.'

'And just because you've brought me here, doesn't mean that you can dispense with the courtesy of calling me "mister", either,' said Spurling as he sat down on the hard chair in front of Hardcastle's desk. For a moment or two the prisoner critically surveyed the scored surface of the desk.

Hardcastle, who rarely made a joke, had on one occasion suggested that the desk was so old that it had probably been purchased when the Metropolitan Police was formed in 1829.

He tapped his teeth with the stem of his pipe and gazed steadily at the man he believed had murdered Rose Drummond. 'What I want to know, Spurling,' he began, 'is why you should have told me a pack of lies the first time Sergeant Drew and I interviewed you?'

'I explained that, Inspector. It was because I was looking to have a little fun with a lady and I didn't want to be seen by any of my friends.'

'That don't hang together in my opinion.' Hardcastle stood up and walked to the window. For a moment or two he studied a pigeon pecking at a piece of gravel on the sill. 'You're a man of some substance, I should think,' he said, turning to face Spurling again. 'Not short of a bob or two, eh?'

'What does that have to do with it?'

'I should have thought you'd've known a few ladies. Ladies who might well be prepared to have a bit of fun with you, as you put it, in the privacy of their own bedroom, so to speak. Or yours, for that matter. But you're telling me that you go all the way to Hoxton to pick up some whore who's more than likely poxed up to her eyebrows. It don't ring true, Spurling. That's what worries me.'

'It takes all sorts, Inspector.'

'Oh yes, and there's none knows that better than me,' said Hardcastle. 'I've had them all through my hands over the years. Stranglers, poisoners, rapists, robbers and thieves, fraudsmen and confidence tricksters.' He returned to his desk and stared at Spurling for a few moments before sitting down again. 'And it's surprising how many of them look like you.'

'Apart from offering gratuitous insults, Inspector, do you have anything else to say?' Spurling half smiled. 'Furthermore, as you haven't actually arrested me, I see no reason why I shouldn't walk out of here. I think it's about time I sent for my solicitor, don't you?'

'When I think you need a solicitor, I'll arrange to have him called,' said Hardcastle. 'And you won't be walking out of here until I decide that you're innocent of the murder of Rose Drummond. In the meantime, you and I are going to have a chat. For a start you can tell me what you were wearing on the night in question.'

'I don't see what relevance that has,' said Spurling.

'You may not, but I do,' said Hardcastle.

'Well,' began Spurling thoughtfully, 'much the same as I'm wearing now. With the addition of a tie, braces, sock suspenders and bootlaces, of course,' he added with heavy sarcasm. 'And a Homburg hat.'

'No overcoat?'

'No, it was a warm night.'

'And you're sure about that?'

'Sure about it being a warm night, or sure about the overcoat?' Spurling gave a truculent smile.

'About the overcoat,' said Hardcastle mildly. He refused to be riled by Spurling's supercilious attitude.

'I was not wearing an overcoat.'

Hardcastle's suspicion about the truthfulness of Spurling's answers began to deepen and for the next fifteen minutes he went carefully over the man's account of his movements on the night of Rose Drummond's murder, but Spurling refused to alter his story. Finally, and with some degree of desperation, Hardcastle slammed shut his day book. 'Well, I'll tell you what I'm going to do, Spurling. I'm going to put you up for identification.'

'And who do you think is going to identify me, and to what purpose, may I ask?' Spurling was still as cool as he had been on the first occasion that Hardcastle and Drew had interviewed him.

'The cab drivers who said that they took you from Hoxton to Chester Mews.'

'I don't see the point of that,' said Spurling. 'After all, Inspector, I'm not denying that I was there or that I took the two cabs I told you about.'

'Take him down, Drew,' said Hardcastle crossly.

When Drew returned to Hardcastle's office, he said, 'I don't see the point of it either, sir. What d'you hope to learn from the two cabbies?'

'Nothing,' said Hardcastle, 'but they might just learn a thing or two from me, like they can't pull the wool over my eyes. Now get them in here, as fast as you like.'

It was two o'clock in the afternoon before the first of the two cab drivers reported to the police station and was shown immediately to Hardcastle's office.

'This is Horace Munns, sir, the cabbie who says he took Spurling from Sloane Square to Chester Mews.'

Munns wore side whiskers, a check coat that appeared several sizes too large and carried a brown derby in his hand. 'Good day to you, sir,' he said, and wheezed.

'So, Mr Munns, you say that you picked up a fare in Sloane Square about two thirty on the morning of Sunday the sixteenth of July and conveyed him to Chester Mews. Is that correct?'

Munns looked furtively round the office. 'On my mother's tomb, sir,' he said.

'Does that mean yes?' snapped Hardcastle. He was always suspicious of witnesses who supported the veracity of their statements by calling upon the Almighty or swearing on the graves of their deceased relatives.

Munns looked momentarily puzzled. 'Of course it does, guv'nor.'

'Now then, you came forward quite voluntarily and told the police at Chelsea that you thought I might be interested in hearing about this gent you picked up in Sloane Square.'

'That's right, guv'nor.'

'And what made you think that had anything to do with the Hoxton murder, eh?'

Munns appeared to be thrown off balance by the question. 'I heard it, like,' he said eventually.

'Oh? And who did you hear it from?'

'It was gossip round the cab shelters, guv'nor,' said Munns, licking his lips. 'There ain't much that misses cabbies, particularly a murder.'

For some seconds Hardcastle gazed at the cab driver, to the man's obvious discomfort, before asking his next question. 'What was he dressed like, this man you picked up?'

'Dark coat, collar pulled up and a felt hat down over his eyes,' said Munns without hesitation.

'How many fares have you picked up between then and now, Mr Munns?' asked Hardcastle.

Munns held out his hands. 'Blimey, guv, I dunno. Must be dozens. Hundreds, even.'

'So what was so special about this man that you remembered him without having to think before you answered my question, eh?'

'Er, well, this gent here'd asked me the same question not four days ago.' Munns nodded in Drew's direction. 'I had to think a bit hard then, I can tell you.'

Hardcastle glanced at Drew and received a nod of confirmation before returning his attention to Horace Munns. 'Did the sergeant explain to you that I am investigating a case of murder, Mr Munns?'

'Gawd bless me, no.' The cab driver looked startled at this revelation. 'He never said nothing about no killing.'

Hardcastle leaned forward menacingly. 'Just now you said you'd heard about the murder from your brother cabbies. Now you're telling me you don't know owt about it.'

'No, well, I put two and two together like.' Munns looked distinctly nervous.

'Is that a fact?' Hardcastle leaned back again. 'Well, you mind what you're saying then, because if anyone tells me any lies about this matter they're just as likely to end up gripping the rail in the dock at the Bailey as the man who did the topping.'

Munns looked decidedly uncomfortable at this pronouncement and licked his lips. 'As God is my witness, guv'nor—' he began.

'D'you reckon you could identify this man, Mr Munns?' Hardcastle interrupted.

Munns looked suitably thoughtful for a moment. 'I'll try, sir,' he said. 'I'll try.'

With Drew bringing up the rear, Hardcastle led Munns down to the cells. After a whispered conversation with the station officer, the three were admitted to the cell passage and Hardcastle slid back the wicket of Number Three cell. 'Have a good look at the man in there, Mr Munns, and tell me if he's the one.'

Munns peered through the small opening and then looked back at Hardcastle. 'That's him, guv'nor, without the shadow of a doubt. D'you want me to make a statement?'

Hardcastle gazed intently at the cab driver. 'What d'you know about making statements?' he asked.

Munns sniffed. 'I had an accident the other day, guv,' he said. 'I had to make one then.'

Hardcastle nodded. 'I see. Well just you make sure you don't have another accident. And no, I don't want a statement.'

Munns pulled a large turnip watch from somewhere within the recesses of his voluminous coat. 'Will that be all then, guv'nor?' he asked optimistically.

'Yes, that'll be all,' said Hardcastle. 'For the moment,' he added ominously.

'What d'you make of that, sir?' asked Drew when Munns had been seen off the premises.

'There's something a bit queer going on here, Drew,' said Hardcastle. 'Your Mr Munns is having us on. He said that his fare, who we reckon is Spurling, was wearing a dark coat with the collar pulled up and a felt hat over his eyes. Now how could he possibly identify a man dressed like that?'

'Well, I suppose it's possible he caught a glimpse of his face, sir, when he was paying the fare perhaps.'

'Don't you listen, Drew?' Hardcastle shook his head. 'It don't hold water. You heard what Spurling said he was wearing: a Homburg and no overcoat. Apart from that, though, the man I showed him was in Number Three cell and his name's Duckett. Sergeant Wood arrested him not two hours ago for burglary.'

'Oh!' said Drew, who was learning more about the investigation of murder every minute. 'So what do we do now, sir?'

'We get a search warrant and have a look round Spurling's house, that's what we do. And when we've done that, I'd better go and see your Mr Quinn. Let him know what we've been up to.'

A uniformed constable appeared in the doorway of Hardcastle's office. 'Excuse me, sir,' he said. 'There's a Mr Arthur Cubbins downstairs, licensed hackney carriage driver. Says you want to see him.'

Hardcastle sighed and tapped out his pipe in the ashtray. 'Tell him to bugger off, lad. I've had enough of cabbies for one day.'

Hardcastle and Drew stepped out into the Whitehall sunshine and Hardcastle stopped to buy a box of matches from a blind and bemedalled ex-serviceman, a box of matches he did not need. 'We'll take a flounder, Drew,' he said, and waved his umbrella at a passing cab.

Using the keys that had been taken from Roger Spurling, and armed with a search warrant from the Bow Street magistrate, Hardcastle and Drew went through Spurling's house from top to bottom. But they found nothing that would have connected him with Rose Drummond's murder.

'What particularly are we looking for, sir?' asked Drew as they descended to the ground floor.

'Well a piece of clothesline that matches the piece found around Mrs Drummond's neck would be handsome, Drew,' said Hardcastle, 'but from what I've seen of our Mr Spurling he'd be a sight too smart to leave aught like that lying about.'

So it proved to be. There were a few pieces of correspondence in a secretaire, but they contributed nothing to the enquiry, save to confirm that Spurling appeared to be a man with a private income derived from investments and inherited family wealth. There was certainly no indication of his profession if, indeed, he pursued one.

It was eight o'clock when the two detectives returned to the police station, but Hardcastle was still not satisfied. 'Get him up again, Drew,' he said. 'We'll have another go at him.'

'I thought you were going to put me up for identification, Inspector,' said Spurling when Drew brought him into the office. He had an expression on his face that was half smile, half sneer.

'Not until I've given you the opportunity to tell me the truth, Spurling,' said Hardcastle. 'You see, we searched your house this afternoon.'

'Oh!' said Spurling non-committally.

Hardcastle leaned back in his chair, surveying the prisoner with an unwavering gaze, and waiting. It was a game he had played often but with only a modicum of success.

Suddenly Spurling leaned forward, his hands linked loosely between his knees. 'It was an accident, Inspector,' he said.

'Then perhaps you'd better tell me about it,' said Hardcastle. His expression did not change, and he remained gazing at Spurling, concealing the excitement he always experienced when he was on the brink of hearing a confession.

'It was as I told you. I went to Hoxton that night looking for a prostitute. I met Rose Drummond in Hoxton Square. At first I thought she was a woman of the street, but then I recognized her—'

'Where did you first meet her, Spurling?'

Spurling appeared mildly irritated at being interrupted. 'I, er, I can't remember exactly. I seem to recollect that it was at a cocktail party in her rooms at Artillery Mansions. Yes, that was it. A friend of mine – an MP – said that he had met her at the House of Commons and that she was having this little get-together and would I go.'

Hardcastle nodded. 'And would this MP be Charles Smith by any chance, the member for Maplewood?'

'Yes, it was.' Spurling raised his eyebrows. 'I must say, Inspector, that you seem to have been very thorough in your enquiries.'

'You were saying that you met her in Hoxton Square, Spurling.'

'Ah, yes, so I was. Well, I was put in an embarrassing position by talking to her as though she was a common streetwalker, but she seemed to think it funny. In fact, she suggested that we should go back to Artillery Mansions and spend the night together.'

'Well, that is what you'd gone looking for, wasn't it?' asked Hardcastle, the trace of a smile on his face.

'Yes, it was, but not with someone I knew. I can tell you, Inspector, I was shocked that a lady of my acquaintance and whom I believed to be respectable, should be doing such a thing.'

'Shocking,' agreed Hardcastle quietly.

'I immediately thought of what would happen to my reputation if Charles Smith got to hear of it.'

'Is there any reason why he should have done?' Hardcastle was having as much difficulty in believing Spurling's latest story as he had experienced in swallowing his first.

'He lives in Artillery Mansions, Inspector,' said Spurling smugly, 'during the week, anyway.'

'Get on with the story then,' said Hardcastle.

'She wouldn't leave me alone. I tried to extricate myself from what I saw as a difficult and potentially embarrassing situation, but she kept insisting that I, er . . .'

'That you bedded her?' Hardcastle raised an eyebrow cynically.

Spurling assumed an expression of distaste at Hardcastle's earthy language. 'Er, yes, I suppose so. However, she was clinging on to me, pawing me in a most offensive way, and imploring me to go with her. A struggle ensued and the next thing I knew, she had fallen to the ground. I stooped to help her up, apologizing as I did so, but she didn't move. To my horror, Inspector, I realized that she was dead.'

'And how did that happen, Spurling?'

'God knows, but when I thought about it afterwards I realized that I must have had my hands around her neck as we struggled. I suppose that I must have inadvertently strangled her. I panicked then and ran off towards Old Street and got a cab.' Spurling looked at Hardcastle apprehensively.

'Is that why you took two cabs then?'

Spurling nodded. 'I was hoping not to be traced to my address by doing that, Inspector.'

Hardcastle nodded. 'Nothing to do with this fanny you were spinning me about being further than six miles, then?'

'No.'

'If this was the accident you say it was, Spurling, why didn't you tell me straight off, instead of drawing the long bow?'

'I was confused, Inspector. I didn't think I'd be believed.'

'What did you do with Mrs Drummond's handbag, after you'd strangled her?'

Spurling was unprepared for that question. 'Handbag?' he said lamely. 'I didn't see any handbag. It must have fallen somewhere near her body.'

Hardcastle glanced at his watch, yawned and picked up his cold pipe. 'Well, I don't think that hangs together too well, Spurling,' he said and glanced at Drew. 'Take him down and tell the station officer that I shall be there shortly to charge Roger Spurling with the wilful murder of Rose Drummond on or about the sixteenth of July 1916.' And then added, somewhat unnecessarily because the station officer knew his business, 'Against the peace.'

'But I tell you, Inspector, it was an accident.' There was desperation in Spurling's voice.

'I think we'll let the jury be the judge of that, Spurling.'

Seven

It was past ten o'clock on the Wednesday evening by the time Spurling had been charged with Rose Drummond's murder, but Superintendent Patrick Quinn was still in his office at Scotland Yard. 'Well, you've not wasted any time, Mr Hardcastle,' he said, when the DDI had finished telling him of Spurling's confession. 'Colonel Kell will be very pleased, I've no doubt.'

'Don't really affect him, sir, does it?' said Hardcastle. 'Murder's not his business.'

'True, Mr Hardcastle, true.' Quinn regarded the inspector with an amused expression. 'But it means he'll be able to get on with his investigations without being concerned that the murderer might have been an enemy agent.'

'But do we know that for certain, sir?'

Quinn looked sharply at Hardcastle. 'And what d'you mean by that, pray?'

'Is Colonel Kell *sure* that Spurling's not been spying, sir? After all, that was a pretty fancy tale he told. And another thing, we still don't know what he does for a living. There was nothing in his house to indicate. Strikes me as a bit of a dark horse, does our Mr Spurling. Frankly, sir, I don't buy that cock-and-bull yarn about going to Hoxton to pick up a doxy. He's a bit of a rum 'un and no mistake.'

'Yes, well, be that as it may, Mr Hardcastle, I don't think you need to worry about it. If Colonel Kell says he's not a spy, then I think you can take it as the case.'

'Won't it upset Colonel Kell's plans when this comes out in the papers, sir?' asked Hardcastle.

'It won't come out in the papers, Mr Hardcastle.'

'But when we go to trial, sir . . .'

'The trial will be in camera, Mr Hardcastle, and for that matter, so will the hearing at Bow Street.'

'But won't that seem a bit odd, sir? I mean, the Old Bailey hacks are sure to be sniffing around and they'll think it uncommon queer if we have a murder trial in camera.'

'Then they'll just have to think it, won't they?' said Quinn. He was growing a little impatient with Hardcastle's theorizing. 'You see, Mr Hardcastle, MI5 want to keep Rose Drummond alive. In a manner of speaking.'

'I'm sorry, sir, I don't—'

'If she was the spy we think her to have been, to create the fiction she's still alive will enable Colonel Kell's people to feed false information to the enemy. And I'll thank you to keep that to yourself.' In fact both Colonel Kell and Patrick Quinn knew that Rose Drummond had been actively spying for the Germans, and they were also fairly certain who her main provider of information was, but the Special Branch chief had no intention of divulging this to Hardcastle; it was, after all, none of his business. Unfortunately for the ambitious plans of MI5, that informant turned out to be Rose Drummond's murderer.

Hardcastle was a little irritated that Quinn seemed to be treating him as though he were a recruit. 'I'm not sure the Bow Street magistrate will wear it, sir,' he said.

'Oh he will, Mr Hardcastle, he will. By the time you get Spurling up there tomorrow the necessary arrangements will have been made.'

Feeling the need for some exercise, Hardcastle, with a reluctant Aubrey Drew in tow, set out to walk to Bow Street police court. At the Strand, they paused at the kerb and doffed their hats as a horse-drawn cortège, its coffin covered by the Union Flag and accompanied by a military escort, wound its slow way from Charing Cross Hospital to St Clement Danes Church.

'D'you know, Drew,' said Hardcastle, 'I've passed one of them every time I've been to Bow Street just lately. And that's only here. God knows how many they're burying across in Flanders. Must be at it all the time.'

The passageway leading from the cells to the prisoners' entrance at Bow Street's Number One Court was crowded with the usual overnight catch of prostitutes and drunks, each with the constable who had arrested them. It was a scene reminiscent of a Hogarth painting.

Hardcastle had no intention of wasting his time and had peremptorily instructed the warrant officer to put Spurling up first. Firmly clasping his prisoner's elbow, he marched past the waiting defendants, ignoring the caustic, and at times bawdy, badinage of the women who saw it as their right to appear before the magistrate ahead of everyone else.

Roger Spurling, his braces, bootlaces and tie now restored to him, stepped into the dock and turned to face the magistrate. He looked around at the unfamiliar scene. The magistrate, high on his bench, head bowed over the large register before him, appeared uninterested in examining the first prisoner of the day. To Spurling's right a number of lawyers – barristers as well as solicitors – thumbed through their papers one last time. Alongside them, a couple of court reporters, sprawling in the press box, appeared equally uninterested in the start of the day's proceedings. Glancing briefly over his shoulder, Spurling was surprised to see that the public part of the court was crowded, but if he had assumed that these idlers were there to see him especially, he was wrong. Having nothing better to do with their time, they crowded into the court every day; to many of them, it was familiar territory and, as like as not, some would find themselves standing where Spurling now stood, perhaps tomorrow.

A barrister representing the Director of Public Prosecutions immediately stood up, quoted briefly from the Defence of the Realm Act, and asked that the hearing be held in camera because of the security implications of the matter now before the court.

The Act was clearly inappropriate in this case, but the magistrate had been briefed and raised no objections to this unusual procedure. 'Clear the court,' he cried in a high-pitched, reedy voice, the order echoing around the high lofted room as it was taken up and repeated by officials and police.

At once there was a buzz of conversation. The two reporters

began to scribble in their notebooks and took several long, hard looks at the prisoner before joining the people shuffling out into the lobby, muttering about the freedom of the press as they went, and annoyed that the morning's entertainment had been disrupted.

'What's this all about then?' asked one of the reporters of a policeman near the door.

'No idea, sir,' said the PC, who would not have told him even if he had known.

Once the court had been cleared of press and public, and others not directly involved, Hardcastle gave evidence of arrest and the barrister asked for a remand in custody. And that was that. The hearing was all over in five minutes and Spurling was on his way to Brixton Prison.

'I don't like it, Drew,' said Hardcastle when the two of them had returned to Cannon Row. 'I don't like it at all. It was much too easy.'

'Well he seemed prepared to stand it, sir,' said Drew. 'There was no beating about the bush with that confession.'

'Hardly a confession, Drew.' Hardcastle shook his head. 'Even though he claimed it was an accident, I've never known a murderer to cough that easy, never in all my service. There's something amiss here, you mark my words. After all, she weren't strangled as such. More like garrotted.'

'What are you going to do then, sir?' Drew could not understand why Hardcastle seemed unhappy at the outcome of his investigation.

'I'm going to shake the tree a bit, Drew, that's what I'm going to do.' And with that mysterious comment, Hardcastle sat down behind his desk and lit his pipe.

'Yes, I know Roger Spurling,' said Charles Smith. He and Hardcastle were standing, once again, in the Central Lobby of the Palace of Westminster. 'What's he been up to?' he asked above the hubbub of subdued chatter. All around them little knots of people were engaged in earnest conversation and Hardcastle recognized two or three MPs whose photographs had appeared in the newspapers.

'Nothing at all, sir. I'm just checking his story. He tells me that you introduced him to Mrs Drummond at her rooms in Artillery Mansions. He said it was a reception of some kind.'

Smith looked thoughtfully into the middle distance before replying. 'Yes, that's right,' he said at last. 'You probably already know that Mrs Drummond was an American and had not been in England very long.' He paused. 'Incidentally, Inspector, I think you may have been wrong about her being a spy. However, she was anxious to increase her circle of friends and when she invited me to her cocktail party, she suggested that I bring someone with me. I took Roger.' Since his last interview with Hardcastle, Smith had consulted the Home Secretary, who, having been briefed by Colonel Kell of MI5, had told the MP exactly what he should say to the tenacious inspector who was investigating Rose Drummond's death. He lowered his voice, adopting a conspiratorial tone. 'Between you and me, Inspector,' he continued, 'I rather think that Roger Spurling and Mrs Drummond had forged a . . . what shall I say . . . a rather intimate relationship.'

'Was this the little get-together that General Levitt was at, sir?'

Smith ran a hand round his chin. 'D'you know, Inspector, on reflection, I'm not sure that General Levitt was there after all,' he said.

'I see. Well thank you, sir,' said Hardcastle as he wondered about Smith's change of heart on the subject of Brigadier-General Levitt. 'I hope you didn't mind my bothering you again, but in a case of this sort I like to eliminate all the innocent parties, so to speak.'

'Not at all, Inspector. Only too glad to be of assistance.'

Hardcastle took a pace away but then turned as though struck by a sudden thought. 'One other thing, sir . . .'

'Yes?'

'D'you happen to know what Mr Spurling does for a living?'

Smith looked searchingly at Hardcastle. 'You mean you don't know?' he asked.

'That's why I'm asking,' said Hardcastle flatly.

The Home Secretary had not said anything about Spurling's occupation, so Smith thought it safe to extemporize. 'My dear fellow, he's engaged in some awfully hush-hush work. Never says a word about it. But I do know you'll find him in the most extraordinary of places. And never an explanation, Inspector, not a word. I'm only telling you because you're a policeman' – Smith smiled patronizingly – 'but if you'll take a word of advice, I shouldn't enquire into his activities too deeply if I were you. Might upset people in high places.'

Hardcastle had been to see Charles Smith by himself. Detective Sergeant Drew, meanwhile, had been sent by Hardcastle to make discreet enquiries in the vicinity of Spurling's Chester Mews house.

'Well, Drew, how did you get on?'

'More or less what I expected, sir,' said Drew. 'Those neighbours who knew Spurling at all said he was a very quiet man. Kept himself to himself. No one seems to know much about him. He doesn't keep what you might call office hours and comes and goes at all times. Certainly no one could tell me what he does.'

Hardcastle nodded and hung up his hat and umbrella. 'Bit of a mysterious cove then?'

'Looks that way, sir. How did you get on with Mr Smith?'

Hardcastle stirred the cup of tea that had been brought, silently, by a constable and broke a ginger snap in two before nibbling at one half. 'He confirmed what Spurling said, that he met Mrs Drummond at a party at Artillery Mansions.'

'Did he have any idea what Spurling did for a living, sir?'

'No,' said Hardcastle, ill-disposed to repeat what Smith had told him. 'No idea at all.'

Drew shrugged. 'Not that it matters. We've got him in Brixton, that's the main thing.'

Hardcastle nodded. 'As you say, Drew, that's the main thing.' He glanced at his watch. 'Well, I think I'll walk across and report to Mr Quinn. Then we'll treat ourselves to an early night. See you in the morning.'

*   *   *

71

Superintendent Quinn listened patiently to Hardcastle's brief account of that morning's hearing at Bow Street police court. 'When d'you think you'll be ready to go for trial, Mr Hardcastle?' he asked.

Hardcastle pondered the question for a moment before replying. 'I should think in about three or four weeks time, sir,' he said.

'As long as that?' Quinn sounded surprised.

'By the time we get all the necessary papers together, sir, yes. Rather depends on what Spurling's counsel has to say about it, and on the Attorney's commitments. I understand from the counsel who was in court this morning that F.E. will be prosecuting the case.'

'Yes,' said Quinn, 'so I've heard.'

'Seems to be a bit heavy for a straightforward murder, sir.'

'Perhaps so,' said Quinn, 'but not uncommon. Now that Casement's appeal has been dismissed and he's set to hang on the third of next month, the Attorney will be free, I should think. Any indication who'll be for the defence?'

'No, sir, but with F.E. Smith prosecuting, I wouldn't be surprised if Spurling weren't to brief Sir Edward Marshall Hall. He likes crossing swords with the Attorney, does Sir Edward.'

Quinn looked up sharply. 'You think so?'

'Just a guess, sir,' said Hardcastle, pleased that for once he appeared to have disconcerted the Special Branch chief.

'Maybe so.' Quinn looked across the office, at the heavily curtained windows. 'Have you found out what this fellow Spurling's profession is yet, Mr Hardcastle?' he asked, suddenly turning back and fixing his gaze on the inspector.

Hardcastle had, by now, deduced that something was going on to which he was not being made privy, and that annoyed him. 'No, sir, no idea, but my enquiries are continuing.'

Quinn nodded. 'Thank you, Mr Hardcastle,' he said. 'You'll keep me informed, of course.'

'Of course, sir.'

Drew had already left when Hardcastle returned to Cannon Row, and that suited him. He walked into the main office and gazed around its gloomy interior. Several detectives were compiling reports and a thick pall of cigarette smoke hung in the air. Detective Sergeant Marriott was bent over his desk at the far end of the room.

'Marriott. A moment of your time.'

'Yes, sir.' Marriott stood up, slipped on his jacket and buttoned his waistcoat. Hardcastle turned on his heel and went back to his own office.

'Close the door, Marriott,' said Hardcastle. 'I've got a job for you.'

'Yes, sir?'

'I don't like being made a monkey of, Marriott,' said Hardcastle angrily. 'You know that, don't you?'

'Yes, sir, but—' Marriott was alarmed that Hardcastle might have been accusing him of some disloyalty.

'I'm not talking about you, Marriott. I'm talking about that Special Branch lot over there.' Hardcastle jerked a thumb in the general direction of Scotland Yard. 'They'll have to get up much earlier than they do if they're to sell Ernie Hardcastle the pup, I can tell you. Much more of this and I shall be knocking on the door of Sir Edward Henry himself.' Hardcastle glanced at Marriott's frowning face. 'Sit down, m'boy,' he said, 'sit down.'

'What's been going on then, guv'nor?' Marriott, sensing that Hardcastle intended embarking on a little informal chat, lapsed into the familiar form of address.

Hardcastle began by telling Marriott what had happened so far in his investigation of Rose Drummond's murder and finished up by saying, 'It don't hang together, m'boy. It don't hang together.'

'What are you going to do, then, guv'nor?'

'It's more a case of what you're going to do, m'boy. And when you've done it, I shall front Mr Quinn with it and see what he has to say. Just because there's a war on and these clever fellows are arresting spies, they seem to think that a topping don't matter. Well, I'll tell 'em different. Now listen carefully.' Hardcastle listed the tasks he wanted Marriott to undertake and then added a caution. 'And when you report back, make sure that Detective Sergeant

Drew of Special Branch isn't hanging around earwigging. All right?'

'Right, sir,' said Marriott as he stood up. 'When d'you want me to start?'

Hardcastle pulled out his watch and stared at it. 'First thing tomorrow.'

Hardcastle spent much of the following morning writing his own statement and preparing the first draft of the report for the Director of Public Prosecutions. Drew had been sent on some fool's errand to Hoxton.

At about noon, Marriott returned to Cannon Row and made straight for Hardcastle's office.

'Well?' Hardcastle put down his pen and knocked the dottle from his pipe before beginning to refill it with his favourite St Bruno tobacco.

'I went all round Chester Mews, sir,' said Marriott, 'and none of them have seen a detective officer. It looks very much as though Aubrey Drew didn't make any enquiries there at all.'

Hardcastle nodded slowly. 'I thought as much, Marriott,' he said. 'This is a rum do and no mistake.' He stood up and walked to the window, puffing furiously on his pipe so that clouds of smoke filled the office. 'Right then.' He turned to face the detective sergeant. 'I want you to get those two cabbies in here, but one at a time, mind. And we'll have them in the order they were supposed to have taken Spurling from Hoxton to Pimlico. Arthur Cubbins first and then Horace Munns.'

'Won't Aubrey Drew be here, though, sir?'

'No, Marriott, he won't. Now that we've arrested Spurling, the case is as good as wrapped up, so I'll send him back where he came from. Mr Quinn won't want him soiling his hands with ordinary things like statements and all the other police work that goes with putting a case together.'

'Right, sir.' Marriott stood up to leave.

But Hardcastle had not quite finished. 'And when we've had a bit of straight talking with the cabbies, we'll go across to Brixton Prison and have another word with Spurling. There's

74

something queer going on here, Marriott,' he added, not for the first time. He walked across to the hatstand and seized his hat and umbrella. 'But now I'm going to see Mr Quinn to tell him to take Drew off my hands.'

'It's all but done, sir, so I thought that I'd send Sergeant Drew back to you. There's no point in him kicking his heels about at Cannon Row. We've only got the paperwork to take care of now.'

Superintendent Quinn looked doubtful. 'Are you sure, Mr Hardcastle?' he asked.

'Oh yes, sir. I mean a highly qualified officer like him'd just be wasting his time. Particularly when there's all these spies around that your chaps have got to investigate. And I suppose there's the Irish too. They must be a bit upset after their little Easter do in Dublin went all amiss.'

Quinn looked piercingly at Hardcastle, wondering whether he was being facetious, but the DDI's face remained impassive.

'Very well, Mr Hardcastle, if that's what you think. Incidentally, Mr Thomson was very pleased that you made an arrest so quickly. He asked me to pass on his congratulations. I'm sure that your diligence and devotion to duty will stand you in good stead when the question of promotion arises.'

'Thank you, sir, very kind I'm sure,' said Hardcastle, but he wondered if Quinn was indulging in a little fulsome flattery; he knew that advancement in the Metropolitan Police depended on more than merely doing the job for which one was paid.

Eight

Detective Sergeant Charles Marriott was much more of a practical policeman than Aubrey Drew of Special Branch, and when he needed to get hold of a cab driver, he knew exactly how to do it with the minimum of effort. Strolling out to the cab shelter on Victoria Embankment, he put his head round the door to be confronted by a thick fug of tobacco smoke and the smell of frying sausages.

One of the cabbies rose to his feet. 'Where to, guv?' he asked, wiping a sleeve across his mouth.

'I'm Detective Sergeant Marriott.' A hush fell immediately. 'Let Arthur Cubbins know I want a word with him, sooner rather than later, at Cannon Row nick.'

Within the hour, Cubbins presented himself at the front office counter of the police station and asked for Marriott.

'Well now, Mr Cubbins,' said Hardcastle, when the cab driver was shown into his office. 'You and I have some talking to do about this murder.'

'Murder, guv'nor?' Cubbins looked shocked. 'Whose murder?'

'Don't give me none of your flim-flam, Mr Cubbins. It's the murder what we talked about last time you was in here.' Hardcastle began to fill his briar with St Bruno. Something about the DDI's expression told Cubbins that there would be no point in attempting to acquire another free fill of tobacco as he had done on the first occasion he had been in the inspector's office. 'You told me, when you came in here the other day, that you picked up a man in Old Street in the early hours of the morning a week ago last Sunday. Is that right?'

'True as I stand here, guv'nor,' said Cubbins.

'True is it?' Hardcastle at last got his pipe alight and blew a cloud of smoke into the air above his desk before looking up at the cabbie. 'D'you know who licenses motor hackney carriage drivers in London, Mr Cubbins?' he asked in a conversational sort of way.

'It's the PCB, ain't it?' Cubbins looked distinctly nervous at this change in the tenor of the conversation.

'The Public Carriage Branch merely arranges the testing of cab drivers and the *issuing* of their licences, Mr Cubbins. They don't actually license them.'

'Oh, don't they?' Cubbins gave his cap a few twists. He failed to understand why Hardcastle was delivering this little homily on the licensing of hackney carriages, and understood even less the subtleties involved.

'It is Sir Edward Henry, the Commissioner of Police of the Metropolis, who licenses cab drivers, Mr Cubbins, and he can take those licences away . . .' Hardcastle flicked his fingers, the noise sounding loud and sharp in the silence that followed this awesome announcement '. . . just like that. All I've got to do is walk across the road to Scotland Yard and knock on his door, and the deed's done.'

Cubbins licked his lips and gave his moustache a brief tug. 'Oh!' he said, in the absence of a more constructive comment.

'And if a cab driver was so foolhardy as to obstruct me, a divisional detective inspector, in the pursuance of my investigation into a case of murder, that cab driver would be without a licence before he could say Jack the Ripper. You follow my drift, Mr Cubbins?'

'Oh indeed I do, sir,' said the anguished Cubbins.

'So, I think we'd better start all over again, don't you?' Hardcastle peered menacingly at the unfortunate cab driver.

'I dunno what to say, guv'nor.' Cubbins was thoroughly alarmed by this sudden aggression.

'The truth, Mr Cubbins, just the truth,' said Hardcastle mildly. 'Now, you didn't pick up no fare in Old Street that morning at all, did you?'

'No, guv.' Cubbins looked extremely sorry for himself.

'Well, I'm waiting.' Hardcastle picked up a dead match

and used it to tease out some loose ash in his pipe which he shook gently into the ashtray before leaning back in his chair and surveying the hapless cabbie.

'I never picked no one up, sir.'

'Aha!' Hardcastle put down his pipe and leaned forward. 'So why did you come in here telling me a pack of lies? Obstructing a police officer in the execution of his duty is a very serious matter,' he added, as encouragement.

'I was approached,' said Cubbins.

'Oh, approached was you? Who approached you?'

Cubbins looked quite wretched now. 'I dunno his name, guv'nor, straight I don't. But he said as how it was very important and it was something to do with winning the war. He said a sergeant would come asking questions and I was to tell him as how I'd picked this gent up at Old Street at a quarter to two on that Sunday morning and taken him down Sloane Square. Very particular about the time he was.'

'And did a sergeant come asking questions, Mr Cubbins?' Hardcastle knew very well that Drew had replaced Catto on the cab enquiry on the express instructions of Superintendent Quinn.

'He was the one what was here last time.' Cubbins's mind was not agile enough to cope with Hardcastle's probing questions. 'Sergeant Drew, I think was his name.'

'So, a mysterious gentleman turns up out of the blue and tells you to lie to the police, and you do it. That's the up and down of it, is it?'

'Well, I mean if it was something that might have helped our brave lads over the other side—'

'Oh shut up, Cubbins,' said Hardcastle crossly.

'Yes, guv.' Cubbins lapsed into silence and gazed mournfully at the cap in his hands.

'Where did this man approach you with this patriotic proposition?'

'On the rank down Victoria Station.'

'When?' Hardcastle's question came out like a whiplash.

Cubbins looked pensively at the ceiling. 'Round about the Wednesday following, I s'pose.'

'The Wednesday following what?'

'The Wednesday following the Sunday when I was s'posed to have picked this gent up.'

'What did he look like, this man who approached you?'

'Looked a right toff he did. A military sort of gent, I s'pose you'd call him. Trim moustache and a bowler hat. Spoke very posh an' all.'

'Know him again, would you?'

'Like as not I would, guv'nor, yes,' mumbled Cubbins, his distress now very apparent.

'And how much did he give you for this favour that you were going to do for him, Cubbins?'

Cubbins glanced at Hardcastle with a foxy expression. 'A flimsy, guv'nor.'

'Five pounds, eh?' said Hardcastle, raising his eyebrows. 'I can see you set a very high price on patriotism, Cubbins. Must have been important.'

'Well, like I said, this gent said as how it was to do with—'

'Yes, I heard you the first time.' Hardcastle shook his head wearily. 'Well, consider yourself lucky, Cubbins, but if you breathe a word of this conversation to anyone, including Sergeant Drew and this military gentleman who kindly gave you five pounds, I shall come looking for you. And the next thing you know, you'll be on the dole, because you won't have a cabbie's licence any more. Come to think of it, you'll more than likely get conscripted under Lord Derby's little scheme and finish up in the army. D'you understand?'

'Oh yes, guv'nor.' Cubbins looked mightily relieved despite having gone several shades paler at the prospect of finishing up in the trenches.

'Because if you do say anything, you could well be damaging the war effort, d'you see?'

'Oh, yes, I do, sir.' Cubbins's cap had now been twisted so often that Marriott, watching from his standpoint in front of the fireplace, thought that it would now be unwearable.

'Right, my lad, you'll now put all that down in writing and sign it. And my sergeant here'll make sure you do.'

'Well, that's half the battle,' said Hardcastle gleefully,

once Cubbins had made his statement and departed. 'Now get Horace Munns . . .'

Hardcastle wasted no time on the second cab driver. 'How much were you given to say that you picked a man up in Sloane Square at two thirty on the morning of Sunday the sixteenth of July, Munns?'

Munns was clearly stunned that Hardcastle knew about the bribe he had been given. 'I, er, well I—' was all he managed to mutter before Hardcastle held up a hand.

'I'll tell you what I told the other cabbie, Munns. Tell me any more lies and you'll be without a licence, and you'll be charged with obstructing the police.'

'How did you know about it, guv?' asked Munns.

'Because I'm a detective and I'm paid to find things out, Munns, that's how. The man you identified down in the cells the other day wasn't the man you picked up because you never picked anyone up. Now, how much were you given?'

'Five pounds, guv'nor,' Munns admitted miserably.

'What did this man look like, the one who obligingly bunged you this fiver?'

Hesitantly Munns described a man who was clearly the same one who had approached Cubbins. 'He said it would be all right, guv. Said it was official an' that. Something to do with the War Office and the defence of the . . .' Munns lapsed into silence, his brow furrowing.

'The defence of the realm is what he probably said.' Hardcastle gazed reflectively at the cabbie sitting hunched on the chair opposite his desk. 'And this man told you the address in Chester Mews you were to pass on to me, did he?'

Munns nodded. 'Yes, guv. An' he made me repeat it, so's I wouldn't forget.'

'Very well.' Hardcastle stood up. 'Take a statement from Mr Munns, Marriott, and then show him out,' he said and, as Munns reached the door, added, 'You will repeat this conversation to no one, d'you understand, Munns. Not to any other police officer and particularly not to this military-looking fellow, should he approach you again.'

80

'Don't you worry on that score, guv'nor,' said the chastened Munns. 'I won't even breathe a word to my old woman.'

'Good,' said Hardcastle. 'By the way, there's a collecting box on the counter of this police station. It's for the widows and orphans of policemen. I get the impression you might like to put some of that five pounds in it.' And he cursed himself for not having made the same suggestion to Arthur Cubbins.

When Marriott came back into the office, there was a wry expression of amusement on his face. 'Well, sir, and what about that?'

'It's no laughing matter,' said Hardcastle. 'I doubt that we'll ever find this military chap, because I don't think he'll want to be found. But the way I see it is that we're deliberately being sold a dummy. I've said it before and I'll say it again. This Spurling came across too easy.'

'So what now, sir?'

'Like I said, Marriott, we're going to pay Spurling a visit, that's what.'

Spurling was as unruffled as ever when he entered the interview room at Brixton Prison, somehow conveying the impression that the escorting warder was a manservant rather than a gaoler. 'Inspector,' he said cheerfully, 'how good to see you.' He sat down and gazed around the sterile room, its drab brown paint made shiny in places where countless people, prisoners and warders, had brushed against it, and then up at the narrow slits of dirty windows beyond the bars at the very top of the walls.

'I've spoken again to the two cabbies who originally claimed to have carried you from Hoxton to Sloane Square and from there to Chester Mews, Spurling,' said Hardcastle, 'and they now deny the story.'

'Then you must have got the wrong cab drivers, Inspector.' Spurling, who as a prisoner on remand was still wearing his own clothes, took a cigarette from a silver case; Hardcastle was surprised when the warder stepped forward and struck a match for him.

'I don't make mistakes of that sort, Spurling,' said Hardcastle, 'not unless someone intends me to make them. Tell me again about the way you accidentally killed Mrs Drummond.'

'I'm not sure that I should, not unless my solicitor is here.' Spurling narrowed his eyes as the smoke drifted up from his cigarette, and then smiled sardonically. 'But I don't mind helping you out.' Slowly, he repeated the story he had originally told Hardcastle. It was word perfect, almost as if he had learned a script.

'Don't take me for a fool, Spurling. Rose Drummond was strangled with a rope, not manually.'

'Then perhaps I didn't kill her after all, Inspector. Perhaps she was still alive and someone else came along and murdered her after I'd taken my cab to Sloane Square.' Spurling seemed quite unperturbed by Hardcastle's revelation.

Hardcastle refused to be riled by the other man's glibness. 'I might have made that mistake, but Dr Spilsbury wouldn't have done,' he said. He had not told Superintendent Quinn about the rope, and it looked as though Quinn's sergeant, Drew, had not done so either. 'Who are you covering up for, Spurling?' Hardcastle leaned forward.

'Covering up, Inspector? What *do* you mean?'

'You know perfectly well what I mean. A mysterious military gentleman approaching cab drivers and suggesting some cock-and-bull yarn that they should spin me. You claiming to have killed Rose Drummond but not having the faintest idea how she met her death. What's going on, Spurling?'

'I don't wish to insult your intelligence, Inspector, but I do think that you've gone off on some flight of fancy. I mean, what more d'you want? I've confessed to killing Rose Drummond, albeit accidentally, and that's that.'

Hardcastle shook his head slowly. 'Oh no, Spurling,' he said, 'that is far from being that, I assure you. But as you've been remanded in custody, you can stay here. And you'll be allowed no visitors apart from your counsel and your solicitor.' He stood up. 'Come along, Marriott, there's work to do.'

In the cab from Brixton to Whitehall, Hardcastle, obviously thinking deeply about the recent interview, remained silent.

But in his office once more, he told Marriott to close the door and take a seat. 'What d'you think, then?' he asked the sergeant.

'He didn't do it, sir.'

'No, Marriott, he didn't. So why did he confess?' Hardcastle shook his head. 'It's all so ham-fisted,' he continued. 'Why have they set me up with a story so thin you could shoot peas through it? I'll tell you this much, Marriott, it's bloody insulting. Do they think I came up the Clyde on a bicycle?'

Marriott declined to be drawn into that particular argument. 'I think they don't want you to get to the real murderer, sir,' he said. 'It seems to me that one of the cloak-and-dagger lot went about bribing cabbies to trot out this cock-and-bull yarn about picking up Spurling, hoping that you'd fall for it. But that still doesn't answer the main question of why they did it. And who is Spurling really? Is he one of them?'

'One of them?'

'Yes, sir. Is he one of the MI5 lot too?'

'You could be right, Marriott,' said Hardcastle thoughtfully, recalling that Charles Smith, the MP, had hinted at it. He began to fill his pipe slowly and methodically. 'I'm getting near the end of my service and I don't expect to be made chief inspector, so I'm fireproof. More or less. But you've a long way to go, m'boy. I don't want you to get in between me and the Special Branch or MI5. They're powerful people, all of them, and a mere detective sergeant could easily be sacrificed if they thought he was getting in the way. I'm going to take them on, but I don't expect you to.'

Marriott grinned. 'I'm game, guv'nor,' he said. 'After all, we're real detectives aren't we? They'll have to get up early to see us off.'

A suggestion of a smile played around Hardcastle's lips and he rubbed his hands together. 'Good,' he said. 'In that case, we'll do two things.'

'And what would they be, guv'nor?' asked Marriott.

'Firstly, we're going to leave Spurling locked up in Brixton Prison. And if necessary, we'll take him all the way to the

Old Bailey and let him stand trial for murder. Just to see what happens.'

'And the second thing, sir?'

'The second thing, Marriott, is that we'll now start looking for the real murderer of Rose Drummond.'

Marriott stood up. 'Or murderess, sir,' he said quietly.

Hardcastle nodded slowly. 'As you say, Marriott, or murderess. But as I've said before, strangling's not a woman's game.'

'There is a war on, sir,' said Marriott jocularly. 'Women are doing all sorts of men's jobs these days.'

Hardcastle did not see the joke. 'We had our chimneys swept yesterday,' he mused. 'D'you know, Marriott, a woman chimney sweep turned up. I thought Mrs Hardcastle was going to have a blue fit. It's bad enough our girl Kitty working on the buses, but a woman chimney sweep. Well, I ask you. Mrs Hardcastle reckoned she was no better than she ought to be.'

Nine

The rain of recent days had given way to sunshine and the temperature in Hardcastle's office had risen quite dramatically. He had opened the windows – startling a lethargic pigeon that had been roosting on the sill – but the lack of a breeze had made no difference to the stifling atmosphere. He ran a finger round the inside of his stiff collar and regretted the convention that required him to wear a waistcoat whatever the weather. 'According to our friend Sergeant Drew,' he said, 'MI5 have been over Rose Drummond's rooms in Artillery Mansions with a fine-tooth comb, so I don't suppose there's any point in our doing it again.'

'I once heard about a bloke who was looking for half a crown in the gutter in Piccadilly Circus, sir,' said Marriott, 'and when someone asked him where he'd lost it, he said Shaftesbury Avenue. So the bloke asked him why he was looking for it in Piccadilly Circus and he said because there was more light there than in Shaftesbury Avenue.'

Hardcastle stared blankly at his sergeant. 'What the blue blazes are you talking about, Marriott?' he asked.

Marriott grinned. 'Well, sir, if MI5 were looking for evidence of spying, they might not have seen something that was connected with the murder.'

Hardcastle ran his hand round his chin and continued to stare at Marriott for some time. Eventually he stood up. 'You might have something there, Marriott,' he said. 'We'll go and have another look.'

There was no sign of Perkins, the porter, but DC Henry Catto was still at the flat.

'Well, lad?' said Hardcastle, 'anything happened?'

'No, sir,' said Catto. 'Nobody's been near the place.'

'Who's covering night duty?'

'DC Wilmot, sir, and he's seen nothing neither.'

Hardcastle nodded. 'Don't think we're going to find any-one coming back here now.' He paused. 'I'll have to think about scrubbing this observation,' he said in an aside to Marriott. 'Perhaps in a week's time,' he added.

Catto, who thought he was about to be released from one of the most boring assignments ever to come his way, groaned inwardly.

On a whim, Hardcastle, followed by Marriott, made for the woman's bedroom and looked around. The bed was made and on the dressing table were an array of the late occupant's scents and cosmetics together with a silver-backed hairbrush and comb. The only evidence of untidiness was a pair of silk stockings draped over the back of a boudoir chair. Hardcastle opened the wardrobe. 'What d'you know about women's frocks, Marriott?' he asked, as he began to move Mrs Drummond's clothing along the rail.

'If my missus is anything to go by, sir, they're expensive, and no matter how many she buys, she always reckons she's never got anything to wear.'

Hardcastle permitted himself a rare smile. 'Just you wait until your daughter grows up, Marriott,' he said, and con-tinued with his examination. 'Now here's an unusual speci-men.' He pulled out a cheap cotton frock and looked at it. 'How tall was Mrs Drummond?' he asked.

'Five feet five,' said Marriott promptly. Unlike Detec-tive Sergeant Drew, he was familiar with the ways of his DDI and knew that he needed to have such facts at his fingertips.

'Bit short for her, isn't it?' Hardcastle handed the frock to the sergeant. 'And there's four more of the same in here. There's some pretty fancy underwear on them shelves, too. I've never seen the like of it in Mrs Hardcastle's wardrobe, I can tell you that. Hold the frock up, Marriott, so's I can have a gander at it.' He surveyed the garment, trying to estimate what it would look like on a woman slightly less than five and a half feet tall. 'What d'you reckon?'

'I'm six feet tall, sir,' said Marriott holding the frock against himself. He pushed one leg out and frowned as he concentrated on the mental arithmetic of the problem. 'That's a good fifteen inches from the ground on me, sir, so on Mrs Drummond it would have been about eight inches off the deck.' He frowned again. 'I'd never let my missus out of the house in a frock that short.'

'No,' said Hardcastle reflectively, 'and Mrs Hardcastle wouldn't have let our girls out in one like it neither.' He continued to gaze at Rose Drummond's frock. 'It's cheap and it's gaudy,' he said, 'and that neckline'd leave a lot on view in a well-built woman. And she was a well-built woman.' He sighed. 'It looks as though she was well at it, wouldn't you say, Marriott?'

'It don't hold water, sir.' Marriott spread the frock on the bed and gazed at it. 'We know she was dressed in something like this when she was found, but if she was the spy that MI5 reckon, there must have been a reason for her getting all dolled up like a dog's dinner. P'raps she was trying her hand at getting a Tommy to talk. After all, Hoxton Square's very near Finsbury Barracks.'

'Have you got some theory about all this, Marriott,' asked Hardcastle, 'or are you just thinking on your feet?'

'Well, sir, forgetting what Spurling told us, which we now know is a load of bunkum, there's no arguing with the fact that she was found dead in Hoxton, and she was dressed like a prostitute.'

'It so happens you're right, Marriott. Colonel Kell said she'd made rough notes about picking up swaddies and getting information out of them. It might be a good idea if we had a word with the military at Finsbury Barracks and see if anyone there remembers having seen her. Could be the topping's down to a Tommy after all. And don't forget that Dr Spilsbury said she'd had recent sexual inter-course.'

'Trouble is, sir,' said Marriott, 'they're like as not over the other side now. Might even be dead after the first day of the Somme.'

Hardcastle glared at his sergeant. 'You're a bloody Job's

comforter, Marriott, that's what you are,' he said, 'and no mistake.'

An immaculate sentry stood at the gate of Finsbury Barracks. Having cast a sly glance at the two detectives, he dismissed the likelihood of their being officers and brought his rifle to the port. ''Alt, who goes there?' he demanded.

'Police,' said Hardcastle tersely.

'Report to the guardroom, pal,' said the sentry out of the corner of his mouth, and brought his rifle down to the 'order' again before standing at ease.

Hardcastle, who did not care to be called 'pal' by anyone, gave the sentry a hostile glare and led the way to the small brick-built structure just inside the gate.

The sergeant of the guard sat behind a desk in the highly polished, sterile guardroom and he also surveyed the two policemen critically; although the younger one might have been a volunteer, the other was clearly too old for military service. 'Help you, gentlemen?' he enquired.

'I want to see whoever's in charge,' said Hardcastle, wrinkling his nose at the overpowering smell of carbolic and floor polish.

'Oh really?' There was an element of sarcasm in the sergeant's voice. 'And what might that be about?'

'I'm Detective Inspector Hardcastle of the Whitehall Division, attached to Scotland Yard, and what it's about needn't concern you, Sergeant,' said Hardcastle, and produced his warrant card; he was in no mood to joust with petty jacks-in-office.

'Ah!' said the sergeant, rising to his feet. 'If you cares to hold on a mo', gents, I'll get a runner.' He turned towards the open door at the rear of the guardroom. ''Oskins,' he bellowed, 'come 'ere.'

A soldier appeared, buttoning up his tunic. 'Yes, sarge?'

'It's sergeant, not sarge,' said the guard commander automatically. 'Put yer bleedin' titfer on and take these gentlemen across to battalion HQ, smartly now. They're to see the CO.'

Lieutenant-Colonel Crombie was an elderly officer who had been 'dug out' from retirement at the beginning of the war and was now responsible for processing recruits to what was still called Kitchener's Army. 'What can I do to assist you, gentlemen?' he asked in a booming voice when Hardcastle had introduced himself and Marriott. He indicated that the two policemen should sit down.

'I'm investigating a murder that took place in Hoxton Square a week ago last Sunday, Colonel,' Hardcastle began.

Crombie nodded. 'Heard something about that,' he said.

'The woman concerned was a prostitute' – Hardcastle had no intention of telling Crombie the real truth about Rose Drummond – 'and her body was found at about two o'clock in the morning—'

'Forgive me for interrupting,' boomed Crombie, 'but is there some suggestion that a soldier from these barracks might be involved in this murder?'

'I don't know who's involved, Colonel,' said Hardcastle, secure in the knowledge that because the police court hearing had been held in camera, it would not be known that Spurling had already been charged with the crime. 'That's why I'm making enquiries.'

'Quite so,' said Crombie.

'May I ask how many soldiers you have here, Colonel?'

Crombie glanced out of the window of his office, across the forest of bell tents that covered Artillery Ground to the south of the barracks. 'In addition to the headquarters staff, about a thousand or so, I imagine,' he said vaguely. 'And I daresay that most of them'll be dead before Christmas.' He sounded resigned to the decimation of the British Army on the fields of Flanders. 'Why, d'you want to interview them all?' The colonel raised an eyebrow and a half-smile played around his lips at such a preposterous thought.

'No, Colonel, just those who may have been out of barracks at the relevant time.'

Crombie grunted. 'Well none of the recruits will have been out. They're granted a walking-out pass from time to time, but they're obliged to be back in barracks by twenty-two-thirty hours. The staff have a permanent pass, of course, and they can stay out until first parade.'

'So they could be out all night on a Saturday,' mused Hardcastle.

'Unless they're on duty, yes.' Crombie leaned forward slightly. 'D'you really think it might have been one of my men, Inspector?'

Hardcastle shrugged. 'Like I said, Colonel, I don't know. That's the point of me being here. Me and Sergeant Marriott, that is. But perhaps I could talk to your permanent staff.'

Crombie raised his eyebrows. 'There's a hundred and twenty of them, Inspector,' he said, 'discounting the officers. I presume you don't suspect the officers.'

'In a murder enquiry, Colonel, I don't discount anyone,' said Hardcastle curtly.

'Mmm! Quite so,' said Crombie. He glanced at the clock on the wall of his office. 'It'll take about half an hour to arrange,' he added, hoping that the delay would dissuade Hardcastle from his intention.

'I daresay it will,' said Hardcastle, and sat back in his chair.

Colonel Crombie picked up his walking stick from where it lay across his desk and rapped sharply on the wall with the crook.

A staff sergeant appeared in the doorway of the colonel's office. 'Sir?'

'Be so good as to give Captain D'Arcy my compliments, if you please, Staff, and ask him and Mr Runciman to see me straightaway.'

Moments later, in a flurry of stamping feet and saluting, the ramrod figure of Regimental Sergeant-Major Runciman appeared in Crombie's office. 'Sah!' he screamed at the top of his voice. The RSM's uniform was immaculate, its creases razor-sharp. Above his left-hand tunic pocket was an array of medal ribbons, and his ammunition boots shone like black glass beneath his tightly wound puttees.

'Mr Runciman, these two gentlemen are from the police.'

'Very good, sir,' roared the RSM, and glanced suspiciously at the two detectives.

'They wish to talk to the permanent staff, as soon as you can arrange it.'

'What, all of them, sir?'

'All of them, Mr Runciman.'

'Sir, very good, sir.' The RSM saluted again, executed a textbook about-turn and marched out of the office.

'Good man, Runciman,' said Crombie. 'Fought in South Africa, you know, and was wounded at Mons. Aching to get back to the front, of course, but I'm afraid he's not really fit enough. Like most of the staff.'

'Really?' said Hardcastle. To him, the RSM had seemed to be bursting with health.

The languid figure of the adjutant, Captain D'Arcy, appeared next. 'You wanted me, Colonel?' he enquired in a tired voice.

'Be so good as to gather the officers together in . . .' The colonel paused momentarily. 'In the mess, I think, in, say, three-quarters of an hour from now, Gerald. The police wish to talk to them.'

'Very good, Colonel.' Evincing no surprise at Crombie's order, D'Arcy nodded and turned on his heel.

For the next fifteen minutes, the colonel made polite conversation about the progress of the war and the disastrous losses at the Somme.

'Permanent staff paraded in the drill shed, sir.' Again stamping and saluting, the RSM reappeared. 'Present and correct and awaiting your inspection.'

'Thank you, Sar' Major.' The colonel picked up his cap and walking stick and led the way out of the office, along corridors and down the stairs. Hardcastle noticed that he had a slight limp. Crossing the parade ground, he finally conducted the two policemen to a large hangar-like building at the edge of Artillery Ground.

The RSM roared a command and the assembled troops crashed to attention.

'Seems a bit unnecessary, all this stamping and shouting, Marriott, don't you think?' whispered Hardcastle in an aside to his sergeant.

Marriott grinned. 'Nearly as bad as Peel House, sir,' he whispered in reply, referring to the training school in Victoria where police recruits were put through a rigorous programme of foot-drill and little else.

'Stand the men easy, Sar' Major,' said Crombie, mounting

91

a low platform, and waiting while Runciman bellowed further orders. 'This is Detective Inspector Hardcastle of Scotland Yard, men,' began the colonel in a voice that carried to the rearmost ranks of the assembled troops, 'and he wishes to ask you some questions.' He turned to Hardcastle. 'It might be better if you came up here, Inspector.'

Hardcastle mounted the rostrum and stared down at the sea of expectant faces, most of them adorned by a waxed moustache. 'A week ago last Sunday, at about two a.m., the body of a young woman was found in Hoxton Square. She had been murdered.'

There was a brief buzz of conversation.

'Stop talking,' roared the RSM.

'My detective sergeant here will now describe the woman to you.' Hardcastle turned. 'Marriott.'

Marriott took out his pocketbook and coughed. 'The woman in question,' he began, 'was aged thirty, or thereabouts. She had a full figure and wore a revealing, red velvet dress with a hem about eight inches off of the ground—'

An anonymous voice said, 'Blimey!' and a lance-corporal whistled quietly. The RSM frowned, and once more screamed, 'Stop talking!'

'She had long brown hair taken up, brown eyes and an oval face.' Marriott went on to list the woman's other salient features before shutting his book and putting it back in his pocket.

'I'm interested to know' – Hardcastle continued – 'if anyone saw this woman loitering near the barracks here, or frequenting public houses in the vicinity.' He whispered to Crombie and received a nod of approval before continuing. 'I'd also be grateful if you could ask around to see if any of the men who were under training here at the time might have seen her either.' He knew it was a vain hope, but in the past he had solved murders with a less encouraging start. 'Thank you for your help, Colonel,' he said, turning once more to Crombie.

'I hope it's been of some assistance, Inspector.' Crombie turned to the RSM. 'You may dismiss the men, Mr Runciman,' he said, and touching the peak of his cap with the crook of his walking stick, led the way to the officers' mess, where Hardcastle and Marriott repeated to the assembled officers what they had just told the men.

'We can find our own way out, Colonel,' said Hardcastle, when he had finished. 'If anything comes of this, perhaps you'd let me know.'

'Of course, Inspector. Good day to you.'

The two detectives had almost reached the gates of the barracks when a corporal caught up with them. 'Beg pardon, sir. Corporal Noakes, sir.'

'What is it, Corporal?' Hardcastle stopped and turned to face the man.

'That woman, sir, the one what you was talking about.'

'What about her?'

'I think I might have spoken to her, sir.'

'Oh? When was this?'

'Must have been a month or more ago, sir.' Noakes looked around as though fearful that he might be seen talking to the 'rozzers'.

Sensing Noakes's reticence, Hardcastle steered him round behind the guardroom where they were shielded from public gaze. 'Go on, Corporal.'

Corporal Noakes relaxed and ran a hand round his mouth. 'I was out on the town, like, sir, a Wednesday it were. I was walking down to the Spread Eagle for a wet, must have been about nine o'clock, I s'pose, when this tart come up to me. I'd swear it was her, sir.'

'Yes, man, and what did she say?'

Noakes grinned. 'She asked me if I was looking for a good time,' he said ruefully, as if somehow he was to blame for being accosted.

'What did you say?'

'I told her to push off, me being a married man an' all.'

Hardcastle smiled inwardly at that. In his experience, soldiers were not usually dissuaded from what they called a bit of 'jig-jig' just because they had a wife and a horde of screaming kids somewhere far away. 'And she went?'

'After a while, sir, yes. She said as how she liked soldiers and was prepared to cut the price, or even do it for nowt. She

93

was going on about how she admired "our brave boys", all that sort o'crap, sir.'

'Did she ask any questions, Corporal?'

Noakes pondered that for a few moments. 'Come to mention it, sir, she did ask when I was going over the other side.'

'And what did you say?'

'I said as how I was permanent here and that with any luck I wouldn't be going no place.' Noakes looked a little guilty. 'It's not as if I ain't done me bit, you see, sir. I got a Blighty one at Neuve Chapelle, that's why I'm here, like.' He tapped his right leg with his swagger cane as if to imply that he had received a wound there. 'Then she asked me when the present intake was moving out, sir.'

'Did you tell her?'

''Course not, sir. Not that I knew, but I wouldn't have let on even if I had.'

'What did she say to that?'

'Seemed to lose interest, sir. Muttered something about having no time for white-feather men and then she told me . . .' Noakes lapsed into an embarrassed silence.

'Then she told you what?'

'Then she told me to piss off, sir, or she'd call the law and say I'd been a-pestering her.'

'What did she sound like?' asked Marriott. 'What sort of voice?'

'That's the strange thing, sir,' said Noakes. 'She never sounded like the ordinary sort of tart. Not common like. It was more of a foreign accent.'

'What sort of foreign accent?' asked Hardcastle sharply.

'Sounded like she was American, sir,' said Noakes.

In the sweltering heat of Finsbury Square, a barrel organ was churning out 'Pack Up Your Troubles', both its operator and his monkey – dressed in red fez and braided waistcoat – looking hot and expectant as the detectives passed by on their way back to Westminster. Hardcastle ignored the pair of them and continued to scour the street for a cab.

'You didn't tell them anything about Rose having had

sexual intercourse just before she was topped, sir,' said Marriott.

''Course not,' said Hardcastle. 'They wouldn't have owned to it, even if they had. Probably have put them off saying anything, specially if they'd worked out that we thought whoever had enjoyed her favours might have done her in.'

'I s'pose so, sir,' said Marriott, 'not that I think we'll get anything out of the soldiers, even so.'

'Probably so, Marriott, probably so,' said Hardcastle gloomily, 'but we've got to cast our bread on the waters, haven't we?' Waiting until two military ambulances had turned out of Chiswell Street, he added, 'Looks like Moorgate and the Underground, Marriott. There ain't a cab anywhere in sight.'

'It's the petrol shortage, sir,' said the sergeant.

'I know what it is, Marriott,' said Hardcastle testily.

Ten

'I really don't know why you found it necessary to speak
to the army at all, Inspector.' Superintendent Quinn
regarded Hardcastle with a disagreeable expression on his
face. 'You've a man in custody for the murder, have
you not?'

'Yes, sir.'

'Well then, why should you want to have Mrs Drummond's
passport so that you can show this corporal her photograph?
We know that she occasionally tried to get information from
soldiers, so it'll take you no further forward.'

'All I have at the moment, sir, is Spurling's confession that
he was the one who topped Mrs Drummond. I don't reckon
as how that'll stand up in court without some corroboration.'
Hardcastle stared truculently at the head of Special Branch.
'Not if Sir Edward Marshall Hall starts having a go at it.'

'But what were you trying to achieve by talking to – what
was it, a hundred and twenty soldiers – about the murder?'

'I was seeking witnesses, sir,' replied Hardcastle stonily.
'Can't have too many witnesses when you're dealing with a
murder,' he added, half to himself.

'You don't seem to realize, man, that you could have
jeopardized a very delicate operation. Colonel Kell's men
aren't fools, you know. They're perfectly aware of what
they're doing, and so am I. You've got your man, so just
concentrate on taking him to court.'

'But don't you think that the gentlemen at MI5 might be
interested in the fact that I found another soldier who Mrs
Drummond was attempting to obtain information from, sir?'
asked the abashed Hardcastle.

'So you say, Inspector, so you say.' Quinn dismissed that

snippet with an impatient wave of the hand. 'But the question your soldier says he was asked is the sort of question anyone might have asked. People are interested in the war, you know. It'll be better for all concerned if you leave spies and spying to those who know what they're about.'

'I don't like it, Marriott,' said Hardcastle. 'I don't like it one little bit. There's something funny going on here.'

'We're not likely to find out what it is, neither, sir,' said Marriott. 'It's almost as if they don't want us to track down the real murderer. Seems like they're willing to send an innocent man to the gallows so's they can play their games.'

Hardcastle grunted. 'We'll see about that,' he muttered, but realized that he had been indirectly criticizing a super-intendent, and that would not do. That would not do at all. 'We'll just have to get on as best we can, Marriott,' he said. He glanced at his watch. 'I think we'll have a walk across to Artillery Mansions, see how young Catto's getting on.'

Yet again, the pair crossed Parliament Square and made their way to Artillery Row. News that a combined force of Australians and British had captured Pozieres was being shouted by a paper boy outside the new Middlesex Guildhall. Despite some of the bitterest fighting so far – by the time it was over the Australians had lost 23,000 officers and men – the crowds seemed to have been imbued with a lightness that had not been apparent during the preceding dreadful weeks.

'It's all very well them cheering, Marriott,' said Hardcastle, 'but it's far from over.' He paused to hand the newsvendor's boy a halfpenny in exchange for the latest edition of the *Star*. At home he had pinned a map, provided by the *Daily Chronicle*, to the kitchen wall and every night brought it up to date with little paper flags representing the warring nations. He had complained when it had become covered in fat splashes but Mrs Hardcastle had been unsympathetic. *If you don't like it, Ernest Hardcastle,* she had said, *move it some place else. I can't be doing with you under my feet when I'm in the kitchen. It gets me all of a doodah.*

As usual, Catto peered suspiciously round the door before opening it fully. 'Oh, it's you, sir,' he said.

97

'Yes, Catto, it's me,' said Hardcastle as he strode into the apartment. 'Well, anything happened, lad?'

'Not a thing, sir. Quiet as the grave.'

'Hmm!' Hardcastle looked displeased at that.

'Are you thinking of taking the observation off, sir?' asked Catto hopefully.

Hardcastle fixed the DC with a grim stare. 'If and when I decide it's going to stop, Catto,' he said, 'you'll be among the first to know. There's been no visitors so far though, is that right?'

'Yes, sir.'

'Well, Marriott,' said Hardcastle, turning to his sergeant. 'Looks as though we're wasting our time hanging about here, though I'm blessed if I know what we're going to do next.'

Marriott suddenly laid a hand on his inspector's arm. 'Listen, sir,' he whispered.

The three figures in the room froze at the sound of a key being turned in the lock of the front door. Silently, Hardcastle indicated to the other two that they should follow him into the bedroom and, once there, he closed the door until there was but the narrowest of gaps between it and the stile. 'Be prepared to pounce,' he whispered, 'when I give the signal.' He applied his eye to the gap but could see nothing. There was the sound of voices, a man and a woman.

Hardcastle threw open the door and, remarkably fast for a man of his bulk, sped into the sitting room. 'And what's going on here, then?' he demanded.

'Who are you?' A tall man wearing a trench coat and carrying a bowler hat was standing in the centre of the room. Beside him was an elegant woman of about thirty attired in a navy blue serge costume with a wide, flared skirt and button gaiters over her shoes.

'We are police officers, and I'm Detective Inspector Hardcastle of the Whitehall Division. Who are you?'

The man appeared slightly disconcerted at discovering three policemen in Rose Drummond's apartment. 'I, er, that is to say, we are from the War Office.'

'Is that a fact?' Hardcastle cast his eye over the two intruders. 'And how did you get a key, might I ask?'

'I don't really think that's any of your business, Inspector,' said the man smoothly.

The woman smiled condescendingly at the three detectives.

'Well, it so happens that breaking and entering *is* my business,' said Hardcastle sternly, refusing to be moved by the man's lofty disdain, 'and right now, I'm minded to run the pair of you in.'

As if to emphasize that he had no intention of being taken anywhere, the man divested himself of his trench coat and laid it across one of the armchairs. The woman slowly withdrew the pins from the large Spanish straw hat she was wearing before taking it off and laying it carefully on a table.

'I think there's been a misunderstanding here, Inspector. I'm Major Fellowes of the War Office.'

'Are you indeed? And why should I believe that?' Hardcastle had no doubt that what Fellowes said was true, but he was irked by the man's high-handed attitude.

Wearily, Fellowes withdrew an official-looking document and handed it to the inspector. 'That should satisfy you,' he said.

Hardcastle examined the paper which testified that Major Cuthbert Fellowes was engaged in special duty at the War Office, and bore the facsimile signature of no less a person than Sir Edward Henry, the Commissioner of Police. Grudgingly Hardcastle returned it. 'That seems to be in order,' he said, 'but what are you doing here?'

Fellowes smiled. 'I'm afraid that's a question you'll have to put to Sir Edward, Inspector,' he said.

'I shall,' said Hardcastle, 'don't you vex yourself about that.'

He glanced at his DC. 'You stay here, Catto. Come, Marriott,' he added, picking up his bowler hat and umbrella.

'I don't think that's a very good idea, Inspector,' said Fellowes to Hardcastle's retreating back.

Hardcastle stopped at the door and turned to face Fellowes. 'When Sir Edward tells me that, I'll have the constable withdrawn, Major,' he said and, irritated that his authority in matters of policing was apparently being flouted, turned once more and marched out followed by Detective Sergeant Marriott.

Hardcastle was in no mood to be browbeaten by Quinn, superintendent or not. 'It's an outrage, sir,' he said.

The Irish policeman gave Hardcastle a tired look. 'I thought I'd made it clear, earlier this morning, Inspector, that there are things going on that you need know nothing about. Anyway, what were you doing in the Drummond apartment?'

'Visiting the constable who's stationed there, sir,' said Hardcastle huffily.

'But you specifically asked for the Special Branch officer I'd assigned to that duty to be withdrawn.' Quinn regarded Hardcastle with a pained expression. 'So why did you consider it necessary to put one of your own men in there?'

'Very simply, sir, because I don't think Spurling's our man. Rose Drummond's keys haven't been found, and Spurling didn't have them in his possession. Not on his person nor in his house at Chester Mews, sir. They was almost certainly taken from her body when she was topped, and whoever killed her must have 'em. My officer was waiting for him to return to Artillery Mansions.'

'And why should he do that?'

'To remove incriminating material, sir.'

'Such as?'

'Such as the little red book which MI5 is at pains to prevent me from seeing.'

Quinn stood up and began to pace around his office. 'Sit down, Inspector,' he said, indicating a chair with an impatient wave of his hand.

Hardcastle seated himself and waited.

Having eventually decided how much he was going to tell Hardcastle, Quinn sat down behind his desk again. 'There is more to this affair than you've been allowed to know so far, Inspector,' he began, 'but it's quite obvious that you'll continue to interfere unless you are acquainted with the facts. Colonel Kell's men know that Rose Drummond was spying for Germany. As I told you earlier, they were within an ace of gathering sufficient evidence for us to prosecute her, when she was murdered. But there was more to it than that. In cases of this nature it is necessary not only to arrest the principal but also anyone with whom she may have been communicating. Now it may be that her murder was unconnected with the espionage, but we cannot be sure. You have Spurling in custody for the killing and that's your job over and done with. But just so you won't go blundering about spoiling a difficult operation, I'll tell you what MI5 are doing. Miss Edith Sturgess – that's the lady you met in Artillery Mansions – works for MI5 and is assuming the identity of Rose Drummond, and Major Fellowes is overseeing what she's doing.'

'And what is she supposed to be doing, sir?'

'She will continue to send information to the German Intelligence Service by the routes employed by Mrs Drummond,' said Quinn. 'Except that it will be false information designed to mislead them.'

'Might she not be at some risk, sir?' Hardcastle wished that he could light his pipe, but he knew that Quinn would never allow it.

'Possibly, but I'm told she's a resourceful woman. In any case, some of Mrs Drummond's informants have been identified and a close watch is being kept on them.' Quinn paused, wondering whether to go further. Eventually, having told Hardcastle so much, he saw no harm in taking the inspector fully into his confidence. 'MI5 have located a hairdresser in Woolwich, close to the Arsenal, and an import-and-export agent in Kingston upon Thames. The man in Kingston lives in Cowleaze Road, which, if you know V Division at all, you will know is almost next door to the Sopwith aircraft factory.' He leaned back in his chair, hands folded across his waistcoat. 'I take it the significance of those addresses does not elude you, Inspector?'

'No, sir, it don't,' said Hardcastle. 'But do you think that Spurling's the man for the topping?' He was still fretting that he had the wrong man in custody.

Quinn afforded Hardcastle one of his rare smiles. 'No doubt of it, Inspector. No doubt of it whatever.' He leaned forward, arms on his desk, fingers interlocked. 'I hope that satisfies you,' he said.

'If you say so, sir,' said Hardcastle, but he was far from convinced that the man sitting in Brixton Prison awaiting trial at the Old Bailey was guilty of the murder of Rose Drummond.

'Very well. You will, of course, say nothing of our conversation to anyone, Inspector. And you will have your man Catto withdrawn from Artillery Mansions immediately.'

'If you say so, sir,' Hardcastle said again and stood up, surprised that Quinn had remembered the name of his detective; he had mentioned him but once, at their first interview, and that was in connection with the fruitless cab enquiries.

'I do,' said Quinn.

'There's just one thing that puzzles me, sir.'

'What is that?'

'How did these MI5 people get hold of a set of keys to Mrs Drummond's apartment?'

Quinn stared into the fireplace. 'There are ways and means, Inspector,' he said mysteriously. 'Ways and means.'

Superintendent Patrick Quinn had not been taking a risk in telling Hardcastle about the two agents identified by Colonel Kell's operatives. At the very moment he was imparting the news to the head of A Division's detectives, Special Branch officers were arresting the two men. By the time Hardcastle had crossed the road from Scotland Yard to his own office at Cannon Row police station, the German spies were safely in custody at Woolwich and Kingston police stations respectively.

'Marriott!' Hardcastle bellowed the first-class sergeant's name as he strode angrily down the corridor. He placed his hat and umbrella on the hatstand and sat down behind his desk, pausing only briefly before pulling out his pipe and scraping at its bowl with a penknife.

'Sir.' Marriott appeared in the doorway.

'Come in and shut the door, Marriott.' Hardcastle stuffed

his pipe with tobacco, a little too firmly he later discovered when he found it would not draw satisfactorily. 'Get across to Artillery Mansions, as soon as you like, and tell Catto to get back here smartly. And tell him I want to see him straightaway.'

'D'you want him replaced with another man, sir?' asked Marriott.

'No, I don't. And warn Wilmot he's not to report there for night duty neither.'

'What's going on then, sir?' Marriott was convinced that Superintendent Quinn had ordered the withdrawal of the observation and was curious to know what had transpired at Hardcastle's interview.

'Nothing's going on, Marriott, that's what,' said Hardcastle testily. 'Them lot across at Special Branch are playing some fancy game that the likes of you and me are not to be made privy to. Now cut along and get hold of Catto.'

It was half an hour before DC Henry Catto reported to Hardcastle, a half-hour during which the inspector had tried vainly to get his pipe to draw. Despite several attempts with a paper clip to clear the stem, he had eventually given up and put the pipe down. It had not improved his temper.

'What happened after Sergeant Marriott and me left there, lad?' he demanded.

'We had a cup of tea, sir,' said Catto innocently.

'Tea, lad, tea?' Hardcastle appeared nonplussed by the detective's reply. 'What d'you mean, you had a cup of tea?'

'Well Major Fellowes went almost as soon as you did, sir, and Edith and me—'

'Edith? Who the hell's Edith?' asked Hardcastle, well knowing who she was, but interested to know how Catto knew.

'Miss Sturgess, sir. She's the lady what was with the major, sir.'

'You seem to have got on friendly terms with her a bit *jildi*, lad.'

Catto grinned. 'She's a very nice lady, sir.'

'And did this nice lady tell you what she was supposed to be doing in Rose Drummond's apartment?'

'Not exactly, sir.'

'Don't fence with me, Catto. Now what did she say? Spit it out, lad.'

'She wouldn't say, sir, except she said it was to do with the war. She said as how she was working for the War Office and it was secret like.'

'Did she indeed? And that's all?'

'Yes, sir.'

'Right, you can go.' Hardcastle picked up his pipe again.

'Back to Artillery Mansions, sir?'

'No, Catto, not back to Artillery Mansions. The observation's off, finished.' Hardcastle stared suspiciously at his subordinate. 'I hope you weren't making a play for Miss Sturgess's favours, lad,' he said menacingly.

'Well, she is a single lady, sir, and I'm unmarried too.'

'I don't give a fig if you're a Trappist monk, Catto,' said Hardcastle, 'you don't go mixing duty with pleasure. Not on my division. Not if you want to stay a detective. Understood?'

'Yes, sir.'

'Right then, bugger off.'

Insofar as the detectives of the Whitehall Division were concerned, that would have been the end of the matter, had it not been for a tragedy that took place three days later.

Eleven

The seventeen constables comprising the early-turn relief of the Rochester Row sub-division in Victoria marched out of the police station at six o'clock precisely. The sun was up already and sweat was forming inside the men's tunic collars, promising a sore neck before the day's shift was out.

'Six beat, fall out,' cried the section sergeant, and Police Constable Albert Travers detached himself from the snaking line of policemen and made for Great Peter Street.

Occasionally trying padlocks and handles in the more deeply recessed doorways, Travers made his slow way along Perkins Rents to Abbey Orchard Street and finally to Victoria Street. For five minutes, he stood on the corner occasionally exchanging good-natured badinage with Whitehall office-cleaners on their way to and from work. He turned left and made his way towards Victoria Station.

At Artillery Mansions, just past the shop where he bought his weekly supply of Old Holborn tobacco and his Rizla papers, Travers was confronted by a man in porter's uniform staring up and down the street.

'Constable, Constable.' The porter started running towards Travers.

'Hold up,' said Travers. 'What are you all in a two-and-eight about?'

'There's been a killing, guv'nor, upstairs.'

'Now just you hold on,' said Travers. 'Who are you for a start?'

'Alf Perkins, I'm the porter here.' Perkins waved a hand towards Artillery Mansions.

'What's all this about a killing, eh?' Legs apart and thumbs tucked under the buttons of his breast pockets, Travers gazed impassively at the porter.

'There's a woman upstairs in the flat where that Rose Drummond lived afore she was murdered. She's dead, I'll swear it.'

'How d'you know about the Drummond woman then?' asked Travers, still disinclined to move until he was in possession of the full facts.

'Had some of your bosses round here, didn't I, a week or two back,' said Perkins breathlessly. 'Poking about they was, and then there was a "busy" sitting in the place for about a week.'

Travers sighed. 'S'pose I'd better take a look,' he said reluctantly. A murder before breakfast was something he could do without. Apart from having to stay there until the CID moved themselves to arrive, it would undoubtedly involve him in the writing of a statement; and Travers wasn't very good at writing.

Perkins led the policeman up to the fourth floor by which time Travers was puffing laboriously. 'Strewth!' he said, 'that was some climb.'

'Soon get used to it when you does it a dozen times a day,' said Perkins, showing no sign of physical distress.

'Now then, hold on,' said Travers when they reached the door of the late Rose Drummond's apartment. 'Before we goes barging in, just tell me what you done to find this body you reckons is in here.' The policeman leaned against the wall, still attempting to recover his breath.

'I was doing me rounds like,' said Perkins, 'what I always does first thing in the morning, when I comes across this door. Open it were.'

'What did you do then?'

'I went in, didn't I? I mean, it was a bit odd finding the door open at that time of the morning.'

'And what time would that be then?'

Perkins pulled out a cheap watch and stared at it. 'Must have been about twenty minutes ago,' he said. 'Round about six o'clock, give or take.'

Travers ran a hand round his chin. 'Well, I s'pose we'd

better have a gander then.' He peered closely at the door jamb. 'No sign of a forced entry,' he said, and pushed the door ajar. 'And mind where you're putting your hands. The CID won't want to find your fingerprints all over the shop.'

There was no sign of a body in the sitting room and Travers turned to Perkins. 'Where's this body of yours then, matey?' he asked.

'In the bedroom, guv'nor.' Perkins pointed at a door on the other side of the room.

Travers pushed it gently so that it swung silently on its oiled hinges. In the centre of the bed, on top of the counterpane, was the body of a fully dressed woman. Her eyes stared sightlessly at the ceiling and her tongue was protruding. 'Gawd save us,' muttered Travers, tugging at his moustache as he moved a step closer. He took hold of the woman's wrist, feeling for a pulse he knew instinctively would not be beating. 'Yeah, she's a dead'un all right,' he said. 'Pretty-looking thing an' all.' He turned towards Perkins. 'You connected to the telephone?' he asked.

'Yeah, got one in me office,' said Perkins.

'Right then. You got a key for this place?'

'No,' said Perkins. 'Your boss took the only one what I had.'

'In that case, you'd better nip downstairs and call the station for me while I wait here. Tell 'em PC one–one–four's got a murder on his hands and to get someone round here a bit sharpish.'

'There's another rasher of bacon going begging, Ernie,' Mrs Hardcastle called from the kitchen. 'Do you want it?'

Hardcastle had just finished his breakfast and was sitting in his shirtsleeves casting an eye over the depressing headlines of the *Daily Mail*, propped against an HP Sauce bottle, when there was a knock at the door.

'No thanks, love.' Hardcastle rose from his chair, wiping his mouth on a table napkin.

'You're wanted at Cannon Row straightaway, sir.' A constable from Kennington Road police station stood on the doorstep.

'Is that a fact?' said Hardcastle. 'What's it about, did they say?'

By way of an answer, the constable handed Hardcastle a message form. 'Something about a murder, sir,' he said.

Hardcastle grunted and ran his eye over the sparse details the message contained. 'Well I'll be buggered,' he said, as he recognized the Artillery Mansions address.

'Ernest!' Mrs Hardcastle only used her husband's full name when she was offended by him, and that included when he swore. 'I'll thank you to keep your barrack-room language for your police station.' Alice Hardcastle had never set foot in a barrack room, but her father had served as an artillery man in India.

'Sorry, dear,' said Hardcastle over his shoulder, and handed the form back to the constable. 'Righto, lad,' he said, but paused as he turned from the door. 'Best call me a cab, there's a good chap.'

'Very good, sir.' The constable saluted and set off to find a taxi.

By the time Hardcastle had donned his jacket and bowler hat and had given Mrs Hardcastle a perfunctory peck on the cheek, the cab was waiting outside. 'Cannon Row police station,' he said. 'No, better still, make straight for Artillery Mansions in Victoria Street.'

Marriott, who lived in police quarters in Regency Street, five minutes walk away from the scene of the murder, was already there.

'Well, Marriott, what's this all about?'

Briefly, Marriott outlined what PC Travers had found and what the police had done so far, which in fact amounted to little more than calling the divisional surgeon.

'Who is it, d'you know?' asked Hardcastle.

'Yes, sir. It's the woman who turned up with that Major Fellowes the other day when we was here.'

Hardcastle nodded. 'I thought as much,' he said, and began to mount the stairs to the fourth floor. 'Morning, doctor. What d'you make of it?' He shook hands with the surgeon and then glanced at the body.

'My first thoughts are that it's manual strangulation,' said

108

the surgeon, waving a hand at the body. 'There doesn't seem to be any signs of a struggle. I'd say it was a strong man who killed her.' He began packing his instruments back into his Gladstone bag.

'Any ideas about the time of death?' Hardcastle knew that it was asking a lot of the divisional surgeon to give such an estimate before the post-mortem examination, but at least he might be imposed upon to make a broad guess.

'Rigor mortis is fully established,' said the surgeon with a shrug. 'That means anything between twelve and twenty-four hours. Given that she's a slender woman, it might be less. Sorry I can't be more helpful than that. I'll let Dr Spilsbury have my findings of course.' He paused. 'I suppose he'll be doing the PM, will he?'

Hardcastle turned from his study of the body and nodded to the divisional surgeon as the latter made to leave the apartment. 'Yes,' he said, at that moment having made up his mind on the point. 'Marriott, see if you can get hold of Dr Spilsbury, tell him we need his attendance as soon as he can get here, because I'll wager this is going to cause a bit of a stink. And find Catto. Where is he, d'you know?'

Marriott looked at his watch. 'Likely arriving at the nick now, sir,' he said. 'I'll get a message sent.'

Having searched the apartment previously, Hardcastle was familiar with what should be there and where it should be, and he spent the next thirty minutes looking around. Nothing was out of place and, as the divisional surgeon had said, there was no sign that a struggle had taken place. Neither, as Police Constable Travers had discovered, was there any sign of the apartment having been broken into, and that worried Hardcastle more than anything else. He came across a handbag that he presumed belonged to the dead woman, but it contained no details of her identity; in the circumstances, that was not surprising. Not that it mattered; he knew who she was.

When DC Henry Catto arrived, Hardcastle took him straight into the bedroom. 'Someone's topped Edith Sturgess, Catto,' he said.

'Oh my oath!' said Catto, staring at the dead woman. 'What a waste.'

'Did you have any contact with her after you left her the day you were withdrawn from the observation?' asked Hardcastle.

'No, sir.'

'Sure?'

'Certain as I'm standing here, sir.' Catto wondered whether the DDI was harbouring suspicions about him. 'Never had no cause to, sir,' he added.

'And she never got in touch with you?'

'No, sir. I know I said she was a good-looking woman, but you said I shouldn't go mixing duty with pleasure.' Catto paused reflectively. 'Pity that Major Fellowes never agreed to having me stay here, sir,' he said. 'Might have prevented this happening.'

'You might be right, Catto,' said Hardcastle. 'But any way up, Major Fellowes is going to have a bit of explaining to do.' He looked round as Marriott came back into the room. 'Well?'

'Dr Spilsbury's on his way, sir.'

It was with a certain misguided and vindictive relish that Hardcastle waited outside Superintendent Quinn's office later that morning. At twenty-seven minutes past nine, a detective constable wearing a tight-fitting blue serge suit and a celluloid collar came hurrying along the corridor. 'Mr Quinn's just arrived, sir,' he said.

Minutes later, the bearded figure of Quinn, attired in the raincoat and silk top hat for which he was renowned, came striding down the corridor towards his office, umbrella tapping the floor with every second pace. 'Ah, Mr Hardcastle,' he said, not slackening his progress, 'and what brings you here so early?'

Hardcastle forbore from mentioning that, in his book, half-past nine was not exactly early. 'There's been another murder, sir, one I think you might be interested in.'

'Is that so, Inspector? You'd better come along in then.' Quinn seemed in a jovial mood and, as he handed his coat and hat to the duty DC, told him to bring an extra cup of tea. 'Well now, you'd better sit yourself down and tell me all about it,' he said, and settled himself behind his huge desk. 'Sit down, man, sit down.'

'At approximately six twenty this morning the constable on six beat, on Rochester Row's ground, was called to the apartment previously occupied by Mrs Drummond in Artillery Mansions, sir,' began Hardcastle.

'Oh?' Quinn's face suddenly assumed a serious expression. 'Go on.'

'And he found the dead body of Miss Edith Sturgess, sir.'

Quinn's mouth opened as he stared disbelievingly at the inspector. 'Holy Mary, mother of God!' he said eventually. 'And what are your initial conclusions, Inspector?'

'She'd been strangled, sir.'

The duty DC reappeared bearing a tray with two cups of tea on it. It was a requirement that the superintendent's tea was always brewed at exactly nine thirty each morning. 'I didn't know if you took sugar and milk, sir,' he said to Hardcastle, 'so I've put some of each on the tray.'

'Don't bother with that now,' said Quinn sharply. 'Who's the duty officer this morning?'

'Detective Inspector Gibson, sir.'

'Send him in, now.'

Moments later Gibson knocked on the door and entered. 'You wanted me, sir?'

'Ah, Gibson. Get on to MI5 at the War Office and tell them that I wish to see Major Fellowes in person as a matter of great urgency.'

As the door closed behind Gibson, Quinn started to stir his tea. 'This is going to cause a great deal of trouble, Inspector,' he said, echoing the comments that Hardcastle had earlier made to Marriott. 'A great deal of trouble indeed.'

'I imagine so, sir.' Hardcastle derived no great pleasure from Quinn's obvious agitation; he knew that, as divisional detective inspector of A Division, it would fall to him to investigate this latest murder.

Quinn took a sip of tea. 'Tell me everything you know, Inspector,' he said, and for the next few minutes listened carefully as Hardcastle described the actions of the police from being called by the porter at Artillery Mansions, to the arrival of Dr Spilsbury.

Detective Inspector Gibson had obviously stressed the urgency of Quinn's request; when the head of Special Branch said that he had something of grave importance to discuss with an officer of MI5, it was taken seriously.

A quarter of an hour later, Major Fellowes strode into the office. 'Good morning, Superintendent.'

'Good morning to you, Fellowes,' said Quinn. 'I think you've met Hardcastle.'

'Yes,' said Fellowes, and afforded Hardcastle the briefest of nods before sitting down, uninvited, in the only other vacant chair. 'Your man said you wanted to see me urgently.' Something in Fellowes's attitude implied that he did not take kindly to being summoned by a mere superintendent. In common with the public at large, he had been misled into believing that Basil Thomson was the head of Special Branch, whereas he was the assistant commissioner in overall charge of the whole of the CID.

'Edith Sturgess has been murdered, Fellowes,' said Quinn without preamble.

'What?' Fellowes was clearly stunned by this news. 'Murdered? What d'you mean, murdered?'

Quinn sighed. 'Hardcastle's investigating it,' he said. 'He'll tell you what the police know so far.'

Briefly, Hardcastle related, yet again, what he knew of the death of Edith Sturgess.

'My God, this is terrible news. She was a trusted agent,' said Fellowes, his face ashen. 'There is something extremely sinister in all this,' he gabbled on. It was very apparent that he feared Colonel Kell was going to lay the greater part of the blame for Edith Sturgess's death on his shoulders and he was trying desperately to recall everything he had done and said since her installation in Rose Drummond's apartment. 'This is going to set us back quite a way,' he continued, as his mind worked furiously, attempting to retrieve something from the wreckage of his plan to delude the German Intelligence Service. 'It's a disaster,' he muttered.

'I can see that,' said Quinn, 'but what concerns the police

at the moment is to discover the identity of her murderer, and Hardcastle here is going to need all the help he can get.'

Hardcastle was cheered by that statement. It seemed that, at last, Quinn was becoming a little weary of the shadowy escapades of the cloak-and-dagger branch of the War Office. He decided to take advantage of it immediately. 'When did you last see Miss Sturgess, Major?' he asked.

'What?' Fellowes looked distractedly at the head of A Division's CID. 'What did you say?'

'I asked when you last saw Miss Sturgess, Major.'

'Yesterday morning, Inspector, at about ten thirty, I suppose.'

'And where was that?'

Fellowes shot a glance in Quinn's direction.

'You may confide in Hardcastle,' said Quinn. 'He's a trusted officer.'

'I met her in St James's Park, near the bandstand,' said Fellowes. 'To give her instructions.'

'Why St James's Park? Why not at the apartment in Artillery Mansions?' Hardcastle knew the answer to that, but he too was becoming a little tired of Fellowes's hole-and-corner antics, had, in fact, taken a dislike to him from their first meeting.

'So as to preserve Miss Sturgess's cover,' said Fellowes reluctantly. 'It wouldn't have done for me to be seen entering her apartment.'

'Well, someone's destroyed her cover now, with a vengeance,' said Hardcastle, with a certain measure of delight, and noted the brief smile that crossed Quinn's face. 'Anyway, if you were so concerned about her cover, why did you go there with her in the first place?'

'Procedure,' said Fellowes curtly.

Hardcastle smiled at that; it was evident that Fellowes was floundering. 'What did you see her about, Major, at this meeting of yours in St James's Park?'

'Operational matters,' said Fellowes loftily. Clearly he was not going to be drawn further on that.

It was of no importance anyway and Hardcastle let it go.

'Did she say anything about having met anyone, or having had any visitors at the apartment?' he asked.

'No, not at all.' Despite Quinn's assurance, Fellowes was still very reticent about discussing secret activities with an ordinary detective inspector.

'I may have to see you again later on, Major Fellowes,' said Hardcastle.

'Yes, of course,' said Fellowes. 'Incidentally, I'd be grateful if you'd keep me informed, Inspector, of the progress of your enquiries and particularly of anyone who becomes a suspect. It may well be someone who has already come to our notice.'

Hardcastle stood up. 'Well there's one thing we can be sure of,' he said.

'Oh?' said Fellowes.

'Yes,' said Hardcastle. 'At least Roger Spurling's not a suspect, because he's still sitting on his arse in Brixton nick. And sure as eggs is eggs, he won't have been let out for a night on the town.'

Twelve

Hardcastle had no sooner returned to his own office above Cannon Row police station than he was sent for by the assistant commissioner. With a sigh, he donned his hat, snatched up his umbrella and crossed the courtyard yet again.

Basil Thomson's large office, off the main corridor of Scotland Yard, enjoyed a magnificent view over the river. Thomson was staring out of the window at a string of barges making their ponderous way to the Pool of London when Hardcastle was shown in.

'Ah, Hardcastle, take a seat.' Thomson turned from the window.

'Thank you, sir.' It was the first time that Hardcastle had been in the assistant commissioner's office and he looked around at the ornaments on the high wooden mantelshelf, at the pictures on the walls and at the various certificates and gifts that Thomson had accumulated over the years.

Thomson sat down behind his desk. 'Well now, tell me all about the murder of Miss Sturgess, Hardcastle,' he said, and leaned back in his chair, an expectant expression on his face.

For the third time that morning, Hardcastle repeated his account of the investigation so far.

Thomson listened intently, nodding from time to time, and occasionally pulling at one of the pendulous lobes of his large ears. 'And what are your thoughts about this dreadful affair, Hardcastle?' he asked, when the DDI had finished.

Hardcastle took a deep breath. He knew how many detective officers were senior to him and he knew how much service he had left to complete before he was obliged to retire, and he had deduced that, come what may, his chances of promotion to detective chief inspector were extremely slim. He decided to speak his mind. 'I think I'm being obstructed in my enquiries, sir,' he said.

Thomson's bushy eyebrows shot up a fraction of an inch. 'Really? What d'you mean by that?'

'Well, I speak as I find, sir, and first off I wasn't allowed to see the names in the book that was found in Rose Drummond's rooms. I was fed bits of it, and then I had Spurling steered in my direction as a likely suspect for the topping, but I've been a CID officer for too long to fall for that.'

'Fall for what?' asked Thomson, an amused expression on his face.

Hardcastle explained about the two cab drivers and their stories of the mysterious military-looking man – he was certain now that it had been Major Fellowes – who had bribed them into making false statements to the police. He mentioned that Spurling's account of how he had supposedly killed Mrs Drummond was at odds with the evidence; and the fact that Spurling did not seem at all concerned when charged with murder. No longer caring what he said to the assistant commissioner he told him what Spurling's neighbours had said of his arcane activities and that Sergeant Drew of Special Branch had clearly not made the enquiries he had claimed to have made.

When he had finished there was a long silence, during which Hardcastle decided that he had probably just put paid to his career.

Thomson smiled and leaned forward. 'I know,' he said.

Hardcastle stared at the assistant commissioner in disbelief. 'You *know*, sir?'

'Yes. You see, Hardcastle, we – that is to say, MI5 and Special Branch – were at pains not to endanger a particularly delicate operation that was being conducted jointly by our two departments. It was imperative that Mrs Drummond's death was kept a secret, and you helped enormously in that regard, until such time as we were able to arrest the two spies now awaiting trial.' Unbeknown to Hardcastle, even now he was being told only half the story.

'Would that be the hairdresser in Woolwich and the man at Kingston, sir?'

'The same.'

'Does that mean that Spurling is innocent, sir?'

'Roger Spurling – Commander Spurling of Naval Intelligence, to give him his correct title – was deliberately used as a decoy, Hardcastle. We didn't want you arresting a murderer who was going to make a fuss and send for his solicitor or get in the papers, all that sort of nonsense. We can't pretend that a murder didn't occur, you see, not even these days. There had to be a murderer, so, just in case it did get out, we had to have a suspect who was reliable. If it's any consolation, I'm sorry that we found it necessary to delude you. It's not that we underestimated your intelligence, or for that matter, your detective ability, but we couldn't afford to take any risks.'

Hardcastle was furious that he had been made to look a fool. 'But that means that the man who murdered Rose Drummond is still at liberty, sir. And very likely he murdered Edith Sturgess, too.'

Thomson nodded gravely. 'I don't doubt that you're right, Hardcastle,' he said, 'but in time of war the rights of the individual must be subordinated to those of the State, d'you see?'

Hardcastle shook his head. 'I don't see the point of it all, sir,' he said.

'Perhaps not, but I can assure you it was essential to safeguard the operation. Unfortunately, it was not visualized that the killer would go to Artillery Mansions and murder Miss Sturgess. At first, it was thought that Rose Drummond had fallen victim to someone she had met at Hoxton, a soldier perhaps, and I think possibly that was your view too. At the outset, there was no indication that her murderer might have known where she lived—'

'Whoever he was stole her handbag and her keys, sir,' interrupted Hardcastle, 'and it looks as though he used those keys to gain entry.'

'Assuming that she was carrying either in the first place,' said Thomson smoothly.

'Don't see how else she was going to let herself back into

her rooms, sir,' said Hardcastle churlishly. 'We looked under doormats and all that sort of malarkey, just to see if she'd left a key there, but there was nothing. And we know she wasn't in the habit of getting Perkins to let her in.'

Thomson nodded. 'Maybe so, Hardcastle, maybe so,' he said, 'but the important thing now is for you to find this killer and bring him to justice.'

Hardcastle shook his head. It was common knowledge that Thomson, a barrister, had been Prime Minister of Tonga and, later, Governor of Dartmoor Prison before coming to Scotland Yard. If only he had been a detective, thought Hardcastle, he would not have assumed that a murder enquiry could just be picked up weeks after it had happened and solved in the twinkling of an eye. 'I'll do my best, sir,' he said resignedly.

'That's all I ask, Hardcastle. Now is there anything you need in the way of assistance?'

'I would like to know all that was in Mrs Drummond's red book, sir, and I would like my questions answered by these people at MI5 who seem so intent on stopping me from finding the real murderer.'

Thomson stood up and skirted his desk to place a reassuring hand on Hardcastle's shoulder. 'I shall speak to Colonel Kell about it straightaway,' he said.

'And Commander Spurling, sir? What about him?'

'Oh, I think it might help your enquiries if we left him where he was for a moment,' said Thomson with a bleak smile. 'Go and see Mr Quinn this afternoon. He'll tell you what he wants you to do next.'

Hardcastle was in a foul mood when he returned to Cannon Row. The condescending attitude of Thomson, who clearly took him for a Dogberry but pretended he did not, still rankled. The Drummond murder enquiry had gone cold, but he was expected to find her killer just the same. On top of everything else, he was now faced with the killing of Edith Sturgess, a death which in his view need never have happened if only those clever buggers at MI5 – yes, and at the Yard – had listened to him in the first place.

'Marriott!'

'Yes, sir?' DS Marriott's face appeared round Hardcastle's office door.

'What's happening?'

'Dr Spilsbury's doing the PM now, sir, at Westminster Mortuary. Says he'll let us know the moment he's got something.'

'I've got to see Superintendent Quinn at two o'clock and then we'll start.'

'Start, sir?' Marriott was always mystified by Hardcastle's sudden pronouncements.

'Yes, Marriott. Tell Catto to bring Perkins over here. I'm going to give him a talking to, cheeky bugger.'

'Right, sir.' Marriott wondered what the porter at Artillery Mansions had done to upset the DDI.

'And when you've done that, come back here. You can buy me a pie and a pint down the Red Lion.'

'Well now, Mr Hardcastle, I understand that you had quite a frank discussion with Mr Thomson.' Quinn, a half-smile on his face, turned from his bookcase as the DDI came into his office.

'I explained to him what I needed, sir,' said Hardcastle bluntly.

For some moments, Quinn fingered his beard and looked thoughtfully at Hardcastle. 'Yes, well he's asked me to do what is necessary to assist you,' he said. 'Sit yourself down.'

Hardcastle sat stiffly in the chair opposite Quinn's desk and waited.

'There's a problem, Inspector.'

'There is that, sir,' said Hardcastle.

'Oh, not with your murders. I'm talking about MI5's operation.'

'I thought that was all over and done with, sir.'

'Not at all, man, not at all. Y'see, MI5 are anxious to carry on the pretence that Mrs Drummond is still alive, and that she's still gathering information that might be of value to the enemy. There is a particular reason behind it, a particular

119

suspect, and that was the whole point of putting Miss Sturgess in the Drummond apartment, but I've explained all that to you before.'

Hardcastle began to think that he was going to be thwarted yet again. 'But I understood that the two spies, them at Kingston and Woolwich, had been arrested, sir.'

'That they have, Mr Hardcastle, but they were small fry. What's been decided on now, is that a letter will be sent to Mrs Drummond's contact in Ireland' – Quinn shook his head despairingly at the thought that another of his countrymen was a traitor – 'telling him that she's moved. MI5 are going to put their new woman in another part of London and we'll wait and see what happens. Or rather, you'll wait and see what happens.'

'Seems to be a funny way of carrying on, sir,' said Hardcastle.

'Inspector, there's a lot about spying you don't know.'

'I wasn't thinking about spying, sir, I was thinking about solving murders, and I don't see that waiting in an empty apartment is likely to do the trick.'

Quinn waved a deprecating hand. 'Glory, man, I wasn't suggesting that's what you should do. Of course you must go about it the way you think fit. I was just explaining to you what the MI5 officers are doing. As you complained to Mr Thomson that you were being kept in the dark,' he added with a frown.

'I understood from Mr Thomson, sir, that Commander Spurling is to be left in custody.'

'Is that what he said?' Quinn looked mildly surprised at that. 'Well, if that's what he wants, then so be it.' He did not seem in the least concerned about the plight of the naval officer who was still confined in the austere conditions of the remand wing at Brixton Prison. 'It's all in the service of His Majesty and he'll still be getting his pay.'

'I asked Mr Thomson for details of what was in the red book, sir,' Hardcastle continued.

Quinn stood up and walked to the safe. Moving the notorious Casement diaries to one side, he took out a slender file and laid it on his desk. 'There's not much here to whet your appetite, Inspector,' he said, and withdrew a sheet of paper. 'This list turned out to be in two parts. The three names you were given were probably those people in high places that Mrs Drummond had a mind to cultivate.' He paused and the hint of a smile played around his lips. 'In her bed, no doubt. But the rest, and they amount to seven in all, are the names of those she used as informants, or so we believe. As you know, the hairdresser at Woolwich and the man at Kingston have now been arrested.' He glanced up at Hardcastle. 'As for the rest, MI5 are still working on them, but they think that they too are pretty unimportant.'

'Do I get to see the list, or to talk to the people whose names are on it, sir?'

'Within a few days, Inspector. I agreed to give MI5 that long so that they could either arrest the others or eliminate them.'

'Eliminate them, sir?' There was surprise in Hardcastle's voice and he wondered if Quinn had meant precisely what he said.

'From their enquiries, man,' said Quinn testily. 'MI5 don't go around assassinating people.'

Hardcastle was beginning to have doubts about that; from what he had seen of the tortuous workings of MI5, he would not have been surprised at anything they got up to. 'I should like to interview Major Fellowes, sir.'

Quinn, seated behind his desk once again, frowned. 'What for?'

'Because he seems to be the only one who knows anything about Edith Sturgess, sir. And I've got to start somewhere.' Hardcastle decided to put forward a theory that no one else in the esoteric world of espionage seemed to have thought of. 'There is always a chance that Miss Sturgess's murder had nothing to do with her being a decoy, sir. For example, she might have been murdered by an acquaintance.'

For some moments, Quinn stared at the inspector. 'D'you really think so, man?' he asked eventually.

'No, sir, but—'

'Well what, then?'

'I was only suggesting that I've got to go down every road,

sir, that's all. And a surprising number of people have got themselves murdered by someone they knew.'

'Quite probably, Inspector,' said Quinn, only too conscious that a career spent in Special Branch had not fitted him to discuss the finer points of murder. 'Well, you must do what's necessary. I'll arrange for Major Fellowes to make himself available. When would you be wanting to see him?'

Hardcastle made a point of withdrawing his watch from his waistcoat pocket. 'Shall we say eight o'clock this evening, sir?'

'I hope you're not thinking of making things awkward for our friends at MI5, Inspector,' said Quinn, but there was the beginning of a smile on his face as he said it.

'Certainly not, sir.' Hardcastle briefly wound his watch and dropped it back into his pocket. 'But I have a lot to do, to catch up on things which I was stopped from doing before.'

'Quite so, Inspector,' said Quinn. 'Quite so.'

Hardcastle felt much happier back on his own ground and by the time he returned to his office the porter from Artillery Mansions was waiting. 'Well, Perkins, what have you got to tell me?'

'Tell you, guv'nor? What can I tell you?' Perkins seemed less confident than he had been when first he had met the DDI. The daunting atmosphere of the police station and the cold austerity of the interview room – Hardcastle had set their meeting there rather than in his office – appeared to have had their effect on the man.

'Two murders have taken place, Perkins,' said Hardcastle. 'One was in Hoxton Square – Mrs Drummond who lived in your place – and the second actually took place in her apartment. Now then, what d'you know about it?'

Perkins licked his lips. He had a nasty suspicion that Hardcastle was wondering whether he had had any part in it. 'It was nothing to do with me, guv'nor, so help me,' he said despairingly.

'This morning you found a dead body in the late Mrs Drummond's apartment, Perkins, so don't tell me that it's nothing to do with you. Now then, what time was you up and about, eh?'

Perkins sniffed. 'Must have been about five-ish,' he said. 'That's when I'm usually up and about, to let the cleaners in, see?'

'Cleaners? What cleaners are they?'

'There's some chars what comes in about then, guv'nor. There's a couple of regular women what does the halls and the stairs and landings, and then there's some what has a private arrangement with the tenants.'

'Are you telling me that some of your residents have cleaners coming in at five in the morning? They don't strike me as the sort of people that'd be up at that time.'

'No, I never meant that,' said Perkins, already being cowed into making inaccurate statements.

'Well, what *did* you mean, then?' Hardcastle posed the question aggressively.

'Well, the hall, stairs and landing women come in then, and some of them do some of the apartments when they've finished. Much later on. Then we gets others what come in later, like.'

'And who was the cleaner that did Mrs Drummond's apartment?'

Perkins thought deeply for a moment. 'That'd be Daisy Watkins, sir,' he said eventually, and with some reluctance, 'but she never come after Mrs Drummond got herself done in.'

'Who told her to stop coming?'

'I did.' Perkins shot a guilty glance at the inspector.

'Oh? And whose idea was that, then?'

'Well, mine, sir. I mean there'd have been no one to pay her wages, would there?'

Hardcastle grunted. It was difficult to argue with the logic of that. 'This Daisy Watkins, where does she live?'

'Strutton Ground, guv'nor, just round the corner.'

'I know where Strutton Ground is,' growled Hardcastle. 'What number?'

'Fourteen, I think, over the pie shop.'

Hardcastle glanced across the room to where his sergeant

was sitting, taking notes. 'Get her round here and have a talk to her, Marriott. This evening if you can.' He paused. 'No, on second thoughts, we'll go there and have a chat with her after I've seen—' He broke off abruptly, suddenly remembering that Major Fellowes's name ought not to be mentioned in front of Perkins. 'After the interview I've got at eight o'clock.' He returned his attention to the porter. 'I haven't finished with you yet, my lad,' he said. 'We'll be having another little chat, tomorrow most likely.'

Perkins thought that might be the case, but said nothing. He was nervous at what might come out of Hardcastle's interview with Daisy Watkins and wished he had not mentioned her, but his concern had nothing to do with the murder of Edith Sturgess.

Thirteen

'I do have another appointment, Inspector,' said Major Fellowes, even before Hardcastle had invited him to sit down.

Hardcastle was in no mood for MI5 officers who thought that they were superior to policemen. 'Major Fellowes,' he said, 'I am investigating the murders of Rose Drummond and Edith Sturgess, and I have had enough of being buggered about by people who think they know my trade better than I know it myself. And don't forget that Miss Sturgess was one of your own officers, or so I've been told.'

'I don't need reminding of that, Inspector,' said Fellowes as he hung his hat and umbrella on Hardcastle's hatstand. 'But you have to remember that we're fighting a war and Miss Sturgess was another casualty of it, as are the thousands at present being killed at the Somme.' He sat down opposite the DDI and crossed his legs. 'D'you mind if I smoke?' he asked, and took out a gun-metal cigarette case as if to brook no refusal.

'Not at all.' Hardcastle picked up his pipe and worried the ash with his letter opener. 'I must say that you seem to have adopted a rather casual attitude to this business,' he said, 'and although you might think that Miss Sturgess was a casualty of war, as you put it, I'd remind you that she was murdered. She didn't fall in action.'

'Do you know that for a fact, Inspector?' Fellowes selected a Turkish cigarette and lit it with a lighter fashioned from a rifle cartridge case. 'What can I do to assist you?' Although his attitude softened a little, he sounded as though helping Hardcastle could not have been further from his mind.

'You can start by telling me something of Miss Sturgess's background.'

Fellowes raised an eyebrow. 'Of what possible use could that be to your investigation?' he asked.

Hardcastle puffed out a cloud of pipe smoke and leaned back in his chair, surveying the army officer opposite him with an expression of near sympathy. 'How long have you been with MI5, Major?' he asked.

For a moment it appeared that Fellowes was not going to answer, but then he relented, probably because Colonel Kell had emphasized the need for co-operation with the police. 'Almost a year,' he said gruffly.

Hardcastle nodded. 'Well, I've been a detective for twenty years, and four years as a beat-duty man before that,' he said, 'and during that time I've investigated nearly every crime in the calendar, not a few murders among them. One of the things I've learned is that you can't leave any stone unturned, something you people at the War Office might bear in mind when you're thrashing about looking for spies.'

'Inspector, I didn't come here for a lecture,' said Fellowes, 'and, as I said earlier, I do have another appointment.'

'Then let's not waste time, yours or mine,' snapped Hardcastle. 'Tell me about Miss Sturgess.'

'What exactly d'you want to know?' asked Fellowes mildly, still refusing to be unduly ruffled by Hardcastle's irritable hostility.

'Everything you know about her. For a start, who are her people?'

'They live in Hampshire, just north of Aldershot. Got a house out at Rushmoor somewhere. Her father was in the army, you see.'

'I suppose they've been told of her death,' said Hardcastle.

'Of course.'

'Was it you who told them, Major?'

'No, it wasn't. We got someone from Aldershot to inform them.' Fellowes was extremely grateful that that unpleasant duty had fallen to another.

'What can you tell me about her friends? Was she walking out, for instance?'

'I really have no idea,' said Fellowes. 'Ours was a purely professional relationship, and I saw no reason to enquire too

126

deeply into her background. Others had done that, I imagine,' he added mysteriously.

'Pity,' said Hardcastle meaningfully. 'How did she come to work for MI5 then?' He was becoming weary of his attempts to extract even the barest of details about Edith Sturgess.

'She was recommended.'

'Who recommended her?'

'Someone at the War Office, I suppose, I don't know who it was.'

'Whose idea was it to use her as a decoy then?'

'Mine. It was approved by Colonel Kell, of course. I think that Superintendent Quinn probably advised you of the plan.' Fellowes leaned forward and stubbed out his half-smoked cigarette in Hardcastle's ashtray.

'Yes, he did,' said Hardcastle. *Only when it was too bloody late*, he thought. 'Very well, Major, it seems that you're not in a position to help me very much further. Thank you for taking the time to come in,' he added acidly.

'Not at all, Inspector.' Fellowes, apparently impervious to Hardcastle's sarcasm, rose from his seat and reached for his hat and umbrella. 'I hope you catch whoever was responsible for this terrible deed.'

'Don't you vex yourself about that, Major, I will.'

Welcoming a breath of fresh air, Hardcastle and Marriott strode across Parliament Square to Strutton Ground as the silent Big Ben showed nine o'clock. Even at that hour the heat was oppressive and there were a lot of people about, many of them in army or navy uniform; and the omnibuses grinding their noisy way up Victoria Street were full. News vendors' shouts of 'Another Zeppelin raid on the East End!' ensured a brisk sale of their papers.

'The House is still sitting,' said Marriott, glancing up at the Union Flag above Victoria Tower.

'Serve the buggers right,' growled Hardcastle. 'A spell in the trenches is what they need.' He was not a supporter of the Liberal Party and had recently heard that his sister's only son, Harold, had perished on the first day of the Battle of the Somme. The whole family had been stunned

127

by the news, Hardcastle particularly so; his nephew had talked enthusiastically about following his uncle into the Metropolitan Police when the war was over. Hardcastle was grateful that his own son, Walter, was too young to volunteer, and Mrs Hardcastle had warned the boy that if he attempted to put up his age to enlist she would be down the War Office quicker than that and have him out again.

During the ten-minute walk from the police station Hardcastle fulminated about the intransigence of MI5 officers in general and Major Fellowes in particular. 'I don't know what's the matter with the man,' he said. 'Anyone'd think he didn't want us to catch Miss Sturgess's murderer.'

'You said as how he's new to the job, sir,' said Marriott, 'and I reckon he's come a cropper over this business. I wouldn't mind betting that Colonel Kell gave him a right bollocking over it.'

'And he'll have bloody well deserved it,' said Hardcastle savagely. 'If you or me'd done something like that, we'd be looking at the sack, my lad.'

'You don't think he had anything to do with it, do you, sir?' asked Marriott.

'Had crossed my mind, Marriott, I must admit, but he ain't got it in him. And why would he have wanted to top her, any road?'

'No telling, sir, but I'll wager her death was nothing to do with his secret operation. There's no reason to it.'

Hardcastle shot his subordinate a sideways glance. 'How do we know that?' he asked. 'Not with these buggers refusing to tell us anything. I think all this spying malarkey has gone to Fellowes's head. He's terrified of saying anything to anyone. I'll bet he's told his missus he's a bloody postman or something.'

'D'you reckon it was the same man as topped Rose, sir?'

'Possibly,' said Hardcastle cautiously. 'I s'pose that whoever done for Mrs Drummond could have gone back to Artillery Mansions and got surprised by Edith Sturgess being there when he thought the place was empty. Wouldn't have happened if they'd let me keep Catto in there.'

'Could have been someone she knew, sir, and he had

128

to top her or be found out,' said Marriott, warming to Hardcastle's theory.

'I must admit it seems like a chance killing, but until we get to know a bit more about her we don't have a ghost of finding out.'

'What's next then, sir?'

'What's next, Marriott, is that we go and see her parents down in Aldershot. But first we'll see what Daisy Watkins has to say for herself.'

Hardcastle hammered on the door of the flat over the pie shop in Strutton Ground and looked around as he waited impatiently. Most of the street-market traders had packed up for the night, but there were still one or two left, their makeshift stalls, bathed in the ghostly light of hurricane lamps, lining the opposite side of the narrow street. There was litter everywhere: discarded cabbage leaves, screwed-up paper bags, rotten apples; it was the usual detritus from a day's trading. The smell of fish mingled with that of vinegar as the remaining stallholders took advantage of the last of the cockles and whelks. Passing in front of them, an optimistic muffin man, his wares balanced precariously on a tray on his head, rang his bell as he walked slowly towards Horseferry Road. And a distant totter could be heard crying 'Rag-a-bone!' above the raucous sound of 'Nellie Dean' being sung in the public bar of the Grafton Arms to the accompaniment of a worn out piano that was in desperate need of tuning.

Daisy Watkins was about twenty-five years old and pretty in a coarse sort of way. Her hair was gathered into a bun at the nape of her neck. She wore a high-button white blouse and her skirt – as short as it dare be at six inches from the ground – was of a black cotton fabric, and probably home-made.

The smile on her face vanished as she saw the two men on her doorstep, but quickly returned as her eyes lighted on Marriott. 'Oh, I thought you was Mrs Turk from next door. I was expecting her, you see.' She spoke with a rich, Cockney accent.

'Daisy Watkins?' asked Hardcastle.

'Yes, that's right.'

'We're from the police at Cannon Row, Mrs Watkins. It is *Mrs* Watkins, is it?'

''Ere, it's not my Frank, is it?' Daisy Watkins assumed an expression of alarm and then peered up and down the street as though someone might wonder what two strange men were doing at her door.

'It's nothing to do with any Frank, Mrs Watkins. He's your husband, I take it.'

'Yes. He's in France, see, and what with all that's going on over there, I live every day expecting some awful news.'

'No, it's nothing to do with your husband,' said Hardcastle, unconvinced that Daisy Watkins's sudden show of concern for her fighting husband's welfare was genuine. 'It's about Mrs Drummond.'

'Oh, you'd better come up then.' Daisy turned and led the way, lifting her skirt a little higher than necessary as she ascended the narrow staircase and affording the detectives a sight of her shapely calves.

It was a small sitting room on the front of the building and although the furnishings had seen better days, they were scrupulously clean. The empty fireplace was filled with a newspaper carefully folded into a fan and the brass fire irons were highly polished. A photograph of a soldier stood in a place of honour on the mantelshelf.

'Do have a seat, gents,' said Daisy. 'I was about to put the kettle on for a cup of tea. Like one, would you?'

'No thank you,' said Hardcastle, his gaze straying wistfully out of the window and across the road to the Grafton Arms on the corner of Victoria Street. 'I understand from Mr Perkins, the porter at Artillery Mansions, that you cleaned for Mrs Drummond.'

'That's right,' said Daisy, perching on the edge of a hard-back dining chair and folding her hands demurely in her lap. 'And then she was murdered, o'course, the poor dear.' She shuddered. 'Don't bear thinking about, do it?'

'And when did you start there, Mrs Watkins?'

Daisy glanced at the mirror over the fireplace. 'About six or seven months ago, I s'pose it must have been.' She paused for a moment. 'Yes, that'd be right. Started not long after Christmas.'

'How did you come by this job?'

'Alf, er, Mr Perkins that is, told me that Mrs Drummond was looking for someone to do for her. Well, I don't normally do that sort of work but what with having Frank in the trenches and money being a bit short, I thought well, why not. And Alf said I'd be doing the lady a favour.'

'How did you come to know Alf Perkins then, Mrs Watkins?'

'Me and Frank met him across the Albert one night.' Daisy nodded in the direction of Victoria Street. 'When my Frank was on his embarkation, end of last year.'

'I see. Did you meet *Mrs* Perkins at the same time?' It was not a relevant question but Hardcastle decided that Daisy Watkins needed a little jolt. He found her too confident for his liking, almost as if she'd been primed by Perkins that the police were going to visit her.

'Wife? He don't have no wife.' Daisy Watkins looked quickly away.

'Yes he does.'

'Well, if he had she weren't there,' said Daisy sharply, recovering her poise almost immediately. 'Anyhow, Alf come round just after Christmas and asked me if I was interested in this job.'

'What sort of woman was Mrs Drummond?'

'A lovely lady, and very considerate. She was always asking after my Frank. Wanted to know where he was and whether he'd been in any of the big battles. After a couple of weeks, she asked for his address so's she could send him a food parcel. Very generous like that, she was.'

'And did he ever get a food parcel, Mrs Watkins?'

'Oh yes. He wrote and asked who this Mrs Drummond was. As a matter of fact I've got his letter here.' Daisy rose from her chair and crossing to a cupboard in the corner took down a bundle of letters. 'He usually only writes stuff like how much he's missing me and what he's going to do when he gets home. He reckoned the second thing he was going to do was take his pack off.' She gave a coarse chuckle and darted a cheeky smile in Marriott's direction before sitting down again, the letters on her lap. 'I've got it here somewhere. Oh yes, here it is.' She unfolded the cheap paper and began to read. '"Dear Daisy, We are in rest for a few days and very welcome it is too, but there's a big push coming, another one. We had a nasty pasting last week at—"' She broke off. 'The censor's cut that out,' she said apologetically before continuing. '"And we lost twenty-five out of our company alone K and W—"' Daisy looked up. 'That means killed and wounded,' she explained.

Hardcastle nodded. 'Yes, I know,' he said.

'Ah, this is the bit.' Daisy lifted the notepaper a little higher to catch the fading light from the window. '"A funny thing happened a couple of days ago. I had a food parcel from some woman called Rose Drummond. At first I thought she was something to do with the Red Cross, but she said in her letter as how you're charring for her. I don't know that I like the idea of you doing cleaning, Daisy dear, but I suppose needs must where the devil drives."' She raised her head and smiled. 'He reads a lot you know, does my Frank, that's where he gets these sayings from.' She looked down at the letter again and carried on reading. '"But I was a bit puzzled when she asked me where I was and whether I was going to be in the thick of it again. She asked whether there was a lot of us and hoped that Fritz wasn't putting up too much of a show. She asked me to be sure and let her know because she was v. interested in the war. Well, Daisy, I didn't like the sound of that and I had a word with my officer about it. He seemed to be v. interested and he took a note of her address. Must close now. Hoping this finds you as it leaves me. Your loving husband, Frank."' She folded the letter and put it back in its envelope. 'Then he put four kisses. That's one for each year we've been married.'

'What was the date of that letter, Mrs Watkins?' asked Hardcastle.

Daisy pulled the letter half out of its envelope again, sufficient to see the date. 'Seventh of July,' she said, 'but it only got here a few days ago.'

'Did this Mrs Drummond have any visitors while you were in her apartment, Mrs Watkins?' asked Marriott.

It was the first time that the sergeant had spoken and Daisy turned towards him, her hand at her throat in what she believed to be a fetching gesture. 'I was always done by ten in the morning,' she said, avoiding the question. 'Mrs Drummond was hardly ever up by the time I left and I usually took her a cup of tea in bed.' She looked thoughtful for a moment or two. 'Mind you,' she continued, 'I reckon she used to have visitors in the evenings like. There was often a lot of glasses what had to be washed up when I got there. But she always paid me extra whenever I had to do that.'

'And how often did that occur?' asked Marriott.

'No more'an about six times, I s'pose.'

'Tell me, Mrs Watkins,' said Marriott, a smile on his face. 'Was there ever a man in Mrs Drummond's bed when you took her a cup of tea in the morning?'

Daisy contrived, unsuccessfully, to look coy about answering. 'Well, I shouldn't speak ill of the dead, but I think she did have one or two fancy men,' she said.

'How many? Any idea?' Hardcastle took the questioning back again.

'Only three what I knew of,' said Daisy.

'Who were they, d'you know?'

'No, 'course not, I never said nothing about it to Mrs Drummond and she never said nothing about it neither.'

'Would you know any of them again, Mrs Watkins?'

Daisy laughed, a harsh unbridled laugh. 'Not likely,' she said. 'They always stayed under the bedclothes when I went in and I'd always left afore they went. Mrs Drummond made sure of that.'

The two detectives thanked Daisy Watkins for her help – although she seemed not to have realized that the most important information had been contained in the letter from her husband – and made their way across the road to the Grafton Arms.

Hardcastle ordered two pints of beer and laid sixpence on the bar. He drank a good half of the weak ale and wiped his moustache with the back of his hand. 'Bloody disgraceful,' he said. 'It's as poor as piss.' He set his glass down. 'Well, what d'you make of that, Marriott?'

'Our Mrs Drummond didn't seem too worried about asking for information, did she, sir?'

'I wonder whether Frank Watkins's officer ever passed that on,' mused Hardcastle as he felt for his pipe.

'And I wonder whether Daisy's "loving husband Frank" knows she's being free with her favours in Alf Perkins's direction, sir,' said Marriott with a grin. ''Cos I reckon she is.'

Hardcastle grunted and took another sip of beer. 'I'll say this for you, Marriott,' he said, 'you don't miss much.'

Fourteen

First thing next morning, Hardcastle instructed Marriott to contact the Aldershot police and ask them to arrange an interview for him with Colonel and Mrs Sturgess at their house at Rushmoor. That done, he filled his pipe and sent for a cup of tea before settling down to review what had to be done next.

He still favoured the theory that Rose Drummond had fallen victim to a casual pick-up, perhaps a soldier from Finsbury Barracks. But then again, she might have been murdered by one of the men whose names appeared in the red book which he and Sergeant Drew of Special Branch had found in her apartment. The MP, Charles Smith, seemed to be beyond suspicion as did the two civil servants, Hollins and Foster, and Brigadier-General Levitt, but Hardcastle would not be satisfied until he had interviewed the remaining seven names that Colonel Kell appeared reluctant to release to him, even though two of them were now in custody charged with espionage.

Marriott returned to say that the Aldershot police would telegraph Cannon Row when they had fixed an interview with the Sturgesses.

Hardcastle stood up. 'I think we'll take a turn down to the War Office, Marriott,' he said, 'and see if Major Fellowes knows about this letter that Rose Drummond sent to Lance-Corporal Watkins.'

'Er, didn't Superintendent Quinn say something about only speaking to MI5 officers in his presence, sir?' Marriott sounded unsure about reminding his inspector of the Special Branch chief's caveat, but felt that he had to mention it.

'Special Branch have said a lot of things that turned out to be untrue, Marriott,' said Hardcastle, by now no longer caring whether he criticized Quinn or not. 'I think I'll pretend that was just another of them.' Seizing his hat and umbrella, he led the way out of the office and down the stairs.

Unwilling to take chances, the sentry at the main entrance to the War Office sloped his rifle and afforded the two detectives a butt-salute. Solemnly, Hardcastle raised his bowler hat in return and strode inside.

'Yes, sir?' The doorkeeper, a young ex-soldier with only one arm and the ribbon of a 1914–15 Star on his blue serge jacket, ran an experienced eye over the two visitors.

'I'd like to see Major Fellowes if he's available,' said Hardcastle, leaning on his umbrella and gazing around while the doorkeeper thumbed through a staff list.

'Don't seem to have anyone of that name here, sir.' The doorkeeper raised his head. 'Don't happen to know what department he is, I s'pose?'

'He's with Colonel Kell's lot,' said Hardcastle.

'Ah, I see.' The doorkeeper nodded. 'And who might you be, sir?'

Hardcastle introduced himself and the custodian disappeared into a small, glass-fronted cubicle where he could be seen in conversation with someone Hardcastle took to be the man's superior.

'Won't keep you a minute, sir,' said the doorkeeper when he returned.

In fact, the two detectives were kept waiting for at least a quarter of an hour before, by some arcane process of internal communication, Major Fellowes appeared in the vast, echoing entrance hall.

'Inspector?' Fellowes raised a quizzical eyebrow and then frowned. He was clearly unhappy at having the two policemen call on him.

'I've got some information for you, Major,' said Hardcastle cheerfully.

'I see.' Fellowes looked around, spoke briefly to the doorkeeper, and then led the two detectives into a small room at the back of the vestibule. 'Well?'

Hardcastle explained about his interview with Daisy Watkins

and summarized what Rose Drummond had written to the woman's husband.

Fellowes listened intently, nodding from time to time. 'Most interesting,' he said, when Hardcastle had finished. 'But of little value now, of course, now that the woman's dead. We certainly didn't hear anything from this man's platoon commander. I presume that's who he told.'

Hardcastle shrugged. 'He said he'd reported it to his officer, Major, whatever that means. But then I'm a policeman, not a soldier, so I wouldn't know what he's called.'

'Quite so,' said Fellowes. 'Well thank you for telling me. Incidentally are you making any progress with the murder of Edith Sturgess?'

'A little,' said Hardcastle. In fact, the enquiry was no further forward than it had been the previous evening, the last occasion upon which he had spoken to Fellowes. Certainly the DDI's conversation with Daisy Watkins had yielded little of value about Rose Drummond's murder, other than to confirm that she occasionally entertained men friends in her bed and held parties from time to time. But that was already known to the police.

'He's a snotty-nosed sod,' said Hardcastle, as he and Marriott emerged from the War Office into the warm August sunshine. 'I don't wonder we're losing the war if he's anything to go by. If you ask me, MI5 could do with a few policemen running it.' He cocked a thumb in the direction of the building they had just left. 'Strikes me that lot don't know a shilling from a sixpence.' He pushed open the door of the saloon bar of the Clarence and ordered two pints of bitter.

The following morning, Hardcastle and Marriott caught a tram over the bridge to Waterloo Station. On a road that ran between two platforms, awaiting the next trainload of badly wounded soldiers to arrive from Southampton, stood a long line of khaki ambulances. The drivers stood about in groups. Many of them were women in high-button boots, and skirts cut so unfashionably short that they could safely operate the pedals of the large Crossley vehicles. A separate gathering of businesslike VAD nurses waited nearby, ready to accompany this latest sad collection of broken bodies to Charing Cross Hospital.

All across the concourse were groups of men in uniform, nearly as many sailors as soldiers, but all bidding farewell to wives, sweethearts, mothers and fathers, the little knots of people surrounded by kitbags and rifles. It was a sombre scene. Most relatives of fighting men were now sufficiently aware of the carnage on the Western Front to know that this might be the last occasion they saw their loved ones.

On Platform Five a whistle blew and a locomotive let forth a cloud of steam, shrouding the women who had gathered to wave goodbye to their menfolk.

It was pouring with rain by the time Hardcastle and Marriott arrived at Aldershot in a train that had been packed with the military. Fortunately Hardcastle's rank entitled him and Marriott to travel second class, but even so his compartment had been full of warrant officers and sergeants, and the two detectives' conversation had been confined to mundane matters. At Woking, a quartermaster-sergeant had offered Hardcastle his copy of *John Bull* and the DDI had spent the remainder of the journey reading it.

The station forecourt at Aldershot was packed with army lorries and a depressing number of ambulances. Soldiers, some wearing waterproof capes, milled about in the sheeting rain in a chaotic, amorphous mass while harassed sergeants screamed orders against a background of revving engines and the whistle of a departing steam train. In among the military transport were one or two horse-drawn hackneys, but of a motor cab there was no sign.

'This is a rum do, Marriott.' Hardcastle, standing in the doorway of the station, pointed his umbrella at a run-down horse. 'I don't fancy a mile or two behind one of them.'

'Hang on, sir,' said Marriott, as he spied a military police-man. He crossed to where the man was checking a soldier's leave pass. 'Excuse me, Corporal . . .'

The redcap turned his steely gaze on Marriott. 'And what can I do for you, my lad?' he said, carefully examining the detective sergeant and concluding that his hair was too long for him to be a soldier and that his suit was not what he would have expected of an officer. He could only be a recruit.

'I'm Detective Sergeant Marriott of the Metropolitan Police.'

'Oh, beg your pardon, I'm sure,' said the corporal sarcastically, still looking unconvinced.

Marriott thrust his warrant card at the NCO. He was not much taken with being called 'my lad'.

The military policeman looked at it carefully and then glanced up with a grin. 'Sorry, Sarge,' he said. 'What can I do for you?'

'My detective inspector and me' – Marriott indicated the figure of Hardcastle hunched beneath his umbrella – 'have got to get out to this place in Rushmoor . . .' He produced the piece of paper with Colonel Sturgess's name and address on it. 'Urgent police business. We're investigating a murder. I was wondering—'

'Soon have you fixed up, Sarge. Hang on a jiffy.' The corporal walked across to a staff car that was parked on the far side of the forecourt, spoke briefly to the driver, and then rejoined Marriott. 'He'll take you, Sarge,' he said. 'It's a sort of taxi service what we runs for the brass, but if one ain't there, they'll have to walk, won't they? Won't do 'em no harm,' he added with a chuckle.

'Well, I don't know how you wangled this, Marriott,' said Hardcastle, as he clambered into the back seat of the Vauxhall, 'but it beats one of them hacks.' He nodded towards the cabs, their horses' coats shining with the unceasing rain.

The Sturgesses' house, a large white stone villa, was about a mile from Rushmoor Arena. The garden was immaculately tended, the geraniums regimented in perfectly straight lines as though aware that they belonged to a soldier.

'Only needs a Coldstreamer on the doorstep and it'd look like the guardroom at Buckingham Palace,' said Hardcastle as he tugged at the brass bell pull.

The woman who answered the door was tall and grey-haired – in her late fifties, Hardcastle reckoned – and wore a full-skirted day dress with a tunic over it that came to a point at the bottom. 'You must be Inspector Hardcastle,' she said with a smile. 'I'm Elizabeth Sturgess. Do come in. You must be drenched.' She glanced up at the leaden sky before standing back and opening the door wide.

'Kind of you to see us, ma'am,' said Hardcastle deferentially as he removed his hat. 'This here's my Detective Sergeant Marriott.' The two policemen left their umbrellas on the doorstep and followed Mrs Sturgess into the temple-tiled entrance hall.

Colonel Rupert Sturgess was sixty-two years of age, and wore a black eyepatch; he had lost his left eye at Spion Kop in the Boer War. 'How d'you do?' he said as he seized Hardcastle's hand. 'Sit down.'

'Would you like a cup of tea, Inspector?' enquired Mrs Sturgess, glancing at Marriott to include him in the invitation.

'Thank you, ma'am, that'd be—' began Hardcastle.

'Daresay you'd rather have a whisky, eh, Inspector?' said the colonel, moving towards a cocktail cabinet on the far side of the large room, a room cluttered with military memorabilia, most of which was Indian in character. 'Need warming up on a day like this.'

'Well that'd be very—'

'Thought you would,' said Sturgess. 'Give me an excuse to have one.' He smiled ruefully at his wife.

The drinks were served and the four of them settled down in comfortable chintz-covered armchairs.

'Well now, Inspector, what can we do for you? What is it you want to know about Edith?' Colonel Sturgess crossed his legs and took an appreciative sip of his whisky.

'May I extend my sympathy on your loss, Colonel,' said Hardcastle haltingly. He was not much good at expressing condolences.

Sturgess grunted. 'Mmm, yes, thank you, very kind I'm sure.'

Hardcastle had decided that there was no need to keep anything back from Sturgess, even though he was no longer on the active list. 'I take it you know what Miss Sturgess was doing when she was murdered, sir,' he said.

'Well, nursing, wasn't it? That's what she told us.' Colonel

Sturgess spoke gruffly as though unwilling to be reminded of his late daughter. He looked at his wife who nodded in confirmation. 'But then again, the fellow who came to see us was from Command HQ, here in Aldershot. Rather odd that, I thought, and I must say he was a bit guarded about what he told us. Said she'd been murdered in some apartment in London, but the damned fellow wouldn't be drawn further than that. Claimed he didn't know much about it. Wouldn't have lasted five minutes in my battalion, going out with half a story like that, I can tell you,' he added, before looking directly at Hardcastle again with his single, penetrating eye. 'Perhaps you can tell us more, Inspector.'

Hardcastle took a sip of his whisky and then placed the glass carefully on the side table. 'She was working for MI5, sir,' he said.

'Was she, be damned?' It was clearly news to Sturgess. 'Doing what, d'you know?'

'It was some secret operation—'

'Yes, would have been, I suppose,' muttered Sturgess.

'But we are by no means sure that her death was connected with her war work.'

'What d'you mean by that?'

'The murder took place in Artillery Mansions, in Victoria—'

'Yes, we know that, but what on earth was she doing there, eh?'

'It was some sort of undercover operation, so I understand, sir.' Hardcastle was finding it difficult to talk to the colonel without giving too much away. 'I'm sure you understand that I'm not in a position to say very much. But we don't think that her death had anything to do with what she was working on.'

'You mean that some damned man just walked in and murdered her?'

'Rupert, do let the inspector finish.' Until now, Elizabeth Sturgess had remained silent and composed throughout her husband's exchange with Hardcastle.

'Yes, of course, m'dear. I'm sorry, Inspector. Do go on.'

'I'm afraid we don't know what happened exactly, sir, and

the people she worked for at the War Office are not being particularly helpful.'

'Comes as no surprise,' growled Sturgess. 'Want me to have a word with them? I know one or two people up there.'

'I don't think that'll be necessary, sir, thank you.' Hardcastle was convinced that Colonel Sturgess would have no better luck than he in extracting information from Major Fellowes and his associates.

'Well, what can we do to help, Inspector?'

'I'd like to know more about her personal life, sir. None of the people she worked with seemed to know much about her friends. In fact, they don't even seem very sure of how she got the job with MI5 in the first place.'

'No bloody wonder,' growled Sturgess. 'Not now Lloyd George is in charge at the War Box.'

'Rupert!' cautioned Elizabeth Sturgess.

'Sorry, dear.'

'She didn't have many friends, Inspector,' said Elizabeth Sturgess. 'There were one or two with whom she went to school, in Switzerland as well as here, but usually they only wrote to each other. But when the war started and James was killed—'

'Who was James, Mrs Sturgess?'

'James Furlong. He was her husband.' Elizabeth Sturgess gave Hardcastle a questioning look as though he should have known.

'I didn't know she'd been married.' Hardcastle was beginning to think that there was an awful lot he didn't know about Edith Sturgess.

'James was a captain in my old regiment,' said Sturgess in a tired voice, as though he had explained all this before. 'They met at Henley Regatta in . . .' He paused and glanced at his wife.

'Nineteen–oh–six,' said Elizabeth promptly.

'Yes. It was a regimental thing. We used to hold it every year till the war. Wonderful do: picnic by the river, champagne and so forth.' Sturgess looked wistfully across the room. 'They were married in nineteen–ten. James went across with the BEF, right at the beginning, and the poor chap was killed at Mons, not seven days into the war.' He shook his head despairingly.

'But she was known as Edith Sturgess to the people she worked with at the War Office,' said Hardcastle.

The colonel nodded. 'I know. For some reason she reverted to her maiden name. She was terribly cut up about James's death, naturally enough. I think it was her way of trying to forget. Anyhow, she volunteered for the VADs after that and was nursing at St George's. At least, that's what she told us. As a matter of fact, the last letter she wrote to us was from there.' He looked at his wife. 'When was that, m'dear?'

'A month ago,' said Elizabeth, turning to Hardcastle. 'She'd seemed very happy lately and couldn't stop talking about a man she'd met.'

'Who was he?' asked Hardcastle.

'Someone she'd nursed, apparently. He'd been wounded off Gallipoli, not seriously but enough to bring him home.'

'What was his name, Mrs Sturgess?'

'It's rather strange, but we haven't heard from him since just before Edith died.' Elizabeth glanced at her husband. 'What was his name, Rupert?'

'Roger Spurling,' said Sturgess. 'Commander Roger Spurling, Royal Navy.'

Fifteen

In addition to learning that Edith Sturgess had been a widow, and that she had become close to Roger Spurling, Hardcastle and Marriott had garnered the names of some of the nurses she had worked with at St George's Hospital at Hyde Park Corner.

'Might be worth having a chat with some of them, I suppose,' said Hardcastle, when he and Marriott were back in London, 'but right now, the thing that concerns me is that Spurling, like as not, don't know a thing about his lady friend having been topped, seeing as how it's been kept from the press. Not that they get to see the linen drapers in clink anyway,' he added with a cackle.

'Don't you think that Fellowes might have let him know, sir?'

Hardcastle snorted. 'That one wouldn't tell his own mother the time of day if he could help it,' he said. 'But I reckon we owe it to Spurling to go and tell him. Never know, we might learn something. I'll wager he's none too pleased being left to moulder in Brixton nick when there's a war on.'

'I'll see this prisoner on his own,' said Hardcastle to the warder who conducted Spurling to the interview room at Brixton Prison.

'Are you sure, sir?' asked the warder. 'I mean, he's banged up for murder an' all.'

'I hope you're not suggesting that me and my sergeant couldn't overpower him if he turned nasty,' said Hardcastle. 'It was us who nicked him, you know.'

The warder still looked doubtful. 'Oh well, have it your way, sir,' he said with a shrug. 'Me and my mate'll be outside if you has any trouble. Just give a shout.' With that the warder left the room and closed the door behind him.

'Well, Inspector, this is a pleasant surprise,' said Spurling with an ironic smile. 'And what brings you here? Thought of something else to charge me with, have you?' He looked none the worse for his enforced incarceration.

'It's *Commander* Spurling, I believe,' said Hardcastle, and leaned back in his chair.

'Ah!' said Spurling, and laughed. 'As a matter of fact, Inspector, you never fooled me for a moment with all your bumbling. And it looks as though I didn't fool you either. How did you find out?'

'In unfortunate circumstances, Commander,' said Hardcastle slowly. 'Have they told you about Miss Sturgess?'

'What about her?' Spurling recognized the gravity in Hardcastle's voice at once and leaned forward.

'I'm afraid she's dead.'

'Oh God, no!' Spurling sank back in his chair, a look of utter torment on his face. He remained silent and contemplative for some time and Hardcastle let him be. Eventually he looked up. 'What happened, Inspector?'

As succinctly as possible, Hardcastle recounted the circumstances of Edith Sturgess's murder including the reason for her having been in Rose Drummond's apartment.

'We were to be married, you know.' Spurling spoke in a whisper, clearly distraught by the news that Hardcastle had brought him. 'It's all my fault, too.'

'How's that, Commander?' asked Hardcastle.

'I don't know how much Colonel Sturgess told you, but I was wounded at the time of the Gallipoli landings. Got a shell splinter in my right leg and finished up in St George's. That's where I met Edith, a lovely girl. After I was discharged, we started walking out together, quite regularly. At least, when she got time off from the hospital. After I'd convalesced, I was transferred to Naval Intelligence. It was there that I learned that Colonel Kell was looking for a girl to do one or two odd jobs for his organization. Nothing dangerous, I was told, otherwise I wouldn't have suggested it.'

'Suggested what?' asked Hardcastle.

'I put the idea to Edith that she might like to give a hand and she was absolutely over the moon about it. Said she was tired of nursing and wanted to do something more positive. I think she fancied herself as a spy, but I soon disabused her of that thought. Anyhow, I mentioned her name to the chief.' Spurling shook his head and looked immensely sad. 'But I never thought it would end like this.'

'If it's any comfort,' said Hardcastle, 'we don't think her death was directly as a result of the work she was doing.'

'What was she doing, exactly?' demanded Spurling, his mood changing to one of anger. 'And more to the point, who was responsible for putting her in that position?'

Spurling had obviously been acting a part at the time of his arrest and the brusque and disdainful manner he had adopted then had now vanished. Hardcastle found himself warming to the man, and not only because of the loss of his fiancée. Furthermore, Hardcastle had taken a violent dislike to Major Fellowes and saw no reason why Spurling should not be told the full story. They were, after all, on the same side, although Hardcastle did wonder about that from time to time.

'It was Major Cuthbert Fellowes of MI5.'

Spurling scoffed. 'Now there's an example of the difference between Naval Intelligence and MI5,' he said. 'Although I say it myself, I was selected for NI work because it was thought that I had some talent for it. But Fellowes was picked because he was no damned good for anything else. They wouldn't have dared trust him in the line in charge of men. He'd have got the bloody lot of them killed.' He stood up and started to pace the room. 'God Almighty,' he said, running his hand through his thinning hair. 'What happens now, Inspector? Are they going to keep me locked up in here until the war's over? You know it was all a game, I suppose? They were out to catch someone important who they thought had been giving information to the Drummond woman. But then I imagine you've been told all that.'

'The plan seems to be that you should be left here until Rose Drummond's killer is apprehended,' said Hardcastle, unwilling to divulge just how little he had been told, 'who is probably the same man as did for poor Miss Sturgess.'

'Well, that's bloody pointless. What d'you hope to achieve by that?'

'It's not my idea,' said Hardcastle defensively. 'But my seniors at Scotland Yard seem to think that it'll lull the murderer into a false sense of security. That he'll think we've got Rose Drummond's killer, you, locked up and that we won't connect the two.'

'And d'you think that, Inspector?'

'No, I don't, Commander. They were at great pains to keep your arrest secret, so I don't see the point of it all. It certainly won't help me.'

'Who d'you mean by "they"?' asked Spurling.

'Mr Thomson and Colonel Kell,' said Hardcastle.

Spurling sat down again. 'Will you do me a great favour, Inspector?'

'Anything I can.'

'Will you get in touch with my chief, "Blinker" Hall, and let him know what's going on. I know he agreed to this charade in the beginning, but the murder of Edith puts an entirely different slant on it all. I don't think he'll be at all happy. I wouldn't presume to teach you your job, but I wouldn't mind betting the same man was responsible for both murders.'

'You could be right,' murmured Hardcastle. 'Incidentally where do I find this Mr Hall?'

Spurling grinned for the first time since he had received the news of Edith Sturgess's death. 'He's Captain Reginald Hall, Royal Navy,' he said, 'the Director of Naval Intelligence, and you'll find him at the Admiralty. You can't miss him, he blinks like crazy.'

'I don't like it, Marriott. I don't like it at all,' said Hardcastle as he and his sergeant left the gaunt, dark surroundings of Brixton Prison and stepped into the August sunlight. 'This ain't the sort of police work I'm used to. All this getting involved in spies and spying.' As they reached the top of Jebb Avenue, a tram ground its way up Brixton Hill, the driver ringing his bell at an errant cyclist who was in danger of becoming trapped in the tramlines.

'No, sir.' Marriott, unsure what his DDI was driving at, was non-committal.

'How the bloody hell do I, a divisional detective inspector, get to see this Captain Hall? If Superintendent Quinn finds out, or worse, Mr Thomson, they'll have fifty fits, and I shall be hauled over the coals a bit *tout de suite.*'

'They don't have to know, sir, do they?' said Marriott, peering down the road to see if there was another tram in sight. 'I know they're all in this secret business together, but from what we've seen so far, they never tell each other anything. If you tell this "Blinker" chap the tale, I reckon you could talk him into keeping it to himself.'

'You might be right at that, Marriott. It's worth a chance, I s'pose.' Hardcastle waved his umbrella at a cab. 'I reckon the Commissioner can stand us a growler,' he said as he wrenched open the door. 'Admiralty, cabbie,' he shouted, and settled himself into his seat. 'There was something in the paper this morning about them rationing petrol, so I suppose it'll be back to hacks again soon,' he added with a sigh.

Eventually the cab pulled into the courtyard of the Admiralty in Whitehall and Hardcastle got out. 'I don't have no change, Marriott,' he said. 'You settle the cabbie, will you?' He paused, one foot on the doorstep. 'And when you put in the claim, show the fare as Brixton Prison to Scotland Yard and put down a different plate number, otherwise some nosey parker'll want to know what we was doing at the Admiralty.'

Muttering to himself, Marriott proffered a half-crown and waited for his change, fixing the driver with a stony glare when he mumbled something about a tip.

'Well, here goes, Marriott,' said Hardcastle as he entered the building. 'Funny to think of Nelson coming in through this very door, ain't it?'

'Yes, sir.' Marriott had never taken Hardcastle for an historian.

It proved far simpler to see Captain Hall than it had been to interview Major Fellowes across the road at the War Office, and several minutes later the two detectives were being shown into the Director of Naval Intelligence's workmanlike office.

148

'Blinker' Hall looked most unlike a spy, which is what Hardcastle, in his ignorance, imagined him to be. He was large and rotund, almost like a cuddly teddy bear, with a bald pate, a hooked nose and a pointed chin that made him look like a caricature of Punch.

'You must be one of Quinn's men,' Hall bellowed as he shook hands.

'Not exactly, sir, no,' said Hardcastle, looking around in vain for a hatstand upon which to hang his hat and umbrella.

'Just put your cap and sword on the table, Inspector,' said Hall, 'and come and sit down.' He positioned himself behind his desk and fixed Hardcastle with a penetrating stare. 'Well, what d'you want to see me about?'

'Commander Spurling,' said Hardcastle.

Hall began to blink furiously. 'What d'you know about him?' he asked suspiciously.

'It was me what arrested him, sir,' said Hardcastle. 'And me and Sergeant Marriott here have just left him.'

'I suppose you want to tell me he didn't do it,' said Hall, unaware that Hardcastle had been made privy to the ruse that had set Spurling up as a murderer.

'I know he didn't do it, sir. I have Mr Basil Thomson's word on that.'

'What d'you want of me then?' asked Hall, scratching the side of his beak-like nose. 'Don't want me to interfere in this business, do you? I don't know what you people and Colonel Kell are playing at, but I agreed to lend them Commander Spurling to help out.'

'Did you know that Edith Sturgess has been murdered, sir?' asked Hardcastle.

'Murdered? What, the girl that Spurling put up for a job with MI5?' Hall leaned forward in his chair and started to blink rapidly again. 'You'd better tell me about it, Inspector.'

Once more, Hardcastle outlined the circumstances of Edith Sturgess's death. 'But Commander Spurling's still in custody in Brixton and he's none too happy about it, sir,' he concluded. 'It all seems rather pointless now.'

'It's more than pointless, it's a bloody outrage,' roared Hall. 'Great Scott, what on earth are they doing at the War Office? I tell you, Inspector, you should never let soldiers get involved in a war. It's much too serious.' He remained in thought for some time, chin resting on his chest. 'Spurling's far too valuable to be left wasting his time in prison,' he continued eventually. 'I shall speak to Thomson about it. And Kell.'

Hardcastle fidgeted with his Albert. 'I'd be grateful if you didn't mention me in this business, sir,' he said. 'You see, I'm not supposed to talk to people like you, not without Superintendent Quinn's permission, but, well to be honest, I felt sorry for Commander Spurling, what with him having lost his fiancée an' all.'

'His *fiancée*? D'you mean the fellow was going to marry the girl, God dammit?'

'You see, I wasn't at all sure that even if I told Superintendent Quinn he'd have told you, sir,' said Hardcastle.

'Quite right, Inspector,' said Hall. 'There are times when I wonder if we're all in the same ship in this war. You did right in coming to see me, but you needn't worry. We're very good at protecting our sources of information in the intelligence business.' He stood up and pushed out his hand, seizing Hardcastle's in a vice-like grip. 'Too bloody good at times.'

It was obvious that Captain Hall had wasted no time in dealing with the matter of Commander Spurling's prolonged detention. Shortly after lunch, Hardcastle was sent for by Superintendent Quinn.

It was with a measure of apprehension that he entered the Special Branch chief's office, but he need not have worried: Hall had been as good as his word.

'There's been a change of plan, Mr Hardcastle,' said Quinn tersely.

'Is that so, sir?'

'This Spurling fellow that you've got locked up. He's to be released forthwith. See to it, will you?' Quinn, obviously unhappy at having received the order peremptorily from a somewhat chastened Thomson, saw no reason for explanation when passing the instruction on to Hardcastle. He opened a file and began to read it.

'It's not that easy, sir.'

'Oh, and why's that?' Quinn looked up fiercely, as if surprised to see the DDI still in his office.

'Commander Spurling was remanded into custody by the Bow Street magistrate, sir. We can't just let him out. He'll have to be brought up before the beak again and admitted to bail, or the DPP's man'll have to offer no evidence.'

'Sweet baby Jesus!' Quinn threw down his pen. The swingeing powers afforded him and Special Branch by the Defence of the Realm Act had lulled him into believing that anything could be solved by deploying it. Not for the first time, he realized that his knowledge of the ordinary criminal law was none too deep. 'All right, then, I'll speak to Mr Thomson about it. Wait across at Cannon Row until I've some news. You might be needed at Bow Street.'

In the event, Hardcastle kicked his heels for nearly three hours before he received a call to return yet again to Superintendent Quinn's office.

'This is a magistrate's order for the release of Spurling.' Quinn tossed an official document on to his desk. 'Take it to Brixton and get him out. The DPP's counsel saw the Chief Magistrate in his chambers and explained.' He was clearly unhappy about having been overridden by the assistant commissioner, even though he claimed to have known nothing of the decision to keep Spurling in custody even after Edith Sturgess's murder.

'Very good, sir.' Hardcastle pocketed the blue form and paused. 'Are you able to let me have the other names from Rose Drummond's red book yet, sir?' he asked.

'I'll let you know when, Inspector,' said Quinn crossly.

'Yes, sir,' said Hardcastle, thankful that Quinn was unaware of his visit to Captain Hall. In his present mood, Quinn would undoubtedly have gone into a towering rage if he had discovered that the DDI had been talking to the Director of Naval Intelligence.

*   *   *

151

Commander Roger Spurling stepped out of the wicket in the large wooden gates and sniffed appreciatively at the air which, even in that part of London, was much purer than the urine-laden atmosphere of Brixton Prison. 'I'm most grateful to you, Inspector,' he said.

'Well, seeing as how it was me what locked you up in the first place,' said Hardcastle, 'it was the least I could do.'

'And what did "Blinker" Hall have to say about it all?'

'Not very much, Commander,' said Hardcastle, 'but I did get the impression that he didn't think too much of that MI5 lot.'

Spurling laughed. 'He's not alone in that.' He became suddenly sad. 'Well, I wonder what I'm to do with myself now?' he mused. He glanced across the road at the pub on the other side. 'The least I can do is to buy you gentlemen a glass of ale,' he said.

'That's very kind of you,' said Hardcastle. 'I could use a wet, but not in that one. In my experience it's usually full of screws.' And even as he pointed to another public house, further down the road, a prison warder emerged from the saloon bar of the first one. 'That one down there's a better bet.'

'Well, sir, what happens now?' asked Marriott, when eventually the two detectives returned to Cannon Row police station.

'We'd better start looking for this murderer, Marriott, that's what,' said Hardcastle. 'I'm getting a bit fed up with all this cloak-and-dagger nonsense. Time we got back to some proper police work.' He stood up and glanced at his watch. 'St George's Hospital, I think. See what we can learn from Edith Sturgess's friends.'

The hospital was redolent with the combined odours of ether and carbolic; efficient nurses in starched aprons bustled to and fro in the highly polished, long corridors. The matron, an austere Scotswoman, named three girls who, she assured Hardcastle, had been friendly with Nurse Sturgess, and afforded the detectives a small room in which to conduct their interviews, but the visit was yet another disappointment. Yes, they each said, they had known Edith but only at work. They had discussed all the usual things that nurses talk about. Each had frequently taken a shine to a particular wounded officer but the infatuation had disappeared along with the young man concerned. In short, they knew nothing about Edith Sturgess that would in any way further Hardcastle's investigation into her death.

Sixteen

Another four days passed, during which time countless young men were cut down in the cloying Somme mud around Thiepval, and the survivors prayed for the fall of the Madonna from the basilica at distant Albert. Myth had it that the war would end when that happened.

Hardcastle, his investigation as bogged down as the armies of the Empire, was finally sent for by Superintendent Quinn.

'Colonel Kell has finished looking into the names that were contained in Rose Drummond's red book, Mr Hardcastle' – Quinn fingered the slip of paper in the centre of his desk – 'and he's agreed to let you have them. As you know, two of them have been arrested but the remaining five have been dismissed from his enquiries. His view is that they were merely people that Mrs Drummond had hoped to cultivate at some time in the future.' He eventually, and reluctantly, handed the slip of paper to the DDI. 'They may be of some use to you, but I doubt it.'

'Very good, sir,' said Hardcastle, taking the list of names.

'Of course, should you find in the course of your investigation anything that might be of value to MI5, you will inform me immediately and take no further action. Is that understood?'

'Yes, sir.' Hardcastle had the feeling that he was still being kept from knowing everything about Rose Drummond's activities. He looked down at the slip of paper. 'I see Alf Perkins is on here,' he said.

'He's the porter at Artillery Mansions,' said Quinn, 'but then you'd know that. It's obvious that he's of no importance.'

*   *   *

'Why should Rose Drummond have put the porter's name in her little book, Marriott?' asked Hardcastle. 'There's nothing secret about a bleedin' porter, I wouldn't have thought. So why go to the trouble of writing him down in invisible ink, eh? It don't hang together, not in my eyes. Not unless she was leaving it for someone else to find if she got arrested.'

'Does seem a bit odd, sir,' said Marriott, 'but this spying business is all my eye and Betty Martin if you ask me.'

'Well I'm not happy about it, Marriott, and I reckon we'll have another go at Mr Alfred Perkins.'

'Right, sir.'

Marriott glanced at his wristwatch – it was half-past six – and thought that another evening was about to be ruined.

'What's that you're wearing, Marriott?' Hardcastle asked.

'It's a watch, sir.'

'What, tied on your wrist?' Hardcastle was clearly bemused by the idea. 'That won't catch on. Daft, that is. You'll be forever knocking it,' he scoffed.

The two detectives strode across Parliament Square and down Victoria Street, its pavements crowded with home-going office workers from the government buildings that abounded in the area. Soldiers and sailors, enjoying the peace and tranquillity of a snatched leave in London in late summer after the hell of the trenches or the confines of ironclads, strolled towards St James's Park, more than one of them with a girl on his arm.

Hardcastle rapped on Perkins's door. There was no answer.

A dowager regally descended the staircase and stared at the two policemen. Disdaining the prevailing fashion, she was attired in full-length black bombasine, had a wide-brimmed, black, straw hat and clutched a parasol in her hand. 'He's not there,' she declaimed imperiously. 'I don't know where he's gone but he's not been there all day.'

'When did you last see him, ma'am?' asked Hardcastle.

'Are you the plumber?' the woman asked.

'No ma'am, we're police officers.'

The woman tossed her head. 'Can't say I'm surprised,' she said. 'Always did think there was something fishy about that fellow. I've been waiting all day for him to see to my tap.

The wretched thing's done nothing but leak for three days now. If I've asked him once, I've asked him a dozen times. I shall talk to the landlord's agent about him. Anyway, a young fellow like that ought to be in the trenches instead of wasting his time doing nothing here all day.' She paused. 'I suppose you aren't any good at taps, are you?' she enquired.

'No, ma'am, I'm afraid not,' said Hardcastle, who was, in fact, quite adept at changing the washers on his own taps. 'You said there was something fishy about Perkins. What exactly did you mean by that, might I ask?'

'He was always in and out of that Drummond creature's apartment, the one who was murdered. A most unsavoury person.' Suddenly the woman realized why the police were there. 'Oh,' she continued, 'I suppose that's why you want to see him. Well, when you find him, perhaps you'd tell him that Lady Rivers's tap is still leaking.' Waving her parasol demandingly towards the door, she waited for Marriott to open it and then swept into the street.

'I think Lady Rivers might have the makings of a good informant,' said Hardcastle, with a rare grin, and hammered on Perkins's door once again, but still there was no response.

'Looks like he's run, sir,' said Marriott.

'I wonder what happened to his missus.'

'Did he have one, sir?' asked Marriott. 'I know you told Daisy Watkins he was spliced, but I thought you was just getting her going.'

'You're right, Marriott. We don't know, do we?' Hardcastle leaned on his umbrella. 'In fact, there's a lot we don't know about Master Perkins. I still don't see why Mrs Drummond should have put his name in her little book, though,' he said thoughtfully, 'not unless he was up to something. After all, Marriott, Frank Watkins's name wasn't there, and the Drummond woman wrote to him asking for information. So why Perkins and not Corporal Watkins, eh?'

'P'raps there's another list, sir,' said Marriott, 'but d'you reckon Daisy Watkins might know where Perkins is?'

'Worth a try, Marriott, worth a try,' said Hardcastle, and led the way back into the street, almost colliding with a sandwich-board man whose placards advertised Harry Lauder's appearance at the Victoria Palace.

''Ere,' said Hardcastle. 'Sandwich-board men are supposed to walk in the gutter. Section Seventy-Two, Highways Act 1835.'

The man muttered something about trying to earn an honest living and shuffled off the pavement.

'Well, get yourself down the recruiting office, cheeky bugger,' replied Hardcastle. 'Time you joined up.'

The two detectives had no better luck at Daisy Watkins's place in Strutton Ground than they had had at Perkins's apartment in Artillery Mansions. After Hardcastle had spent a few minutes hammering vainly on her door, he and Marriott entered the pie shop beneath the woman's flat.

'Evenin', gents. A couple of nice hot mutton pies is it? Got some fresh ones just out of the oven.' The pie-shop owner, a large man with a flowing moustache, was wearing a white coat, a striped apron and a straw boater. He rubbed his hands together briskly.

'Police,' said Hardcastle. 'D'you happen to know the whereabouts of Mrs Watkins?'

'What, her what lives upstairs, you mean?'

'Yes.'

The pie-shop owner shook his head. 'She went off in a cab last night. Said something about having a holiday. Had a case with her an' all.'

'Did she say when she'd be back?' asked Marriott.

'No, guv'nor. She never said where she was going neither, but she did say as how she'd pop in from time to time to pick up her letters. You want me to give her a message if I sees her?'

'No,' said Hardcastle. 'And I don't even want you telling her we've been here making enquiries.' He turned towards the door. 'Come along, Marriott.'

The pieman wrapped two hot mutton pies and handed them to Marriott. 'There y'are, guv'nor,' he said. He knew how important it was to keep on the right side of the law. 'On the house.'

'What are we going to do now then, sir?' asked Marriott

157

when they were back at Cannon Row. He wiped the last of the mutton-pie crumbs from his lips. 'Seem to have come to a dead stop.'

Hardcastle licked his fingers. 'Like I said, Marriott, I reckon there's more to this Alf Perkins than we've found out about. He's a crafty little bugger and I reckon he's cunning enough to have run rings round them MI5 blokes. He'd certainly have talked his way out of trouble if it was the bold Major Fellowes what interviewed him, any road. Couldn't catch a cold, that one, let alone a spy.' He picked up his pipe. 'Get hold of Catto for me.'

Detective Constable Henry Catto entered Hardcastle's office nervously fingering the bottom button of his waistcoat. He always felt indefinably guilty whenever he received a summons to the DDI's office.

'Catto, d'you know the pie shop in Strutton Ground, lad? Round about Number Fourteen, I think.'

'I'll find it, sir,' said Catto.

'I hope you do,' said Hardcastle, ''cos you're going to be spending some time hanging around there. There's a woman called Daisy Watkins living over the shop. Well, she used to, but it seems she's gone off, like as not with Alf Perkins.'

'What, the porter from Artillery Mansions, sir?'

'The very same,' said Hardcastle. 'I want you and Wilmot to take turn and turn about to keep a watch on the place. Mrs Watkins, according to the pieman in the shop under her place, says she's coming back to pick up her letters from time to time.'

'You want her arrested, sir?'

'No, Catto, I do not want her arrested. You or Wilmot will follow her and see where she goes. Understood?'

'Yes, sir, but what if it's a long way away. Off the manor, like?'

'I don't give a fig if she goes to Glasgow, Catto. You'll follow her. And dress yourself up, rough like. I don't want you sticking out like a carbuncle on a vicar's nose. Got it?'

'Yes, sir.'

'Good. Well don't hang about. Get on with it.'

'And now, Marriott,' said Hardcastle, when Catto had departed, 'we're going to ask some more questions about them four as we had down for Rose Drummond's fancy men.'

'What, the MP, the general and the two civil servants, sir?'

'Exactly,' said Hardcastle and began to fill his pipe.

The interviews with Lawrence Foster, the Admiralty civil servant, and Donald Hollins at the Ministry of Munitions, proved unproductive. Although Hardcastle, who on that occasion had been accompanied by DS Drew of Special Branch, had spoken to each of them following the death of Rose Drummond, he thought it worthwhile to question them about their movements at the time of Edith Sturgess's murder.

Both the men had apparently unshakeable alibis for the night of the first of August and Hardcastle dismissed them from his list of suspects. At least for the time being; he was sufficiently thorough an investigator not to eliminate anyone until he had secured a conviction.

Hardcastle was a little more circumspect with Charles Smith, the Liberal MP, and questioned him on the basis of being a weekday resident of Artillery Mansions who might have witnessed something untoward. Somewhat ruefully, Smith explained that he had gone from the House to the National Liberal Club in Whitehall Place on the evening of Edith Sturgess's murder. He had dined well, he confessed, got rather drunk and spent the night in one of the club's rooms. Seeing through Hardcastle's ploy, Smith then added that he could provide a list of people 'as long as your arm, Inspector' who would happily testify to having been in his company, including the two who had actually helped him to his bed.

Brigadier-General Humphrey Levitt proved to be as difficult as ever to contact but on learning from one of his aides that the general had been in France from the thirty-first of July to the fifth of August, Hardcastle did not pursue the matter.

*　　*　　*

159

DC Henry Catto was a resourceful detective. Assigned to watching Daisy Watkins's flat by day – Wilmot had fallen for the night stint again – he had arranged with an iron-monger, whose shop was immediately opposite where the woman lived, to keep observation from there. He also had a word with the regular traders whose market stalls lined the road outside and, contrary to what Hardcastle would have wished, explained who he was looking for, but not why. The stallholders, anxious always to stay on the right side of the police, promised to keep their eyes open and be as helpful as possible. His traps having thus been set, Catto settled down to what he believed would be a pleasant few days away from the DDI. His pleasure was further enhanced by the presence of the ironmonger's daughter, a doe-eyed, shapely creature of about twenty, who kept the books for her father and dispensed frequent cups of tea to Catto, for whom she had clearly developed a great liking.

Unfortunately for Catto, the observation in Strutton Ground did not last very long. At about noon on the third day, a fruiterer appeared in the doorway of the ironmonger's shop.

'*Guv'nor!*' The fruiterer addressed Catto in a stage whisper.

'What is it?' Catto put down his cup of tea.

'That dolly you was looking for. I think she's just gone in.'

Catto leaped from his chair and made towards the door. 'How long ago?' he asked, peering across the street.

''Bout two minutes ago, guv'nor. Pretty-looking doxy, she were. Youngish, like you said.'

'Thanks,' said Catto. He stepped into the street and positioned himself against the ironmonger's window so that he could see Daisy Watkins's front door through the gap between the fruiterer's stall and that of the oil-and-lamp vendor next to it. Dressed in an old seaman's sweater, tattered trousers and a cloth cap, he blended easily with the habitués of the street.

Daisy Watkins stayed only long enough to collect her letters, and probably to gather one or two items she had forgotten when she had left three days previously, before emerging into the midday bustle of the market, a shopping basket over one arm. For a moment or two, she paused, glancing up and down the street, and then set off towards Horseferry Road. Stopping at the dairy to have her can filled with milk, she carried on down the road, past the Greycoat School and into Rochester Row, pausing occasionally to look in shop windows.

Catto, skilled in surveillance work, kept his distance but never once lost sight of his quarry, although he came close to doing so when Daisy crossed Vauxhall Bridge Road and almost immediately turned left into Tachbrook Street.

The policeman on point duty waved on the traffic, and Catto, dodging between a tram and a cab, was only just in time to see Daisy turning the corner.

''Ere, you trying to kill yourself, mate?' snarled the policeman.

'I'll do you a favour one day, culley,' mouthed Catto.

'Blimey, never knew it was you, Henry,' said the policeman, his jaw dropping in surprise as he recognized the usually well-dressed detective.

Halfway down Tachbrook Street, Daisy Watkins let herself into a house with a latchkey.

So much for a trip to Glasgow, thought Catto, and with a sigh made his way back to Cannon Row police station.

'Is Perkins there an' all?' asked Hardcastle.

'Don't rightly know, sir,' said Catto.

'Well, you'd better find out, my lad. You won't find him in my office, that's for sure.'

'D'you want him run in, sir?'

Hardcastle sat back in his chair and chewed absent-mindedly on the stem of his pipe. 'Strikes me you're all too fond of running people in, Catto,' he said. 'A sort of easy way of doing things, ain't it?'

'Oh no, sir, not exactly.'

'No . . . ?' said Hardcastle pensively. 'Then you'd better get yourself back round to Tachbrook Street and stay there until you see Alf Perkins. *Then* you can come back and let me know.'

'Yes, sir,' said Catto.

'And Catto . . .'

'Yes, sir?'

'Take a pushbike so you can get back here in double quick time.'

It was half-past seven that evening before Perkins appeared at the end of Tachbrook Street. Twice he walked past the house that Daisy Watkins had earlier entered until, looking furtively up and down, he too admitted himself with a latchkey.

Catto mounted his bicycle and rode furiously back to Cannon Row to impart his news to the DDI.

'Right, Marriott, we'll go and have words with that pair. They're up to something, I'll be bound.'

Marriott glanced at his watch. 'Yes, sir,' he said, 'and right now I can guess what it is.'

Hardcastle pocketed his pipe and tobacco pouch before donning his bowler hat and picking up his umbrella. 'Well, we'll just have to interrupt their slap and tickle, won't we, Marriott,' he said.

Seventeen

Determined to lose no time, Hardcastle took a cab from Whitehall but, not wishing to draw too much attention to his visit, dismissed it in Warwick Way. He and Marriott walked down Tachbrook Street until they reached the house that Detective Constable Catto had seen Perkins and Daisy Watkins enter.

It was a good five minutes after Hardcastle had begun hammering on the door that it opened and the face of Alf Perkins peered round it. 'What d'you want?' he demanded angrily, as he recognized the two policemen.

'So, Perkins, I've found you at last,' said Hardcastle. 'I want words with you.' He pushed the door wide and Perkins retreated into the narrow hall.

Realizing that Hardcastle was not to be dissuaded from asking questions, Perkins opened the door of the front room and then closed it again once the three of them were inside. His hair tousled, and dressed in trousers, a collarless shirt and unlaced boots, he stood aggressively in the centre of the room. 'What about?'

'Lady Rivers's tap's busted,' said Hardcastle, his face belying any amusement.

'What?' said Perkins, his chin dropping.

'I said Lady Rivers's tap needs mending, Perkins. She ain't best pleased with you, I can tell you.'

'Stupid old bat,' said Perkins angrily. 'Bane of my bleedin' life, that silly cow. But you ain't come round here just to tell me that, I'll wager.'

'Well, what are you doing holed up round here? Done a bunk, have you?'

At that point the door opened and a woman's voice asked,

'Who was that at the door, Alf?' The figure of Daisy Watkins entered the room. Her long, brown hair was loose around her shoulders and she was attired only in a floor-length, cotton peignoir from which her bare feet peeped. 'Oh, my Gawd!' she said as she caught sight of the two detectives. Her hand went to her mouth and she clutched the flimsy wrap more closely around her shapely body.

'Well, well, if it ain't Mrs Watkins,' said Hardcastle, affecting surprise. 'And what are you doing here?'

'Look here,' said Perkins truculently, 'I don't see as how it's anything to do with you.'

'When I'm investigating a murder, Perkins,' said Hardcastle, 'everything's to do with me. Now then, shall we all sit down? I want to talk to you. Both of you.'

The four of them sat down, Daisy Watkins perching uncomfortably on the edge of her chair, clearly embarrassed at having been found with Perkins, and in a state of *déshabillé*.

'It's not what it seems,' said Perkins, running a hand round his mouth. 'Me and Daisy, well we—'

'It don't need explaining, Perkins,' said Hardcastle. 'I've got eyes in me head. But I wonder what Corporal Watkins'd think of it all.'

'Frank was killed last week,' said Daisy listlessly.

'I'm sorry to hear that,' said Hardcastle, and was about to say that it had not taken Daisy long to move in with Perkins, but he thought better of it. Nevertheless he was in no doubt that that was the true state of affairs. He looked around the room, taking in the cheap furnishings and, over a cast-iron fireplace, a mantelshelf crowded with bric-à-brac. Judging it all not to be the choice of the couple now sitting opposite him, he asked, 'You renting this place?'

'Sort of,' said Perkins.

'What's that supposed to mean?'

'Well, it's like on loan.' Perkins was obviously unwilling to discuss his living arrangements.

Hardcastle thought that it was probably because the police had discovered enough about them already. 'How long did you know Rose Drummond?' he asked suddenly.

Perkins gave that some thought. 'Since she moved in. Nigh on a year ago, I suppose.' He glanced at Daisy. 'End of September, I think it was.'

That certainly accorded with the entry in Mrs Drummond's false American passport, which showed that she had arrived at Liverpool in September 1915. 'I've heard that you spent a lot of time going in and out of her apartment.' Hardcastle pressed on with his questioning.

'Well, o'course I did. I was the porter, weren't I?'

'Was? Does that mean you've given up the portering job, then, Perkins?'

'Yeah!' Perkins spoke churlishly. 'Had enough of the likes of them what lives round there, so I chucked it. It was Perkins this and Perkins that, all day long. I got fed up with it, I can tell you.'

'So, why did you spend so much time in Mrs Drummond's place?' Hardcastle was determined to get an answer.

'This and that. A very generous woman was Mrs Drummond—'

'So I've heard,' said Hardcastle quietly.

'And she was always grateful when I done odd jobs for her.'

'What sort of odd jobs?'

'Things like fixing her gramophone when it went wrong. She was having a party one time, a soirée she called it, and she said it wouldn't be nothing without a bit of music. An' another time, she'd had wine spilt all over the carpet. Give me a Bradbury for cleaning that up, she did.'

Hardcastle glanced at Daisy. 'Mrs Watkins said that she occasionally had men-friends staying the night. What d'you know about that?'

'Nothing,' said Perkins, a little too promptly.

Hardcastle looked at Daisy once more. 'That is what you said, Mrs Watkins, isn't it?' he asked.

Daisy giggled and clutched her peignoir even more firmly to her throat. 'Yes,' she said, 'leastways I reckoned they must be men. Like I said, they was always under the covers when I took her tea in the morning, an' she wouldn't have been sharing her bed with another woman, would she?'

'I wouldn't know.' Hardcastle looked back at Perkins again. 'You must have seen people coming and going to her rooms.'

'There's a lot of apartments there, guv'nor. Half the time I never knew who was going where.'

'Did she ever ask you for information about the other residents at Artillery Mansions, Perkins?'

'Sometimes.'

'Anyone in particular?'

'What's this all about?' demanded Perkins. 'If you've got a straight question, ask it.'

Hardcastle leaned forward threateningly. 'It's the same question I put to you before, Perkins, when we found out that Mrs Drummond lived there. One of her visitors might have murdered her. And the same man might have killed Miss Sturgess.' He turned towards Daisy. 'What about you, Mrs Watkins? Did you see anyone going in or coming out?'

'No,' said Daisy. 'Never.'

Perkins shook his head. 'No one,' he said, again seeming to give the matter no thought at all.

Hardcastle stood up. 'Well, you needn't think I've finished with you,' he said. There was an edge of menace in his voice. 'We'll be having another little chat again before very long. And if you carry on being awkward, my lad, I'll likely arrest you for obstructing me in the execution of my duty, and we'll see if a few hours in a cell at the nick'll improve your memory. Come to that, I might just run the pair of you in.' At the door, he paused. 'And don't you go running away again, neither.'

Hardcastle waited until he and Marriott had reached the end of the street and had turned into Warwick Way before speaking. 'I want you to hang on here, Marriott. See if either of the buggers goes anywhere in a hurry. I'll leg it back to the nick and get Wilmot or one of the others out to relieve you. But if Master Perkins in particular takes off, you're to keep your minces on him until he settles again. Got it?'

'Yes, sir,' said Marriott, wondering how long it would be before one of the night-duty detectives arrived.

In fact, DC Fred Wilmot had been in the police station doing some paperwork when Hardcastle returned there in a cab, and

166

had been sent straight to Tachbrook Street. The following morning he reported to the DDI.

'Well, lad, anything happen?'

'The man Perkins left the house at half-past nine, sir, just after I'd relieved Sergeant Marriott, and made his way to the Windsor pub, bottom of Vic Street. He went in the "public" and had a pint or two, and spoke to a couple of men.'

'Who were they, any idea?'

'No, sir,' said Wilmot, 'but I took a brief description of the pair of 'em. One of 'em looked a bit of a toff, sir,' he added as he proffered his pocket book to Hardcastle.

The DDI scanned the detective's brief notes and handed the book back. 'Could be anyone,' he said dismissively. 'Righto, lad. Is Catto round in Tachbrook Street now?'

'Yes, sir.'

'I wonder what the bugger's up to, Marriott.' As Wilmot left, Hardcastle settled behind his desk again. 'If he's a spy, he's making a poor fist of it, I'll say that for him. Wouldn't last five minutes in the Department.'

Detective Sergeant Wood appeared in the doorway of Hardcastle's office. 'Excuse me, sir. A message from across the road. You're to see Superintendent Quinn, urgent.'

Hardcastle sighed and stood up, wondering when the Special Branch chief was going to leave him to get on with the two complicated murders he was trying desperately to solve. He seized his bowler hat and his umbrella and, in a fit of pique, walked downstairs and strode across the courtyard to the main entrance of the Commissioner's Office.

'You know Major Fellowes, of course,' said Quinn as Hardcastle entered the superintendent's office.

'Yes, sir.' Hardcastle glanced at the army officer and gave him the briefest of nods. 'Major,' he murmured.

'He wants to talk to you. Sit down.'

'Inspector, I'm told that you saw Perkins last evening.'

'Yes, I did.' Hardcastle wondered how the MI5 man knew of his visit, and the ramifications of his statement brought a scowl to the DDI's face. 'Bit of a dodgy character that. As a matter of fact, Major, I'm thinking of having him in.'

'Mmm!' Fellowes stroked his moustache. 'I'd rather you didn't do that.'

'Why not? As far as I'm concerned, Perkins could have valuable information about the murder of Edith Sturgess, but the little bugger's not coming across. He's playing the dummy with me, is that one, and I'm not having anyone obstruct me in a murder enquiry. I've given him time to think it over, but if he don't come up to snuff, I'll lock him up and sweat it out of him. In the meantime, I've put a man on him, just in case he's thinking of upping sticks again. Him and the doxy he's sharing his house with.'

'You say you've put a man on him, Inspector?' Fellowes sounded quite alarmed.

Hardcastle nodded. 'I have that,' he said.

Obviously disconcerted by this piece of information, Fellowes turned to Quinn. 'D'you think I can take the inspector fully into my confidence, Superintendent?' he asked.

'I think you'll have to, Major,' said Quinn. 'I fancy it'll be the lesser of two evils,' he added with a bleak smile.

Still Fellowes hesitated. 'Your man must have been very discreet,' he said. 'My chap didn't spot him.'

'My men aren't amateurs, Major,' said Hardcastle pointedly, and wondered why one of Fellowes's men had also been watching the Tachbrook Street house.

'Evidently,' said Fellowes drily. Hardcastle's jibe had not been lost on him. 'Well, Inspector, the truth of the matter is that Perkins is in fact Staff Sergeant Perkins of the Royal Engineers Signal Service. Did some very good work in Ypres in early nineteen-fifteen. That's why we pulled him back here for a special job.'

'Well I'll go to the foot of our stairs,' said Hardcastle, infuriated that yet again he had been made to look a complete fool. He glanced at Quinn but was unsure what to make of the smile that was spreading slowly across the Special Branch chief's face. 'What's that all about then?' he demanded angrily.

'You will know from what Colonel Kell told you at the time of Rose Drummond's murder that we had harboured suspicions about her for some time, Inspector,' Fellowes continued smoothly. 'It was decided that to put the man Perkins in there to become as friendly and helpful as possible might just have provided us with sufficient evidence that she was spying to warrant her arrest.'

'And did it?' asked Hardcastle, still fuming at this latest example of MI5 chicanery.

'Alas, no,' said Fellowes. 'But it might have done had she remained alive.'

'So what's the point of Perkins moving to Tachbrook Street?'

'We're going to use him again, to act as support, and as a bodyguard. You see, we're putting another woman into that house and she will send false information to the enemy which we hope they'll swallow. At least, we hope they will once we've convinced the Germans that she's Rose Drummond. Then we'll sit back and see what happens.'

'And who's this new woman going to be?' asked Hardcastle. 'Or is that another of your secrets?' He wondered how Perkins was going to explain the presence of Daisy Watkins to his superiors.

'You know her as Daisy Watkins,' said Fellowes.

Hardcastle glanced at the impassive face of Quinn and then looked blankly at Major Fellowes. 'And I suppose that's why Corporal Watkins, the man who wrote her the letter about Rose Drummond's food parcel, conveniently got himself killed last week,' he said sarcastically.

'There was no Corporal Watkins,' said Fellowes. 'That whole business was a piece of elaborate flim-flam prepared by our officers, and Mrs Drummond took the bait, I'm pleased to say. The idea of the letter was that Daisy Watkins would show it to Rose Drummond when we gave her the signal, in the hope that Mrs Drummond would be panicked into doing something stupid, like trying to escape. Incidentally, Daisy Watkins is actually called Gertrude Frost. The Honourable Gertrude Frost.'

Hardcastle shook his head. 'What was the point of her reading me out all that stuff from the letter she's supposed to have got from Corporal Watkins, then? Who, according to you, never existed anyway.'

Fellowes shrugged. 'Playing a part, Inspector,' he said enigmatically. 'Just playing a part.'

'Well, what happens now?'

'That, Inspector, is up to you,' said Quinn. 'Major Fellowes has only told you all that so that you won't go pestering either of them again. It might interfere with secret arrangements, d'you see?'

'But even so I'm sure that Perkins knows more than he's told me.' Hardcastle was now hopelessly confused by the convolutions of the counter-espionage operations that had been going on beneath his very nose. 'I've still got two murders to solve,' he added plaintively.

'Yes, I know,' said Fellowes, 'and we'll do all we can to assist you. D'you think that another talk with Perkins will help then?'

'I'm sure of it, Major. And Daisy Watkins, or whatever you say her name is.'

'Very well. I'll advise both Staff Sergeant Perkins and Miss Frost that they are to be brought to Scotland Yard, discreetly of course, so that you can talk to them. And I shall tell them that they are to co-operate with you fully. How would that be?'

'Cannon Row would be better, Major.'

'Very well.' Fellowes paused. 'D'you think you could arrange to have them taken there under cover of darkness? I have no wish to compromise them any more than they have been compromised so far.'

Hardcastle, only slightly mollified at having been taken into the confidence of MI5 at long last, nodded. 'We'll get them smuggled in, Major, have no fear of that,' he said. 'I'll have to take my sergeant into my confidence though,' he added. 'Otherwise Marriott might go asking some embarrassing questions.'

Reluctantly, Fellowes agreed. 'Very well, Inspector,' he said, 'but I must ask you to use the utmost discretion in all your dealings with my two agents. I don't have to tell you that their lives may depend upon it.'

'You'll tell them they're to be picked up, Major, will you?' asked Hardcastle.

'Yes, and the sooner the better. Would this evening suit you, at say eleven o'clock? It's just about dark then what with this daylight-saving nonsense that the government's introduced.'

'Eleven o'clock it is,' said Hardcastle. 'I'll collect them myself.'

It was raining when a motor cab, driven by DS Marriott, drew up outside the house in Tachbrook Street. It was a cab that had been acquired by the police for observation work and looked like the hundreds of others regularly plying the streets of the capital.

Complying with the arrangements that Major Fellowes had insisted upon, Hardcastle waited in the cab. No sooner had it stopped than the door of the house opened and two figures swiftly crossed the pavement and got into the vehicle. Neither of them said anything.

'The driver's one of my men,' said Hardcastle. 'So, Staff Sergeant Perkins and Miss Frost, is it? Well, you two have been pulling my leg and that's no mistake. You ought to thank your lucky stars there's a war on otherwise you'd have been locked up, the pair of you, for obstructing a police enquiry. Drive on, Marriott.'

In the dark interior of the cab, neither Perkins nor the woman Hardcastle had known as Daisy Watkins could see that the DDI was smiling.

Ten minutes later, the cab drew into the yard of Cannon Row police station and a constable, specially posted there for the purpose, closed the huge gates behind it.

Eighteen

'So this is the centre of your web, Inspector,' said Gertrude Frost, slowly drawing off her gloves and gazing around Hardcastle's office with a whimsical smile on her face. She slipped off her long cloak and handed it to Marriott, but kept her hat on. Smoothing the skirt of her grey drill costume, she accepted the DDI's invitation to sit down.

Staff Sergeant Perkins sat down also and crossed his legs, unable to prevent himself from smiling at the deception he and Gertrude Frost had perpetrated on Hardcastle.

'I understand from Major Fellowes that you think we may be able to help you.' Gertrude spoke in polished tones; there was no trace now of the working-class accent she had assumed so effectively when playing the part of Daisy Watkins.

Hardcastle was impressed. 'If ever you think about my line of work when the war's over, miss,' he said, 'I'm sure we could find you a job. Where on earth did you learn to talk like a cleaning woman?'

Gertrude Frost smiled graciously at the implied compliment. 'My mother was an actress,' she said. 'Well, a chorus girl really. She was one of the Gaiety Girls when my father married her. She used to tell us wonderful stories about the theatre when we were small, and do all the accents. So it came as no surprise to my father when I followed my mother into the theatre, until the war started, that is. I'm told I do quite a good "common".'

'That you do, miss,' said Hardcastle admiringly. 'You certainly had me fooled.' He took his pipe from the ashtray and held it up, hesitating. 'D'you mind?' he asked.

Sitting at the back of the office, Marriott was silently

172

amazed at his chief's uncharacteristic deference, but he had to admit, now she had shed the persona – and the cheap clothing – of Daisy Watkins, that Gertrude Frost was an extremely handsome woman.

'Not at all,' said Gertrude. 'D'you mind if *I* do?' She smiled again, opened her handbag and took out a cigarette case and a long holder. 'Don't look so shocked, Inspector,' she added, catching sight of Hardcastle's surprised expression. 'It's the influence of the stage, I suppose – and the war – but I do the most outrageous things these days.'

Hardcastle struck a match and stood, leaning over his desk, to apply the flame to the end of Gertrude's cigarette. 'Now then, Sergeant,' he began, sitting down again and directing his gaze at Perkins.

'If you want to use my rank, it's "Staff",' said Perkins mildly. 'But I'm quite happy to be called Alf.' He grinned and stuck his forefingers into his waistcoat pockets.

'Well, er, Mr Perkins,' said Hardcastle, unable to be so familiar with someone whom, until now, he had believed to be at best a villain, possibly even a spy. 'I'll explain what's what.' He paused to light his pipe. 'Rose Drummond had dressed herself up as a prostitute' – he glanced at Gertrude – 'begging your pardon, miss, for speaking straight like.'

Gertrude Frost laughed. 'I'm no stranger to the ways of the world, Inspector,' she said. 'Do go on.'

'Well, like I was saying, Rose Drummond was dressed as a prostitute the night she was murdered and we believe that she'd been hanging around Finsbury Barracks trying to pick up a soldier. She'd certainly been doing it before.'

'Yes, we know that,' said Perkins.

'Yes . . .' said Hardcastle reflectively, and wondered how much more the staff sergeant knew. 'We certainly came across one man from there who reckoned that he'd been accosted by her. According to Colonel Kell, she used to do it quite regular, hoping to get some information from them, troop movements and the like.' Hardcastle glanced at Perkins. 'Anyhow, she was found in Hoxton Square early on the morning of Sunday the sixteenth of July. She'd been strangled with a length of rope.'

173

'D'you think a soldier was responsible?' asked Gertrude, leaning forward to tap the ash from the end of her cigarette into Hardcastle's ashtray.

'No idea, miss, but then, on the second of August, Edith Sturgess, what had been put in to replace her, so to speak, was found by Mr Perkins here in Rose Drummond's apartment in Artillery Mansions. She'd been strangled an' all, but manually of course.'

'How awful,' said Gertrude, shuddering slightly, but her horror at the crime was probably a result of knowing that she was about to take on a similar role as part of Major Fellowes's elaborate plan.

'And right now, I don't have a single suspect,' continued Hardcastle with an honesty rarely revealed to those outside the police force.

'How can we help then, Inspector?' asked Perkins.

'Well, for a start, I think you might know a bit more than you've been telling me, Mr Perkins—'

'I was told to say nothing that might affect the operation,' said Perkins, 'and that stymied me a bit, but now that Major Fellowes has given the all clear, I'll tell you as much as I know. I was there, as he probably told you, to keep an eye on Rose Drummond. I made myself as useful as possible and gained her confidence. As far as I know.'

'I think she had you lined up as a possible agent,' said Hardcastle.

'You mean because my name was in the book you found in the davenport?'

'You knew about that, then?' Hardcastle raised his eyebrows.

'Oh, yes, I knew about that, Inspector, and I got to know about the one or two men who called on her. I reckon she wasn't above sleeping with anyone she thought might be useful to her. Anyhow that was the way I saw it, and Major Fellowes did an' all.'

Hardcastle nodded. 'D'you have any names?' he asked.

Perkins had no need to refer to any notes he might have made. 'Yes,' he said, 'there was the MP, Charles Smith, and a couple of civil servants called Foster and Hollins.'

'Well I'll be—' Hardcastle broke off, infuriated that Foster and Hollins had also shared Rose Drummond's bed but had denied it so vehemently that he had believed them.

Perkins licked his lips. 'And then there was Brigadier-General Levitt.' He chuckled at that. 'Dropped me a florin one night for calling him a cab. Gawd, if only he'd known I was a sapper staff-sergeant, he'd have had a blue fit.'

Hardcastle joined in the laughter. 'I should think he would,' he said. 'What time of the day did these men usually call on her?'

'In the evening, any time after about seven, I suppose. Smith, the MP, often came later but that probably depended on what time he could get away from the House of Commons.'

'D'you know what time they left again?'

'Sometimes I'd see them go, perhaps quite late, but I couldn't say for sure. I wasn't always around. Much as I'd like to help, I couldn't say whether they stayed the night or not. I never saw any of 'em leaving in the mornings, any road.'

'Didn't mean they was giving her information though, does it? Probably no more than just the chance of—' Hardcastle broke off and gave Gertrude Frost an embarrassed glance.

'Inspector,' said Gertrude, 'I do wish you wouldn't let my being here worry you. You were about to say that these men were merely calling in for a little jig-jig and nothing else.'

Hardcastle was astounded at the woman's forthright manner, but attributed it to her having been an actress. 'Well, yes, miss, that's one way of putting it, I suppose. What I mean is,' he hurried on, 'that there mightn't have been any more to it than that. No evidence to say that they was giving Mrs Drummond what she wanted.'

Gertrude Frost giggled. 'Matter of opinion,' she murmured, and then laughed openly at Hardcastle. It was an infectious, bubbling laugh.

'In the way of information, I mean.' Too late Hardcastle tried to redress Gertrude Frost's deliberate misinterpretation, and struggled on. 'Was there anyone else what you knew of, either of you?'

175

Perkins shook his head. 'No, but I wasn't really in a good position to know, being as how I was often doing other things. It wasn't really much cop, putting me in there as a porter, but I s'pose it was the best they could come up with.'

'There's one thing I noticed that might be useful to you, Inspector,' said Gertrude slowly.

'What's that, miss?'

'It was one of the mornings when I took the Drummond woman tea and there was a man in bed with her. I couldn't say who he was because, as I said the first time we met, they'd always be right under the bedclothes, and they always left after I did. But when I was running the Ewbank round the sitting room I came across an officer's red-banded cap. It was on the floor behind the sofa. I don't know whether it had been hidden there deliberately, or whether it had just fallen down and been forgotten. It could have been either because I didn't often pull the sofa out to clean behind it.' Gertrude smiled mischievously at Hardcastle. 'I wasn't a very good charwoman.'

'And d'you think it was General Levitt's cap?'

'I'm afraid your guess would probably be as good as mine, Inspector. There was certainly no name inside it. I looked.'

'And you don't have to be a general to have a red-banded cap,' said Perkins. 'All staff officers wear them, whatever their rank.'

'Oh, well, I seem to have come to a dead end again.' Hardcastle stood up.

'There is one other thing, Inspector,' said Perkins.

'Yes?'

'When I called the constable, the morning of Miss Sturgess's death, I told him I'd found her front door open.'

'So I was told,' said Hardcastle.

'Well, it wasn't.'

'I think you'd better explain, Mr Perkins.'

'Major Fellowes had told me to keep an eye on her, so every morning I'd knock to make sure she was tickety-boo. I never got an answer that morning, so I let myself in—'

'How?' asked Hardcastle sharply.

'I had a set of keys.'

'And where did you get those from?'

'Major Fellowes,' said Perkins with a grin, 'and don't ask me where he got them from.'

'I see,' said Hardcastle irritably, although he knew from his first meeting with Fellowes that he had possessed a key to the apartment. 'Well, thank you both for coming to see me.' He moved towards the door. 'I've arranged for Sergeant Marriott here to see that you get back to Tachbrook Street safe and sound.'

As Marriott ushered Perkins and Gertrude Frost into the corridor, Perkins stopped and turned. 'Inspector, you know when you called at Tachbrook Street yesterday evening . . . ?' he began in hushed tones.

'What about it, Mr Perkins?'

'Well, Gertie and I were—'

'You and Miss Frost were what?' Hardcastle was being deliberately obtuse; it was his way of repaying Perkins for having impeded his earlier enquiries, even though it had not been the soldier's fault.

Perkins ran a hand round his mouth. 'She and I were, er, well, we were enjoying each other's company is the best way of putting it, I suppose.'

'I think I get the idea,' said Hardcastle, retaining a stern expression. 'What Miss Frost calls *jig-jig*, if I remember correctly.'

'Yes . . .' Perkins was clearly embarrassed at having been caught out. 'But I was wondering, hoping, that you'd not mention it to the major if you see him again, 'cos I don't think he'd approve.'

'I'm quite sure he wouldn't,' said Hardcastle, laughing, 'but it's nothing to do with me. Nor him, if you want my opinion.'

Hardcastle had despatched Marriott to make discreet enquiries into the alibis furnished by Foster and Hollins, and by Charles Smith, MP, for the night of Edith Sturgess's murder. All, it seemed, were sound. That left one other.

'This Brigadier-General Levitt, Marriott . . .'

'Yes, sir?'

177

'When we got in touch with the War Office, they said he was in France from the thirty-first of July to the fifth of August.'

'That's right, sir. Why, have you got doubts?'

'I've always got doubts, Marriott. And just because a man's a general don't rule him out in my book.'

'What d'you want done then, sir?'

'We'll go and have another chat with him, Marriott, that's what we'll do.'

'Is that wise, sir? From what you were saying, Levitt's a bit of a bristly character. Might be that you wouldn't get anything out of him. Why not have a word with the Provost-Marshal, see if he can help?'

Hardcastle leaned back in his chair and surveyed his detective sergeant. 'D'you know, Marriott, you're coming on a treat. That's not a bad idea. I wonder where he hangs out.'

Marriott grinned. 'The War Office, sir, and he's called Brigadier-General Edward Fitzpatrick.'

'I'm investigating a murder, General,' said Hardcastle. 'Well, two murders, as a matter of fact, and I was wondering if you could help.'

'Only too pleased, Inspector. What seems to be your problem?' The head of the army's police waved a hand towards chairs and then sat down behind his desk.

Hardcastle explained, in detail, about the deaths of Rose Drummond and Edith Sturgess, and went on to tell the Provost-Marshal of Brigadier-General Levitt's visit to France. 'It's not that I suspect him, General,' he said, 'but I don't like loose ends. I'd like some confirmation that General Levitt was where he was supposed to be on the date in question.' He paused. 'You see, he's already lied to us, saying as how he never visited the Drummond woman, but we now know that he did.'

Fitzpatrick drew a pad towards him. 'What were the dates that he was supposed to be in France?' he asked, and when he had written them down, he added, 'Leave it with me, Inspector. I'll see what I can do, although I have to say that it may not be easy. To be frank with you, the army's

178

movements are often a mystery, even to those of us in it.' He smiled apologetically. 'Are there any other enquiries you'd care for me to make while I'm about it?'

'Not at this stage, General, thank you. If General Levitt was in Flanders, or wherever, then that's an end to it. But if he wasn't then I shall have to see him again and try to get the truth out of him.'

'Yes, of course. There is a possibility that he was on some secret mission and that the details of it are not readily available, but I'll see what I can do.' Fitzpatrick stood up and held out his hand. 'It sounds like a difficult one, Inspector. I wish you luck.'

'Thank you,' said Hardcastle, 'I reckon I need it.'

Three whole days elapsed before Hardcastle got a call to see the Provost-Marshal again.

'It seems that General Levitt was indeed in France, Inspector, but not between the dates you gave me.' Fitzpatrick looked grave. 'He arrived at Fifth Army headquarters for a conference with General Gough on the thirtieth of July. I have no idea what the conference was about and I doubt that it matters, but he left there on the first of August and we do know that he travelled home on a troopship on that date.'

'D'you know where he went when he got back here, General?' asked Hardcastle.

'No,' said Fitzpatrick. He turned over a sheet of paper in a file on his desk. 'The troopship disembarked its passengers at Folkestone at 1645 hours on the first. General Levitt next reported for duty here at the War Office on the sixth of August. One can only assume that he was on leave for those five days, probably at his place at Henley.' The Provost-Marshal flicked over another page. 'Yes, at Bray to be precise.' He looked up. 'I don't know whether that helps or not, Inspector, but it's the best we can do without alerting General Levitt to your interest.'

'Thank you for your assistance, General Fitzpatrick,' said Hardcastle. 'It looks as though we'll have to make a few local enquiries and perhaps talk to General Levitt again.'

*   *   *

Rather than leave such delicate enquiries to the Berkshire Constabulary, Hardcastle sent Marriott and Catto to Bray. According to the policeman responsible for that part of the village where Levitt had his country retreat, the general had been seen there between the first and the fifth of August, but there was no one, except perhaps the general's wife, who could say for sure that he had been there all the time.

The DDI received this news with a measure of cynicism and promptly dismissed any thought of interviewing Mrs Levitt. 'It looks very much as though we'll have to talk to General Levitt again,' he said, echoing what he had said to the Provost-Marshal, 'but we've got nothing to connect him with either murder.' Gently, he knocked the ash from his pipe and began to refill it. 'And I don't want to let him know that we're thinking about him for the toppings, not until we've got something that'll cause him to wriggle.'

'What did he say when you and Drew saw him last time, sir?' asked Marriott.

'He said that he'd only met Rose Drummond the once, at some soirée at the House of Commons, and that he'd never seen her again.'

'Well, if what Miss Frost said about finding a general's cap behind the sofa's true, sir, he's got a bit of explaining to do there.'

'If it was his cap, Marriott,' said Hardcastle. 'But she didn't say it was a general's cap, she just said it had a red band round it. And Perkins said that all staff officers wear 'em. So it don't mean much.'

'I know about that, sir,' said Marriott, 'but don't forget what Staff Sergeant Perkins also said about calling him a cab one night, so we know that Levitt saw our Rose more than just the once. And Mr Smith said that he was at a do at Rose's place, as well. Be interesting to see what the general's got to say when you put that to him.'

Hardcastle nodded slowly. 'He'd probably deny it,' he said, 'and Smith changed his tune about having seen him at Mrs Drummond's place. We can't tell him who Perkins was either, not without blowing Major Fellowes's little plan. Anyhow, we'll find out where Levitt lives when he's in

180

London, Marriott. It might be a start if we can find a neighbour who saw him there round about the time Edith Sturgess was topped. Then we'll have a think about what to do next.' He pulled his watch from his pocket and stared at it. 'I don't know about you, Marriott, but I could shift a pint down the Red Lion.'

Nineteen

Hardcastle had imagined that the simplest way to find out General Levitt's London address would be to ask the Provost-Marshal, but although Brigadier-General Fitzpatrick was his usual helpful self, the answer he gave the DDI did not really assist.

'General Levitt lives in a senior officer's quarters at Chelsea Barracks when he's in London, Inspector.'

'Well, that rather puts the kibosh on that,' said Hardcastle gloomily. 'If I start asking questions around there, General Levitt will find out in no time at all that I'm taking an interest in him.'

Fitzpatrick leaned forward, a purposeful expression on his face. 'D'you really think that General Levitt had something to do with these murders, Inspector?' he asked. 'Because if he did, it could have serious implications for the army, particularly in time of war.'

Hardcastle shrugged. 'I don't know, General,' he said, 'but the fact of the matter is that when I first saw General Levitt he claimed to have seen Rose Drummond just the once, at a soirée at the House of Commons.'

'Well, surely that—'

'However,' said Hardcastle, cutting across the Provost-Marshal's intervention, 'as I told you before, I have since heard that he called on Mrs Drummond at her apartment at least once, possibly more often. And another informant,' he added, being careful to shield Gertrude Frost's identity, 'claims to have seen a man in bed with her who was quite probably General Levitt.'

'But how on earth could someone have seen—?'

Hardcastle held up a hand. 'I'm sure you'll understand,

General,' he said, 'being as how you're in the trade, so to speak, that I can't possibly reveal the name of my informant. Suffice it to say,' he continued, somewhat pompously, 'that I am satisfied as to that informant's reliability.'

'If you say so, Inspector,' said Fitzpatrick, a little piqued at not being taken fully into the detective's confidence. 'If you say so. However, I'd like to ask you a favour . . .'

'And what's that, General?'

'If there is a likelihood of your arresting General Levitt, I'd be grateful for a little advanced notice. I'm sure you know how these things work: at the first intimation of a general officer being charged with a murder, the Chief of the Imperial General Staff would send for me and demand an explanation. And believe me,' Fitzpatrick went on, with a wry smile, 'when General Robertson asks a question like that it behoves one to have a ready answer.'

'And are you going to keep General Fitzpatrick informed, sir?' asked Marriott, as he and Hardcastle left the War Office.

'No I ain't, Marriott. I don't trust any of 'em. They're all officers, you see. Like as not went to the same school. It's a case of you scratch my back and I'll scratch yours. No, Marriott, if Levitt's our man, we'll have him locked up first and then we'll let the army make what they want out of it, but if we tell anyone, then General Levitt'll get to hear of it and he'll be off like a long dog, you mark my words.'

'D'you really think he's mixed up in this, sir?'

'I don't know, Marriott, but he's got some answering to do, that's for sure.' Hardcastle sighed. 'There's only one thing for it,' he added, 'we'll have to see him again and see what he's got to say for himself.'

However, it was only after some considerable delay that General Levitt granted the two detectives a further interview.

'I hope this is not going to take long, Inspector, because I'm extremely busy.' Levitt waved at a couple of chairs with an imperious gesture as he repeated his customary caveat. 'The army is fighting for its life on the Somme and I really don't have time to waste on these footling questions of yours.' He glanced at a huge map of the Western Front that adorned one wall in his office. 'And as for Ypres . . .' He shrugged and then scowled at the two detectives.

But Hardcastle was not about to be cowed by the general's ferocity. He regarded it, in fact, as an attempt to dissuade him from asking his questions. 'When I first saw you, General,' he began, 'you told me that you had met Rose Drummond the once. At a soirée at the House of Commons you said.'

'That's correct,' said Levitt.

'But you also called on her in her apartment at Artillery Mansions on at least one occasion, possibly twice.'

'What absolute poppycock,' said Levitt angrily. 'Where on earth did you get that idea from?'

'Information from a reliable source,' said Hardcastle flatly. He thought it unwise to mention Charles Smith's name to Levitt and he certainly could not disclose Perkins's true identity.

'Really? Well, I would suggest to you, Inspector, that your so-called reliable source is lying, and I shall issue a writ for defamation if I hear such a scandalous slander repeated.'

'So you weren't having an affair with Mrs Drummond, General, is that what you're saying?' Hardcastle had sensed that Levitt's outrage was contrived and he was now, more than ever, convinced that the general had something to hide.

'I'm a married man, Inspector.'

'That don't altogether answer my question,' said Hardcastle mildly, conscious that his very impassiveness was infuriating Levitt even more.

'I think I told you, the last time you came here badgering me, Inspector, that I happen to know Sir Edward Henry rather well.' There was no mistaking the menacing tone of Levitt's voice.

'Yes, you did, General, and I told you *the last time I came here* that the Commissioner insists on his officers being most thorough in their enquiries.' It was apparent that Hardcastle was to get no more out of Brigadier-General Levitt so he stood up. 'And I shall pursue those enquiries until such time as I find the murderer of both Rose Drummond and Edith Sturgess.' He paused. 'Where were you, between coming back from

France on the first of August and the sixth of August when you returned to duty here, General?' He posed the question quietly, almost as if it was an afterthought.

The directness of Hardcastle's enquiry seemed to disconcert Levitt and he did not immediately respond, but then, recovering himself, he said, 'I can't answer that, Inspector. It is a military secret.'

'Can you at least tell me if you were in London?'

'No, I was not,' said Levitt forcefully.

Hardcastle nodded. 'Very well, General,' he said, and then added, 'Well, that looks like it for the time being, but I've no doubt we shall be seeing each other again.'

The following day, Hardcastle was again summoned to the Provost-Marshal's office.

'Seems to me, Marriott,' said the DDI, as the two detectives strode down Whitehall, 'that we're spending all our time going in and out of the War Office.'

'I occasionally dine at Chelsea Barracks, Inspector,' said Fitzpatrick, when Hardcastle and Marriott were seated in the Provost-Marshal's office once more, 'and I took the opportunity to sound out the mess caterer about General Levitt.' He noted the alarm on Hardcastle's face and smiled. 'I'm a policeman too, Inspector,' he continued, 'and I know how to be discreet. It seems that General Levitt dined in mess on the night of the first of August. He must have gone there straight from Folkestone.' He leaned back in his chair, a smile of self-satisfaction on his face because he had discovered something that had, so far, eluded the experienced detective opposite him. 'Does that help at all?'

'It certainly makes a mockery of what the general told me,' said Hardcastle thoughtfully, and deciding to take General Fitzpatrick some way into his confidence, added, 'He claimed that he wasn't in London at all between the first and the fifth of August. Trotted out some twaddle about it being a military secret.'

'That's not necessarily as sinister as it sounds, Inspector,' said Fitzpatrick, an expression of mild amusement on his face.

'The phrase "military secret" is the oldest euphemism there is when it comes to describing a visit to one's mistress, and Mrs Levitt would not take the idea of her husband having a fancy woman lying down. If you don't mind an apt metaphor,' he added with a chuckle.

'I suppose you don't know who this mistress of General Levitt's might be?' asked Hardcastle hopefully.

Fitzpatrick laughed outright. 'Now that *is* a military secret, Inspector,' he said.

Lieutenant-Colonel Crombie was clearly unused to the telephone and Hardcastle was forced to hold the receiver some distance away from his ear or be deafened.

'Is that Inspector Hardcastle?' The booming voice was unmistakable.

'Yes, Colonel.'

'I, er, I have a soldier in custody here at Finsbury Barracks who I think might be able to help you, Inspector.'

'Why is he in custody, Colonel?' Hardcastle immediately wondered if Crombie had, by some quirk, detained the man who had murdered Rose Drummond and Edith Sturgess.

'He's a deserter, Inspector.'

'Why should that be of interest to me?' Hardcastle had formed the opinion, at their first meeting, that Crombie was not very good at getting to the point.

'I think he may be able to shed some light on the murder that you came up here and talked to my men about.'

'Really?' Hardcastle was reserved in his response. A detective of his experience knew better than to get excited simply because an amateur sleuth thought he might have solved a crime; it had happened all too often in the past, but he also knew that it would be foolhardy to ignore it. 'I'll come there and see him, if I may, Colonel.'

'Of course, of course,' said Crombie. 'When?'

Hardcastle glanced at the clock on the wall of his office. 'Shall we say three o'clock?'

Regimental Sergeant-Major Runciman was with Colonel Crombie when the two detectives arrived.

'I've asked Mr Runciman to be here, Inspector,' said Crombie, 'because he is fully conversant with the facts of Sculley's case.'

'I take it Sculley is the soldier you spoke to me about on the telephone, Colonel?'

'Yes, he is. Didn't I mention his name? Oh well, that's who he is.' Crombie glanced at the RSM. 'Perhaps you'd conduct these two gentlemen to the guardroom, Mr Runciman.'

'Sir! Very good, sir.' Runciman stiffened, flicked his pace-stick beneath his left arm and saluted punctiliously.

The RSM led the two detectives across the parade ground, his eyes constantly swivelling from left to right as he marched. 'This Sculley, Mr Hardcastle,' he said, 'is a lairy little bastard. Didn't fancy milling it with Fritz, you see, so he cut and run just after the passing-out parade. Should've been on the one before, o'course.'

'The one before?' Hardcastle could not see what relevance that had to his enquiry.

'Oh yes. He was in the guardroom doing fourteen days for insubordination to an officer and for being late in. And drunk.' The RSM suddenly pointed his pace-stick threateningly at the figure of a soldier in the distance. 'That man here,' he roared, 'brace yourself up, you idle whoreson!' He turned back to Hardcastle and continued in a level, conversational tone as though he had not interrupted himself. 'He was picked up by the provost in Liverpool, day before yesterday. When he gets back here, he comes on with some yarn about knowing something about this murder of yours. Not that he'd say owt to the CO about it. Just that he knew something. Personally, Mr Hardcastle, I reckon he knows sweet Fanny Adams about it. Just trying to save hisself from going across the water, if you ask me. Bloody napoo.'

'We shall soon see, Mr Runciman,' said Hardcastle quietly.

The sergeant of the guard leaped to his feet as Runciman opened the door of the guardroom. 'Sir!'

'Open up Sculley's cell, Sarn't,' bellowed the RSM.

The sergeant seized a large bunch of keys from a hook on the wall and led the way into a dank passageway. He opened the door of the cell and stood back.

'On your feet, Sculley,' screamed the RSM. 'There's two officers here from the police wanting a word with you, my lad, and you'd better be telling them the truth or you'll have me to answer to.'

'Would you mind if we interviewed the prisoner on his own, Mr Runciman?' asked Hardcastle, glancing at the white-faced prisoner.

The RSM tugged at his moustache. 'As you wish, Mr Hardcastle,' he said, 'but mind what I said, he's a lairy little sod.' Somewhat reluctantly, Runciman withdrew to the front office of the guardroom.

Sculley was about eighteen years old and among the first to be caught up by Lord Derby's conscription scheme. Hardcastle imagined that he was terrified both of the RSM and the prospect of going into the trenches. Clad in heavy canvas trousers, a khaki flannel shirt and plimsolls, he remained rigidly at attention by the plank bed – the only furniture in the small cell – even after Runciman had left.

'All right, lad, you can sit down,' said Hardcastle.

'Yes, sir.' Sculley sat down, but remained tense, his fingers intertwined and clenched.

'D'you smoke, lad?'

'Yes, sir.' Sculley looked at the detective hopefully.

'Give him one of your fags, Marriott, and then ask that sergeant out there for a couple of chairs. I'm buggered if I'm going to stand up while I talk to this man.'

Once Sculley was puffing hungrily at his cigarette and Hardcastle and Marriott were seated on the hard-backed chairs that had been brought in by a sentry, the DDI began. 'The colonel tells me that you've got some information about the murder in Hoxton Square on the sixteenth of July.'

'Yes, sir,' said Sculley nervously.

'Well, spit it out, lad. What d'you know?'

'I saw it, sir.'

'What, saw the murder?' Hardcastle, accustomed as he was to surprises, was unable to conceal his astonishment.

'Yes, sir.'

Hardcastle raised his eyebrows and wondered if RSM

188

Runciman had been right about the deserter Sculley: that he was trying it on to escape embarkation. 'Go on, then.'

'I'd been out that Saturday night, sir, down the Crooked Billet for a few wets with me mates. Well, we got split up somehow and I, well I ain't used to too much drinking, sir . . .' Sculley paused, looked round the cell and then carefully tapped his cigarette ash into the palm of his hand and transferred it to one of his trouser pockets. 'Me mum always told me I shouldn't drink on account of me old man always getting pissed on the housekeeping—'

'I'm sure she was right, Sculley,' said Hardcastle, 'but can we get back to this Saturday night you were talking about?'

'Yes, sir. Well, I'd had a skinful and when we was coming back to barracks, through Hoxton Square – I was on me tod by then – I sort of passed out and fell in a bush. Any road, when I woke up I knew I was in bother.'

'How was that?'

'I knew I was late booking-in, see. We has to be in by twenty-two-thirty hours and I reckoned it was well past that. Any road, I got up and I was just about to move when I sees this bit of a fight going on, not but a few yards away from where I was. A man and a judy it were. Then this judy fell over and lay still like and the bloke runs off, straight past me.'

'What was the weather like, lad?' asked Marriott off-handedly.

Sculley did not have to think. 'It'd just started raining and minutes after it was coming down real heavy, sir.'

Hardcastle nodded. 'What did you do then?'

'I scarpered back to barracks.'

'Did you tell anyone about this fight you saw?'

'I tried to tell the officer, sir, but he wouldn't listen. Just went on about me spinning him a yarn to get off the charge of being drunk and over the wall, like. Then he told me to shut up. But I kept trying to tell him and he shoved me in the clink for insubordination.'

Hardcastle sighed, and toyed with the idea of charging the officer concerned with misprision of felony. Only later did he discover that not only had the lieutenant concerned already been posted to France when the DDI had talked to the training battalion's officers, but had been killed within days of his arrival there. 'Can you describe this man you saw, lad?' he asked. He had no hope of getting more than a vague description and that, undoubtedly, would be useless.

'Yes, sir, he was tall and had a moustache and he was . . .' Sculley frowned with the concentration of trying to recall what the murderer had looked like.

'Take your time, Sculley.'

There was silence in the cell, save for a bugler sounding a call somewhere in the distance, followed by a shouted and unintelligible order.

'I saw him again, sir.'

Hardcastle stared at the young soldier. 'You did what?'

'I saw him again, sir,' repeated Sculley.

'Well, where, lad, and when?'

Sculley glanced around his cell, a shifty expression on his face as though fearful of being overheard by someone in authority. 'He come down for the passing-out parade, sir.'

Hardcastle shot a meaningful glance at Marriott and then switched his gaze back to the soldier. 'What was his name, lad, any idea?' He asked the question casually as though it was of no importance.

Sculley shook his head. 'No, sir, except that he was a general.'

'When was the passing-out parade?'

'Can't rightly remember, sir.' Sculley frowned again, desperately anxious to assist. 'It was before I went adrift.'

'Would have been,' said Hardcastle drily, and stood up. 'I'll be wanting a statement from you about all this, lad. But I'm buggered if I'm having it done here.'

Accompanied by much stamping and shouting, and two escorting soldiers and a corporal, Sculley was transferred to an office where Detective Sergeant Marriott took a statement from him. Meanwhile, Hardcastle returned to Colonel Crombie's office.

'The man Sculley, Colonel, claims that he was on a passing-out parade just before he went absent without leave. Can you tell me who the general was who inspected it?'

Crombie rapped on the wall of his office with his walking

190

stick and repeated Hardcastle's request to the staff sergeant who responded to his summons.

A few minutes later the staff sergeant returned. 'The reviewing officer on the parade that Sculley was on was Brigadier-General Levitt, sir,' he said. 'He come down from the War Office, special like.'

Twenty

Immediately upon his return from Finsbury Barracks, Hardcastle urgently sought an interview with Superintendent Quinn and laid before him the details of what Private Sculley had told him.

'And this man definitely accuses General Levitt, does he?' Quinn wanted to be absolutely certain of the facts of the case.

'He's in no doubt of it, sir. Sculley never knew the general's name, but Colonel Crombie confirmed that it was Levitt who came down for the parade.'

For once, Quinn was reluctant to make a decision. 'There's nothing else for it, Hardcastle,' he said, 'if we're talking about charging a general with murder, you'll have to see Mr Thomson.' He glanced at the clock and stood up.

'What seems to be troubling you, Hardcastle?' asked the assistant commissioner. Although he was the most senior CID officer in the force, Thomson had, of late, immersed himself in the workings of Special Branch and seemed unwilling to devote too much of his time to ordinary criminal matters.

Hardcastle explained, in detail, the progress of his enquiries into the two murders. 'It seems to me, sir,' he went on hesitantly, 'that General Levitt's got a few questions to answer if what this swaddy says is true.'

'On the contrary, Hardcastle, I think that the RSM has probably got it right. This man Sculley is obviously trying everything he can to avoid active service. I think you'll find that his story is a tissue of lies.' Thomson leaned back in his chair and surveyed the inspector with a look of sympathy on his face. 'Do you seriously suggest that an Old Bailey jury is going to take the word of an eighteen-year-old white-feather deserter against that of a brigadier-general? You'd get laughed out of court, man. The whole idea is preposterous.'

'But General Levitt hasn't told the truth about his movements on the nights in question, sir.' Hardcastle struggled on. 'I don't like it at all. Mr Smith first of all swore that he was at a party at Mrs Drummond's place and then he changed his tune. I reckon he's covering up for General Levitt.'

Thomson dismissed the Liberal MP's uncertainty, and Hardcastle's implied theory of conspiracy, with a wave of his hand. 'There's probably a quite rational and reasonable explanation for it all, Hardcastle,' he said. 'Levitt's deeply involved in the war – he holds a responsible position at the War Office – and may well have been engaged in some arcane operation that he's ill-disposed to tell you about. Frankly, I can think of nothing worse than the political ramifications that would certainly follow the arrest of a senior army officer for two murders he had not committed.' Having delivered that little homily, the assistant commissioner leaned back in his chair. 'After all, he's under no obligation to answer your questions, and you really don't have a shred of evidence to connect him with the crimes you're investigating.'

'He's not coming across, sir,' said Hardcastle, 'and from what I've learned of him he was more likely to have been in bed with a woman, leastways according to Miss Frost. It's not only the evidence of the man Sculley, you see, sir,' Hardcastle continued, already regretting being obliged to share his doubts with the assistant commissioner.

'You said that Miss Frost told you that she hadn't seen the man's face,' said Thomson mildly.

'But Staff Sergeant Perkins called him a cab one night, sir, from Artillery Mansions, so we know he was there. I don't see why he shouldn't tell the truth, if he's in the clear. Why not tell me what he was up to? If he was in bed with his mistress, he surely don't think I'd go up and down Whitehall telling everyone.'

'I should hope not, Hardcastle,' said Thomson, fixing his subordinate with a severe gaze. He knew that the DDI was a shrewd and experienced detective, but there had been times when his lack of discretion had proved to be an embarrassment to the force.

'We still have a piece of rope, that what Rose Drummond was strangled with, sir, and we ain't married that up yet. If we were lucky enough to find a similar piece at General Levitt's place, it would take some explaining away.'

Thomson scoffed. 'If, and I stress if, a brigadier-general had taken it into his head to murder a prostitute, Hardcastle, I think he would have had enough savvy to dispose of any evidence that might tie him to that murder, don't you? What are you proposing, that you obtain a warrant to search Levitt's house? And his quarters at Chelsea Barracks?' The assistant commissioner's bantering tone clearly indicated what he thought of that idea.

'Well, it'd be a start, sir,' said Hardcastle miserably. The assistant commissioner, a lawyer by profession, was destroying his every argument.

'Out of the question, Hardcastle,' said Thomson dismissively. 'Can you imagine what would happen if you carried out this search and found nothing suspicious, which I'm sure would be the outcome? Not only would the Metropolitan Police become a laughing stock, but the Commissioner would find himself answering some very tricky questions. From Sir Herbert Samuel most likely.'

'I s'pose so, sir.' Hardcastle nodded unhappily. The thought that Sir Edward Henry might have to explain the actions of one of his detectives to the Home Secretary did nothing to improve his confidence.

'There is no question of a search warrant, Hardcastle,' said Thomson, 'but you may continue with discreet enquiries, ideally to *eliminate* General Levitt from the investigation. Then get out and find the real killer. The Commissioner has been quite anxious that we achieve a satisfactory solution to this embarrassing affair, and I need hardly say that Colonel Kell, who also has influential friends, has been asking me questions about the murder of one of his agents.'

'Yes, sir, thank you, sir.' Hardcastle stood up, aware that any overt enquiries into Levitt's movements would undoubtedly bring trouble in their wake, but he was convinced in his own mind that the general was more involved in the deaths of Rose Drummond and Edith Sturgess than had so far been discovered.

Despite the assistant commissioner's strictures, Hardcastle was determined to unravel the mystery of Levitt's reticence and the next day he decided to risk his career in one last attempt at getting a confession from him. If not a confession of murder, at least a confession that so far he had not been entirely truthful in his answers to the police.

It was raining when Hardcastle and Marriott made their way down Whitehall once more. Sheltering under the inadequate portico of the Banqueting House, a man with a barrel piano on a strap round his neck ground out 'Goodbye-ee' and looked hopefully at the two detectives. The newsboys' placards still carried sombre statements about the increasing losses on the Western Front, and the grave faces of the passers-by seemed to reflect the hopelessness of the Allies' repeated attempts to defeat the might of the German Army.

A boy bowling a hoop momentarily lost control of it so that it brushed against Hardcastle's trousers leaving a muddy, wet mark.

''Ere, you want to look out, mister,' shouted the urchin.

'I'll give you look out, you little ragamuffin,' said Hardcastle, and raised a hand to clip the boy's ear, but the child laughed and dodged out of the way.

'Bloody guttersnipe, in Whitehall an' all,' muttered Hardcastle. 'I don't know what the world's coming to, Marriott.'

'No, sir,' said Marriott non-committally, but he knew that Hardcastle's irritation was not really with the hoop-bowling street Arab, but with his inability to solve the two murders that were now occupying his every waking hour.

Hardcastle's mood was not improved when he and Marriott arrived at the War Office. 'I've come to see Brigadier-General Levitt,' he announced to the ageing doorkeeper in a tone that implied that he would brook no refusal. He looked around and then placed his wet umbrella in a stand near the door.

'One moment, sir,' said the doorkeeper, running his finger down the page of a large book. He looked up. 'I'm afraid he's not here, sir.' He glanced at a passing colonel and touched the peak of his cap. 'Morning, sir.'

'D'you know when he'll be back, then?' asked Hardcastle, convinced that he was being deliberately obstructed.

'He ain't here any longer, sir,' said the doorkeeper. 'He's gawn.'

'What d'you mean, gone?'

'Like I said, he ain't here any more, sir.'

'That's not good enough,' said Hardcastle. 'Get hold of someone who can tell me where he is.'

The doorkeeper clearly took umbrage at being told what to do by a civilian. 'You can't just come in here demanding things like that,' he said, puffing out a chest adorned with Boer War ribbons.

Hardcastle held his warrant card in front of the man's face. 'I'm Divisional Detective Inspector Hardcastle of the Whitehall Division,' he said menacingly, 'and you'd better get someone down here a bit quick, culley.'

The doorkeeper took a pace back. 'All right, guv'nor, all right,' he said. 'Won't keep you half a mo.'

The immaculately dressed young captain who appeared, minutes later, in the ornate entrance hall of the War Office seemed, so far, to have escaped the ravages of war. 'Can I help you?' he asked loftily.

'Yes, but only if you can tell me where Brigadier-General Levitt is,' said Hardcastle. He was beginning to tire rapidly of what he saw as military intransigence.

'Somewhere on the Western Front,' said the captain. 'He was given command of a brigade the day before yesterday. Is there anything I can help you with? Would you like to see General Levitt's successor, perhaps?'

'No,' said Hardcastle tersely. 'Where on the Western Front is General Levitt?'

'I'm afraid I don't know,' said the captain, with a condescending smile, 'and even if I did I wouldn't be able to tell you. It's a military secret, you see.'

*   *   *

196

'Looks like we're buggered, Marriott,' said Hardcastle, driving the fist of his right hand into the palm of his left. 'He's cut and run.' He stood at his office window and stared moodily down at Westminster underground station.

'We don't know that for sure, sir,' said Marriott. 'These military people do get posted quite regularly and it might just be a coincidence.'

'Coincidence my backside,' said Hardcastle angrily, turning to face his detective sergeant. 'He's got the wind up. That last time we saw him, he was thrown by me asking him if he was in London at the time Edith Sturgess got topped. He knows we're on to him, Marriott, and he's pulled strings to get himself out of the firing line, so to speak.'

'Looks like he pulled them to get himself *into* the firing line, sir,' said Marriott, and grinned at what he thought was a rather clever joke.

Hardcastle was not amused. 'I wonder if we can pull a few strings of our own, Marriott,' he mused. 'Fancy a trip over to France, do you?' he asked, looking directly at his assistant.

Marriott's mouth opened in astonishment and disbelief at Hardcastle's suggestion. He had a brother-in-law who was a sergeant-major in the Middlesex Regiment and the harrowing accounts he gave of life in the trenches did nothing to encourage Marriott to see it for himself. 'They'd never let us go over there, sir,' he said hopefully.

Hardcastle tapped the side of his nose with the stem of his pipe. 'Don't you bank on it,' he said. 'When Ernie Hardcastle decides to do something, there ain't a lot as is going to stop him.'

Marriott nodded slowly. He knew that to be true.

Brigadier-General Fitzpatrick seemed faintly surprised that Hardcastle should have asked for details of Levitt's present whereabouts.

'I can certainly find out where he is, Inspector, but what d'you propose to do once you know?'

'Go there and interview him, General,' said Hardcastle.

The Provost-Marshal was clearly bemused by that. 'But

there's a war going on over there, man,' he said. 'You could get killed.'

Hardcastle was cynical enough to think that a brigadier-general was unlikely to be anywhere dangerous but, needing Fitzpatrick's assistance, forbore from saying so. 'I have a duty to do, General,' he said.

It did not take long. A major on the Provost-Marshal's staff was sent for and despatched to another part of the War Office. Twenty minutes later he returned. 'General Levitt's brigade is in the Ypres Salient for the time being, sir,' said the major. 'Although how long it'll stay there nobody knows, obviously. I'm informed that he has his headquarters in Poperinghe at the moment. It's about seven miles west of Ypres.'

'I know where Poperinghe is,' said Fitzpatrick sharply.

'Apparently General Levitt requested that he be sent to the Front as soon as possible, sir,' said the major. 'Seems a bit unusual.'

'Well, well, I wonder why he should do that,' said Hardcastle sarcastically.

Fitzpatrick stared at Hardcastle. 'I hope you're wrong, Inspector,' he said, 'but I must say it seems just a trifle suspicious.'

'It seems a bit more than suspicious in my book,' said Hardcastle. 'I reckon General Levitt's trying to get away.'

'I take it you intend to pursue him, then?' said Fitzpatrick.

'Certainly I do,' said Hardcastle.

'Very well,' said the Provost-Marshal, 'then I shall see if I can get you a passage on a troopship. I must say it's a bit irregular though. But if I can fix it, I'll arrange for a military police officer to accompany you.' He shook his head, unable to fathom what drove a detective like Hardcastle.

Basil Thomson, however, was less amenable than the Provost-Marshal had been at the prospect of Hardcastle and Marriott going to France. 'I still think you're wrong, Hardcastle,' he said, 'but I must say that Levitt having volunteered for active service in that way does rather make it look as though he's trying to remove himself from the jurisdiction. However, I'm not prepared to make the decision myself. I shall speak to the Commissioner and to Colonel Kell.'

A week later, a week during which the investigation into the murders remained moribund, Hardcastle was sent for again by the assistant commissioner.

'The Commissioner has, somewhat reluctantly, agreed to let you go to France, Hardcastle,' said Thomson.

In fact, far from being reluctant, Sir Edward Henry had applauded the DDI's devotion to duty and spoken warmly of the splendid qualities of a man who would risk life and limb in the front line in order to track down a possible killer. Sir Edward had dismissed Thomson's proposition that because Levitt was a brigadier-general, he was deemed incapable of committing a murder. When Thomson mentioned that Levitt claimed a close acquaintanceship with the Commissioner, Sir Edward laughed and said that he had never heard of the man until now.

There was, however, more to it than that. 'It so happens, Hardcastle,' Thomson continued, 'that General Levitt's departure has come as a shock to Colonel Kell.'

'Really, sir?' Hardcastle did his best to restrain the spark of interest that Thomson's statement had aroused.

Thomson brushed a hand over the corner of his desk. 'I'm not sure if you know,' he went on slowly, 'but General Levitt was warned by military intelligence that Mrs Drummond was suspected of espionage, and that his continued association with her would not be tolerated.'

'Yes, sir. General Levitt told me that himself.'

'Did he, by Jove?' Thomson looked surprised at that.

'Yes, sir. And I think that's why he told me that he'd never seen her after the first time at the House of Commons. But, of course, we know that he did. Leastways, according to Staff Sergeant Perkins, and possibly Mr Smith, the MP.'

'Yes, quite so.' Thomson looked extremely unhappy that this mere divisional detective inspector, whom he personally had ordered should conduct the murder enquiry, seemed to have found out information that he believed only MI5 and his beloved Special Branch had been made privy to. Hardcastle had turned out to be far more resourceful than Thomson had anticipated and he realized, too late, that the DDI's tenacity had probably alerted Levitt to MI5's continuing suspicions. 'General Levitt was warned by MI5, as you say, and they strongly suspected that he had passed sensitive information to the Drummond woman. Unfortunately, once she'd been murdered there was no way that it could be proved.' He sighed. 'It was well known that Levitt had a weakness for women. An elaborate plan was formulated to put Miss Frost at Tachbrook Street and have her make Levitt's acquaintance in an attempt to seduce him into giving the sort of information that MI5 was convinced he had been passing to Rose Drummond. In that way he could have been arrested. The man had to be stopped, you see, Hardcastle.'

'But it's possible that he already knew Miss Frost in the guise of Daisy Watkins, sir, on account of him having likely been in Rose Drummond's bed when Daisy was there. And I thought that Miss Frost was supposed to be pretending to be Rose Drummond.'

'There's a lot more to this business than you know, Hardcastle,' said Thomson. Too late, he realized that a much better policy would have been to take the DDI fully into his confidence from the outset.

'But wouldn't that have meant Miss Frost acting as *agent provocateur*, sir?'

The assistant commissioner gazed wearily at Hardcastle. 'Yes, it would,' he said, 'but all's fair in love and war.' He smiled bleakly at the fitting aphorism. 'Unfortunately, Colonel Kell's people did not see fit to warn the General Staff – not even General Robertson – of their plans. Had they done so, I'm sure that Levitt's little scheme to get himself posted to active service would have been thwarted. As it happened, no one raised any objections. In fact, it was even regarded as a sign of the man's patriotism.'

'Do I take it that you want him arrested after all, sir?' Hardcastle's face remained impassive, even though he was being proved right almost by the minute.

'Yes, Hardcastle,' said Thomson. 'You see, the fact that he's somewhere in Flanders gives him even greater access to information of a sensitive and secret nature, and God knows what he might do if he's tempted by some woman out there. The CIGS, General Robertson, apparently went into a frightful rage when he heard,' he went on, reluctant at having to tell Hardcastle all this. 'There may be nothing in it, but General Robertson wants him brought back here.'

'Can't the military police do that, sir?' asked Hardcastle, beginning to regret his impulsive plea to go to Flanders himself.

'That was my suggestion,' said Thomson, 'but the Commissioner said that the murder enquiry takes precedence, which is why he agreed to you dealing with it. He seems fairly convinced that you're right in your assumption that Levitt was responsible for the murders of Rose Drummond and Edith Sturgess.' The assistant commissioner shrugged despondently, recalling the uncomfortable interview to which he had been subjected when Sir Edward Henry had asked him what the hell was going on. 'He could be ordered back by the army, of course, but that would give him time to think. And in any case, he might just take it into his head to run.'

'Very good, sir,' said Hardcastle. 'I'll go and get him.'

'You're to take Detective Sergeant Drew with you, Hardcastle,' said Thomson. 'As a Special Branch officer he'll know what to do if you find any evidence of espionage when you arrest Levitt.'

'I was going to take Marriott, sir . . .'

'Well, you'll take Drew instead.'

'That's it then, Marriott,' said Hardcastle when he returned to Cannon Row. 'I'm off, as soon as General Fitzpatrick can arrange it, and I'm to take Drew instead of you.'

'Lucky old Aubrey,' said a relieved Marriott. When he had told his wife that he might be going to France to arrest a murderer, she had thrown a fit of the vapours and even a meal at a restaurant normally beyond the range of Marriott's pocket had succeeded only partly in placating her. Although relieved that he was to be left behind, he now wished – purely for economic reasons – that he had kept the news to himself, at least until it had been confirmed.

Mrs Hardcastle, however, had merely shrugged. 'You take care of yourself, Ernie,' she said, 'and mind you take a stout pair of boots. From what I've seen in the *Daily Mail* there's mud everywhere over there.'

Twenty-One

Despite Brigadier-General Fitzpatrick's assurances that he would do everything within his power to facilitate the visit of Hardcastle and Drew to the Western Front, it was seven days before the DDI was advised that a passage had been arranged in a troopship. Thus it was not until Monday the twentieth of August that the two detectives arrived at Southampton for the long crossing to Le Havre, and the tortuous journey of nearly two hundred miles from there to Poperinghe.

The troops who had been on the same train from London as the policemen flooded out on to the platform at Southampton as a military band began to play popular wartime melodies against a background of shouted orders, train whistles and ships' sirens. Everywhere was pervaded by the distinctive odour of steam trains. Movement-control officers dashed hither and thither attempting to create order out of chaos, while a grinning second mate leaned over the bridge-rail of the Admiralty Transport Service troopship, amused as always at the antics of the military.

When the troops had formed up on the quayside, the mayor of Southampton, in morning dress and mayoral chain, made a speech, the high-falutin, patriotic tenor of which was largely wasted on the soldiers, many of whom were returning to the Front for the second or third time after recovering from wounds.

There was a constant fear of German submarines and the rough crossing was made no more bearable by the captain of the escorting destroyer frequently ordering the troopship to change course. Halfway through the voyage the ship was joined by another merchantman, on its way from Avonmouth to Le Havre. On its deck were large, mysterious wooden crates shrouded in tarpaulins.

Captain Basil Willard of the Royal Engineers, the provost officer whom Brigadier-General Fitzpatrick had assigned to the detectives as escort and guide, excitedly told them that the crates contained a new secret weapon called tanks, which were to be used at the Somme in a week or two's time, and was quite disappointed that the two policemen, both of whom had been laid low by seasickness, had not shared his enthusiasm.

In all, Hardcastle and Drew spent nearly ten hours at sea before arriving in France.

The journey from Le Havre was nearly as bad as the sea crossing had been. The military train stopped often, sometimes even reversing for a few miles for no apparent reason, and it was a whole twenty-four hours before it drew into the railway station at Poperinghe, now little more than a makeshift collection of wooden huts.

Hardcastle, feeling out of place in his heavy Chesterfield coat and bowler hat, stood on the platform and stretched, trying to ignore the depressing sight of heavily bandaged soldiers on rows of stretchers further along, and the constant background thunder of artillery fire. 'Well, Drew,' he said, 'I don't know about you, but I could shift a pint or two right now.' He glanced at the detraining soldiers. 'If those poor bastards fared worse than us, I feel bloody sorry for them.' Despite being accorded the status of officers for their journey, Hardcastle and Drew had dined only frugally since leaving Southampton.

Willard touched Hardcastle's arm. 'I've arranged accommodation for you at an officers' mess on the edge of the town, Inspector,' he said, 'rather than in the senior officers' mess in the Stadhuis. I'm told that General Levitt is staying there and I take it you'd rather not meet him across the breakfast table?'

Hardcastle's face twitched into a grin. 'You're right about that, Captain Willard,' he said. 'I'd prefer our being here was a bit of a surprise, if you take my meaning.'

Willard laughed at the thought of being present when a brigadier-general was confronted by two London policemen who had tracked him all the way to the Ypres Salient. 'I heard you saying something about a pint of beer, Inspector. I think that can be arranged.' He beckoned to a staff car bearing Military Police signs and stood back while Hardcastle and Drew clambered in.

As Willard and the two detectives were driven away from Poperinghe railway station, Brigadier-General Humphrey Levitt, shoulders hunched in his trench coat, was striding swiftly down the narrow, cobbled Gasthuisstraat at the other end of the small town. The divisional commander's briefing had lasted longer than expected and Levitt was hurrying to dinner.

The street was crowded with soldiers, arguing or laughing or singing some familiar wartime song, and somewhere the plaintive notes of a mouth organ picked out the haunting refrain of 'The Roses of Picardy'. Despite being 'in rest', the troops were constantly reminded of the fighting by the low rumble of artillery and the flashes that lit the eastern sky.

As Levitt passed Skindles – the cafe had been given the name by an officer with pleasant pre-war memories of the real Skindles at Maidenhead – a noisy party of officers came out and, surprised to see a general on foot, came to attention and saluted as soldiers had done to mark his progress through the town.

The same thing happened as Levitt crossed the market square and picked his way between the lorries and limbers which stood about in ordered confusion near Ginger's Cafe. Its real name was *De Renke* and it was renowned for its Mazarine tart and its waffles, but the owner was a comely auburn-haired girl and, in consequence, the cafe had been dubbed Ginger's by the soldiers.

Levitt stopped briefly by his staff car, parked in the square, and told the driver and his batman Stallard to get a meal as he was going to have dinner himself nearby. The car had been there for an hour already, waiting to take him to Ypres, but Levitt preferred to walk around the small town of Poperinghe.

He paused to allow a staff car to pass as he crossed the road to the Stadhuis. He glanced briefly at its distinctive Military Police signs and then at the occupants. A man in plain clothes sat next to the driver and in the back was a sapper captain with an 'MP' brassard on his arm. Beside him was another civilian. Levitt stared in shock. The last time he had seen the man was in his room at the War Office.

Suddenly he knew that his desperate attempt to avoid Hardcastle by volunteering for active service again had been in vain. The wretched man had pursued him. Ironically, Hardcastle had been deep in conversation with Willard, and Drew with the driver. None of them had seen Levitt, which, in view of what happened later that evening, was unfortunate.

The officers' mess to which Willard took Hardcastle and Drew was a commandeered hotel at the far end of Hofstraat and the two policemen were agreeably surprised to find that it had comfortable beds and hot water. But their first priority was beer and they and Captain Willard sank two or three pints before considering what was to be done next.

Levitt had first been to the restaurant when he was in Poperinghe at the beginning of the war, and was delighted to find it still open on his return, now five weeks ago. He liked it for its seclusion: it was on the first floor of a disused coach house and, being unmarked, was not easy to find. Most of all, though, he liked it for its owner.

The wood panelling which covered the walls to head height was stained a dark brown and was cracked in places. Above it, on a shelf running all around the room, there were plates and brass ornaments and a few stone beer mugs, and beneath it a picture or two depicting Flemish scenes; but they were no longer typical of the Ypres Salient, long since pulverized into acres of mud and ruins.

The atmosphere of darkness and gloom was made worse by pieces of cardboard fixed into the window frames, outnumbering the remaining panes of glass.

Ingrid Naeyaert was slender and tall, almost as tall as Levitt, and her blonde hair was piled high on her head. Her long, black bombasine dress was nipped in tightly at the waist, emphasizing her hips. She smiled. 'Harry, my dear,' she said, 'I thought you would not come tonight.' Humphrey Levitt was always known as Harry to his friends.

Tossing his cap to one side and taking off his trench coat, Levitt took her in his arms, kissing her passionately.

Releasing her, he unbuttoned his side pocket and handed her a small package.

She smiled shyly. 'What is it?'

'It's only scent.'

'Only scent!' She tore off the wrapping quickly. 'It is my favourite.' Impulsively, she stepped towards him and kissed him again. 'Come, we eat.' She opened a bottle of Chablis and poured it. Then she sat down opposite him with a half-sigh and raised her glass. 'That you may be safe, my dear,' she said.

When they had finished their meal, Levitt leaned back in his chair, gently swirling his brandy around in his glass, and gazed at her. The dancing flames of the candles lit her face, so that she looked younger than her twenty-six years. On his first visit, in early 1915, she had told him that she was a widow: her husband of less than a year had been a soldier for only three months when he was killed. She had shown him a photograph in a silver frame: a sepia print of a soldier, a smiling, boyish head and shoulders, the face shadowed by the distinctive steel helmet of the Belgian Army, the ill-fitting khaki collar standing away from the neck. 'He was a chef, not a soldier,' she had said on that occasion. 'A creator of wonderful food. But the army gave him a rifle. They wouldn't even let him be a cook. It is all tragedy this war.' That night Levitt and Ingrid had made love for the first time.

'You are moving . . . to the Somme, I think?' Ingrid raised a quizzical eyebrow.

'I'm sorry, darling, I can't—'

Ingrid held up a hand and smiled. 'I know, my dear, it is a military secret. You must not tell me. But we know what is happening. In Poperinghe, we always know what is happening.' She stopped talking and they were both aware of gunfire as the Germans began to put down a heavy barrage from their stronghold some seven miles to the east.

'Yes, we're moving. But I can't tell you where we are going. You do understand, don't you?'

She nodded sadly. 'Of course.'

'But not immediately. Not tonight.' The move to the

207

Somme had been ordered for four o'clock the morning after next, some thirty hours hence.

'You can stay then?'

'Yes, darling,' said Levitt, 'I can stay.' He held his brandy glass aloft in brief salute. He had suddenly realized how terribly important this girl had become to him. She was soft and gentle, self-assured and independent, and yet vulnerable. And she represented all the things that two years of war had driven from his mind, and to a certain extent brutalized. Since August 1914, he had thought of nothing but fighting, even during his few brief months at the War Office in London. Of moving men, securing supplies and trying to outwit the enemy.

And burying the dead.

He thought back to the countless men he had known who were now no longer. Mostly young, but some quite old. And of all the letters he had written, as a battalion commander, to grieving relatives. And the irony of it was that the Germans were seated on the Messines Ridge doing exactly the same.

And now this girl had come into his life, reminding him of all the things he had been missing: the regimental balls, the point-to-points, riding to hounds; and boating on Hickling Broads when the weather always seemed fine and sunny, a pretty girl beside him and not a care in the world.

Then came the news of the assassination of the heir to the Austro-Hungarian throne in an unheard-of place called Sarajevo. A couple of shots from a student and for a reason never clear to Levitt, suddenly the whole world was plunged into this pointless war.

'What are you thinking, Harry, my dear?'

'I'm thinking that I've fallen in love with you, Ingrid.'

'Oh!' She pouted a little and flushed, and looked down. 'I think this is not a good time for falling in love,' she murmured.

'Why not? I think it's a very good time.'

'But the war—'

'You can make the war an excuse for not doing anything, or for just doing bad things.'

'Now you are talking riddles again, Harry.'

208

'No, I'm being very serious and very direct. I want to marry you. Do you love me, Ingrid?'

She placed her glass carefully on the table and gazed at him steadily with her piercing blue eyes. 'Of course I love you, Harry.'

Levitt stood up and walked round the table to where she was sitting and kissed her, an arm around her shoulders.

She broke the clumsy embrace. 'Finish your brandy, Harry,' she said, her heart beating so fast she thought it would escape from her breast.

'Hang the brandy.'

'That's a fine way to treat my brandy. And how can you hang it? It is not possible.' She took another mouthful of wine, trying to recover from her breathlessness and attempting to restore normality to her voice. 'But I cannot marry you.'

'Why ever not?'

'It is not right. It is not good. Not with the war going on. Perhaps tomorrow you will be gone. Forever.' There was something awfully final about the way she said that word, and they both knew what she meant.

As if to emphasize that imminent danger there was a sudden succession of explosions, ear-splitting and very close at hand. The curtains billowed inwards and just as quickly were sucked out again through windows from which the blast had removed not only the last remaining glass, but the cardboard and the very frames themselves. There was a secondary clatter as the ornaments around the room were swept from their high shelf, and pictures were snatched from the walls to shatter on the floor.

Levitt leaped up. 'My God!' he said, 'they've registered on the market place.' He peered out of the window, down Ieperstraat, saw the flames, and heard the familiar shouts and screams, and saw too the insidious Flanders rain. 'Are you all right?' he asked, quickly buckling on his Sam Browne and revolver.

'Yes. You must go and help.' Ingrid handed him his trench coat and he struggled into it as he hurried through the kitchen and the deserted restaurant.

He ran down the road towards the square, oblivious to the

rain and regretting having left his cap behind. Several lorries and wagons had been in the market place, and medical orderlies and stretcher-bearers were seeking out the wounded. Men were running everywhere, and Levitt glimpsed a veterinary sergeant despatching a severely wounded horse.

As he peered helplessly around for his staff car, another salvo struck the square.

In the officers' mess in Hofstraat, Willard, Hardcastle and Drew had just finished dinner.

'Bloody hell,' said Willard as the first salvo struck, 'that was a bit too close for comfort. I'd better go and have a look.' He stood up and grabbed his cap and Sam Browne from the table. 'Sorry to have to abandon you, Inspector, but I imagine there are a few casualties. Unless I'm much mistaken, they've got the market place.'

'We'll come with you,' said Hardcastle as he and Drew stood up.

'Rather you didn't, Inspector,' said Willard. 'Could be a bit grisly.'

Hardcastle laughed and picked up his coat and hat. 'I was dealing with dead bodies before you were born, Captain Willard. Now, lead the way.'

Other soldiers were running towards the market square as Willard and the two detectives dashed into the street.

A string of three shells had left large craters in the pavé, while a fourth had demolished the front of a cafe near the corner of Gasthuisstraat. Soldiers were pulling at baulks of timber and digging into the debris with bare hands. The dead body of an officer, a gaping wound in his chest, was dragged clear and left near a gun limber.

There was little that Willard or the two detectives could do. The non-commissioned officers were in charge, and clearly much better at dealing with such commonplace emergencies than they. Orderlies from the field ambulance had appeared with stretchers and were applying tourniquets and administering morphine, meticulously marking the foreheads of the wounded with a large letter M before carrying them away to the field dressing station. Some were beyond earthly

210

help, and they were put aside in favour of the living even by Tubby Clayton, the padre from up the road at Talbot House, hatless and helping a gun crew to right a limber to release a trapped sergeant.

Outside the Stadhuis was the scattered wreckage of what had once been a staff car. It had received a direct hit and there now remained only twisted metal, shreds of uniform and unrecognizable pieces of human body – bones and flesh – to indicate what had once been two men and a Vauxhall car.

'Who was in it?' Willard demanded curtly of two soldiers standing nearby. The authoritative tone and the Military Police brassard commanded instant respect.

'It looks like some general and his driver, sir,' said one of the men, a garrison artillery bombardier, 'but there's no telling. Could be anyone, but I reckon it was one of the brass.'

'Whose car was it?'

A sergeant turned and saluted. 'Brigadier-General Levitt's, sir,' he said. 'He was the brigade commander, but there ain't much left of him, that's for sure.'

Willard shrugged and turned away. 'Carry on, Sergeant,' he said.

'Yes, sir,' said the sergeant, and when Willard was out of earshot, added, 'What did the bloody fool think we were going to do?'

Willard had managed to arrange an immediate passage back to England and had even secured places for himself and the two detectives on the troop train from Folkestone Harbour.

Hardcastle had been in a foul mood for the whole of the journey back to England, and his mood had not improved by the time the trio reached Charing Cross railway station in London. 'Well, Drew, that's that, I suppose,' he said. 'Now we shall never know. Two bloody murders unsolved and the main suspect buried in Flanders, what was left of him.' Irritably, he reached for his pipe and began to fill it. 'I'll tell you this much, Drew, I never want to get involved with MI5 again, nor your bloody lot neither. Bungling bloody amateurs the lot of them.'

They stepped out into the autumn sunshine and turned along the Strand.

'What's going on in Trafalgar Square?' asked Drew, glancing across at the crowds.

'Looks as though Horatio Bottomley is holding another of his recruiting rallies,' said Captain Willard as the band on the square began to play 'It's a Long Way to Tipperary'.

Twenty-Two

It was the eleventh of November 1945. The sound of a Guards band playing 'It's a Long Way to Tipperary' as ex-servicemen marched past the Cenotaph, was muffled and distant to the military policeman as he watched the stooped figure painfully ascending the steps of the Central London Recruiting Office at Great Scotland Yard.

The old man's dark suit was clearly unfashionable now, but the creases in his trousers were razor sharp. His well-brushed bowler hat was frayed in places around its braided brim, squarely placed but tipped forward slightly.

As he climbed slowly upwards, the old man paused at intervals to lean on his stick and recover his breath.

'Another Old Contemptible got lost,' said the military police corporal to his colleague. 'And he's got a few gongs.' The corporal's own array of medal ribbons testified to service in North Africa and Italy. 'That's a DSO, an MBE, an MC, Pip, Squeak and Wilfred *and* a mention in despatches. Blimey! I reckon he's seen a bit of action,' he added, his practised eye rapidly identifying the old man's decorations.

At the top of the steps, the old man stopped again, waiting until he had summoned the strength to push open the heavy door, but the corporal opened it for him, at once stepping back and saluting. The visitor's appearance indicated that he had been an officer and the medals confirmed it.

'Yes, sir? Can I help you?'

'D'you mind if I sit down, Corporal?' The old man nodded towards a wooden bench seat in the entrance hall.

'Please do, sir.' The corporal waited until, unsteadily, the aged officer had sat down, leaning forward on his stick and wheezing a little as he got his breath back. 'What can I do for you, sir?'

The old man looked up at the corporal, his pale grey eyes flickering briefly over the younger man's medal ribbons. 'I am Brigadier-General Humphrey Levitt,' he said. 'This is the headquarters of the military police for London District, isn't it?'

'Yes, sir,' said the corporal.

'Is there a military police officer here who I could speak to?'

As it was Remembrance Day, a Deputy Assistant Provost-Marshal, a youngish artillery major called Goddard, was on duty. Immaculate in service dress, complete with Sam Browne, he came downstairs and conducted Levitt to his office.

'What can I do for you, Brigadier?' asked Goddard.

'Brigadier-*General*.' Levitt corrected the major's omission automatically; the suffix 'general' had been dropped in 1921, but as far as he was concerned his own rank had not changed. 'I wish to surrender myself for desertion from military service in 1916, Major,' he said. 'And for other crimes.'

'Desertion, sir?' Goddard raised his eyebrows in surprise. Although officers had occasionally absconded during both world wars, he had never come across a brigadier who had done so.

'Is that so strange, Major?' Despite his age, Levitt still managed to conjure an authoritative stare.

'I have to admit I've not come across a similar case before, sir.'

'I'd better explain, then. While I was serving at the War Office, just before the start of the Battle of the Somme, I was foolish enough to become involved with a woman called Rose Drummond. Unfortunately, and unbeknown to me, she was suspected of being a spy and I was warned off by military intelligence, but not before, somewhat unwisely, I had revealed some confidences. We had an affair, you see, and in those circumstances one is apt to say things which one should not.' Levitt gazed balefully at the young major. 'I was a bloody fool, I'm afraid,' he admitted. 'However,

214

when I tried to break it off with her, she threatened to tell my superiors that I had given her information of value to the enemy. I need hardly say that I wouldn't have dreamed of doing such a thing intentionally, but I realized that I had perhaps been a little careless about what I had told her. I knew what the outcome would have been had she gone to the War Office or, worse still, the newspapers. It would have been a general court martial and I would have been cashiered and disgraced – imprisoned even – no matter how much I'd protested my innocence. There was a war on, you see, and "Wully" Robertson – he was the CIGS – would have made an example of me. The end of a promising military career. Not that that mattered in view of what I did later.' Even after all these years he was still unable to tell the truth; he knew that he had been guilty of treason – all because of that damned woman – and might well have been shot at dawn. For a moment, he looked piercingly at Goddard as if defying him to disagree, and then he smiled ruefully. 'And as if that wasn't enough, I then learned that she used to pick up soldiers from barracks in the London area, Finsbury Barracks in particular, I suppose with a view to obtaining information.' He shook his head as if unable to credit his stupidity at having got mixed up with such a woman all those years ago. 'To put it simply, Major, I followed her one evening from Artillery Mansions – that's where she lived – and I murdered her. In Hoxton Square. I thought that to kill her there would allay suspicion, that the police would think that it was a soldier who had done it.'

There was a bemused smile on Goddard's face now. 'Really, sir?'

'Yes, Major, really,' snapped Levitt, irritated that the military policeman appeared to be doubting his word. 'Then, of course, I realized that, if she was the spy that MI5 said she was, she would probably have made notes about our relationship and I knew that if the police found them, I'd immediately become a suspect for her murder.'

'Quite likely, sir,' murmured Goddard, himself a pre-war policeman.

'After I'd killed her, I threw her handbag in the river, but

215

I kept her keys. I had no idea that she'd been identified, that her body had been identified, I mean. There was nothing in the papers about it. But then I had a visit from some damned policeman. That gave me quite a shock, I can tell you. The police had learned that I'd met Mrs Drummond at a junket at the House of Commons. Then I heard through the War Box grapevine that someone had been arrested for the murder.' Even now, Levitt did not appreciate that that information had been fed to him deliberately. 'A few weeks later, when I thought that the coast would be clear, I went to Mrs Drummond's flat and let myself in with the keys I'd taken.'

'But what for, sir?' Major Goddard was finding the story so bizarre that it beggared belief.

'To see if there was any incriminating evidence there, of course,' snapped Levitt. He was becoming increasingly irritated by Goddard's apparent inability to follow the narrative. 'But if I'd thought about it, I'd've known that the police would have found it already.'

'Undoubtedly,' murmured Goddard.

'To my horror I found a woman there,' Levitt continued. 'I learned later that her name was Edith Sturgess. She'd been a nurse at St George's Hospital originally, but Colonel Kell had later taken her on to his staff—'

'Colonel Kell, sir?'

'Dammit, man,' growled Levitt, annoyed at being interrupted again, 'the head of MI5.'

'Oh, I see.' By now Goddard was convinced that he was dealing with an old soldier suffering from senile dementia and that his only course of action was to humour him until he could contrive to get him out of his office. 'Do go on, sir.'

'I tried to bluff my way out of it, pretending that I'd come to see my mistress, but then she said, "I know you, you're General Levitt." She said something about having been on duty at St George's when I paid an official visit there. Then the real reason for my being there dawned on her, and she accused me, straight out. "It was you who murdered Rose Drummond," she said. I knew then that the game was up, so I strangled her too.' Levitt related the macabre events of

216

nearly thirty years ago in a monotone, almost as if he had been a casual observer rather than the principal participant. 'I had no alternative, really, d'you see? The trouble was that this damned detective – from Scotland Yard, I think he was – a fellow called . . .' He paused, his brow furrowed in thought. 'Harker, Harmsworth, Hargreaves, some name like that.' His face cleared. 'Ah! Hardcastle, that was the chap. Well, he was convinced that I'd done for these two women, you see, and of course he was right. He kept pestering me, so I got myself posted back to Flanders, in command of a brigade, just to get out of the way, but the wretched man pursued me there. I can tell you it gave me the most awful shock when I caught sight of him in the market place at Poperinghe.'

'Why didn't he arrest you, sir, if, as you say, you'd killed these two women?'

'He was in a car and I was on foot, Major. He didn't see me, but I saw him. Then I had a bit of luck, although it sounds heartless to call it luck. It wasn't often that the German artillery registered on Poperinghe – and even when they did it was usually the railway station they hit, just as they were loading casualties – but this particular night they put a salvo down on the market place, yards from divisional headquarters.'

'Good targeting,' murmured Goddard, his professional interest aroused.

'My staff car, which was parked on the square while I was having dinner nearby, received a direct hit and was destroyed completely, killing my driver and my batman. Stallard – he was my batman – shouldn't have been there at all, but he always insisted on accompanying me wherever I went, and I was going into Ypres later that evening to visit each one of the headquarters of my three battalions. Everyone thought that Stallard was me. So, to cut a long story short, I took advantage of the situation and deserted. In all the confusion I raced back to the restaurant—'

'I'm sorry, sir, but what does a restaurant have to do with it?' asked Goddard, still trying to absorb the unlikely tale that the old officer was relating.

'There was this girl, you see, Major, Ingrid Naeyaert, who

217

kept the restaurant – it was in Ieperstraat in Poperinghe – and we'd fallen in love. I told her what I'd done and we ran away together. We caught a train to Courtrai and then on to Brussels – no one ever queried where a general officer was going, or why – and we got married there. And we've lived there ever since, at least until Ingrid died in January.' Levitt shook his head wistfully. 'It was a bigamous marriage of course. I had a wife in Bray at the time. God knows what happened to her. Not that Ingrid ever knew about Maud. There was no point in telling her, really.'

By now, Goddard was beginning seriously to doubt the old brigadier-general's story – it seemed too fantastic to be credible – but on the other hand, he asked himself, why should anyone wish to make up such a tale? Despite the major's first amateurish diagnosis of senile dementia, Levitt was quite lucid in the way in which he was recounting these events.

'I felt very badly about Stallard though, still do as a matter of fact,' mused Levitt.

'Stallard, sir?'

'Yes, man, he was my batman,' said Levitt irritably. 'I told you. He'd been in the car with my driver. They were both killed. The authorities undoubtedly thought that he was the one who'd deserted. You see, Major, he has no grave; the poor devil was blown to smithereens. His name doesn't even appear on the Menin Gate, but mine does. It's quite a shock, I can tell you, to see your own name listed among the fallen with no known graves.' Lost in thought for a moment or two, Levitt looked across the office towards the tall windows. 'I really must do something about that,' he mumbled.

'That MBE that you've got, sir, how did you come by that?' The DAPM knew that the Order of the British Empire had not been instituted until 1917, the year after Levitt claimed to have deserted.

Levitt looked down at his row of polished medals. 'Tried to make up for it, Major,' he said. 'I changed my name to Latham, Harry Latham, when Ingrid and I were married. When the second show started in '39, we tried to get back home, here, but we'd left it too late. I'd learned to speak Flemish fluently so I changed my name again, to Jozef Vanderwegen this time. *Mijnheer* and *Mevrouw* Vanderwegen . . .' He paused to chuckle at that. 'We stayed in Belgium throughout the second war and I got involved with the Resistance. At my age, there wasn't much I could do, but I helped out in one or two minor operations and I managed to work a secret radio.' He dismissed his actions – actions that could have got him shot as a saboteur, ironically by the Germans this time – with a deprecating wave of a hand misshapen with arthritis. 'Last month the King was gracious enough to invest me with the MBE. As Harry Latham, of course.'

'Well, sir,' said Goddard, after listening to Levitt's story, 'I've never come up against anything quite like this before.' He pushed aside the notes he had been making. 'I'm sure you understand that there's no question of my placing you in custody . . .'

'I suppose not,' said Levitt. 'But what happens now?'

'Well . . .' Goddard hesitated. 'Report the matter to the Provost-Marshal, I suppose, sir. I imagine that he will consult the Army Legal Service, or the civil police, and then . . .' He shrugged.

Levitt managed a wry grin. 'Admit it, Major, you don't know what to do, do you?'

Goddard smiled. 'I'm sure you'll believe me when I say that there aren't too many precedents for this sort of thing, sir. But we'll be in touch with you once a decision has been made. Where can we find you?'

Levitt gave the address of a seedy hotel in the back streets of Pimlico and then slowly stood up. 'I shall be there, Major,' he said. 'I'll not run away. Not again.'

Twenty minutes later there was a knock on the major's door and the corporal entered, stamping and saluting.

'Yes, Corporal?'

'That brigadier, sir . . .'

'Yes, what about him?'

'He collapsed when he got to the bottom of the steps, sir, just as I was about to put him into a cab.'

'Yes?'

'He was dead when the ambulance arrived, sir. They've

219

taken the body to Westminster Hospital in Horseferry Road, but no doubt it'll be put straight into the mortuary.'

'Thank you, Corporal,' said Goddard. 'A very suitable day for the old man to go, wasn't it?'

'Beg pardon, sir?'

'Remembrance Day, Corporal.'

'Oh yes, sir. Quite so, sir.' The corporal saluted once more and turned to leave. Then he paused. 'What was it he wanted, sir, if you don't mind my asking?'

Major Goddard picked up the notes he had made, tore them into little pieces and dropped them into the wastepaper basket. 'Just wanted someone to have a yarn with about his war, Corporal,' he said. 'You know what these old soldiers are like.'